The Power
of the
Serpent

Peter Valentine Timlett

THE POWER OF THE SERPENT
A Bantam Book | September 1976

ISBN 0–553–02370–5

Published simultaneously in the United States and Canada.

Bantam Books are published by Bantam Books, Inc. Its trade-mark, consisting of the words "Bantam Books" and the por-trayal of a bantam, is registered in the United States Patent Office and in other countries. Marca Registrada. Bantam Books, Inc., 666 Fifth Avenue, New York, New York 10019.

PRINTED IN THE UNITED STATES OF AMERICA

DEVIL-SPAWN
FROM THE MISTS
OF TIME

As the last of the fog rolled away Ramin realized that he was in a small underground cave, no more than a dozen yards across.

The stench was appalling, a musty, disgusting smell. The rocks under his hand were wet, but not with water—a sticky, revolting slime. He felt as if he was in the lair of some foul and loathsome creature of the half-world.

As that thought entered his mind he saw that the entrance to the cave was blocked by a spider web, and there in the center of the web was the spider itself, a huge bloated monster as big as himself.

The spider moved slightly on its web, and those gigantic eyes turned in his direction, and Ramin knew that he was doomed.

Chapter One

The great earthworks that surrounded the stone circle of Cor Gaur was already littered with dead priests, both Wessex and Druid, and the early morning sun had not yet even cleared the horizon. The young Druid battle commander, Melkor, stood athwart the topmost level of the earthworks, his sword still in his hand. He seemed mesmerized by the blood that was already drying along the blade. A few months earlier he had not believed it possible that he could have knowingly taken a human life in any way at all, let alone in such a brutal, bloody, and savagely primitive fashion—and yet in the last hour he had killed not once but many times as the screaming, frenzied Wessex priests had stormed the Druid defences. The memory of it sickened him. He thrust the sword back into its scabbard, and adjusted the white robe of his rank as a full fourth-degree initiate. The robe had blood on it, too, and it seemed to him a sacrilege, a crime against the Earth Spirit itself, that the white robe of Druidry could have become thus tainted. The red smear was a violation of everything that Druidry stood for—a denial of all that he personally held sacred. The revulsion was so strong in him that he almost vomited.

A young blue-robed neophyte of the Bardic Degree, the probationary degree, came up to him. "Greetings to Melkor," the boy said nervously. Three months ago he had been a cattle-boy on his father's estate. The Druid Master of the Outer Court had called to see his father and the two men had talked far into the night, and at dawn the boy had been led away as a likely candidate for the priesthood. In the following three months he had barely spoken to any of the white-robed senior priests save his own Master, let alone one of such exalted rank as Melkor. "I am commanded by my Master," he stammered, "to inform you that the Arch-Mage, Druthin, requires your presence." The carefully rehearsed words came tumbling out in a nervous rush.

Melkor smiled. "Greetings." he said softly. "I will come at once." He stared north across the plain to where the Wessex warrior-priests were regrouping. There was obviously no danger for a while. He put his hand on the boy's shoulder. "Come, we will walk down together."

As they picked their way down to the great standing stones, Melkor studied the boy. How old was he —ten—eleven? There was blood on his robe also. "What is your name, Bard?"

"Zelta, my Lord."

"And how old are you, Zelta?"

"Eleven, my Lord—at least I think so. My father was not a great one for reckoning the years."

Melkor shook his head wearily—eleven! "There is blood on your robe, young one—yours?"

The boy hesitated. "No, my Lord—it's Wessex blood."

The senior priest stopped short and turned the boy to face him. "You have shed Wessex blood?"

The boy hung his head. "No, my Lord. I tried to but the sword was too heavy." He paused but the battle-commander did not speak, just stared hard at him. "I was commanded to stay at the rear, but my Master was being driven back by two warriors." The eyes bore into him. He shuffled his feet nervously. "I went to aid him but the sword was too heavy, and I stumbled and fell against their knees. And they staggered, and I was knocked down, and then my Master killed them both right there above me, and the blood spurted . . . and it fell on my robe," he finished lamely.

A boy's foolish bravery, Melkor thought, probably saved his Master's life. "Who is your Master?" he said sternly.

"Cludin, my Lord."

Ah yes, Cludin—born of the stones—a good name for one of such honor. "And what did he say to you, Bard?"

The boy's eyes widened. "He was angry, my Lord. I have never seen him so angry. He was trembling with rage. He pointed and I ran!"

Melkor struggled to hide his smile. The silent, stone-willed Cludin trembling with rage? A rare sight. "A rage born of love for you, I think," he said. "The next time your Master gives you a command, obey it! There is no room for disobedience in the priesthood. Come." He took the boy's arm and they continued on down. The boy would do well in the priesthood, he thought, if he lived long enough. A great deal can be done with courage, and precious little without it.

As they drew near the cluster of priests at the great King Stone at the center of the circle, Melkor pushed the boy slightly forward. "Go to your Master. You and I will speak again when this is over." The boy ran and Melkor stepped through the outer circle and strode forward through the double circle of bluestones, the Holy Stones, and came to the great Sarsen Trilithons. At the very center of Cor Gaur, the Elder Council waited for him, with Druthin seated on the King Stone itself.

Melkor stopped a few paces short of the King Stone and raised his right fist aloft in salute, three fingers extended—the three Rays of Light upon which all knowledge is inscribed. "From Melkor to Druthin, Arch-Mage of all Druidry, greetings!"

The old man's eyes were sharp and ice-green. "Greetings," he said simply. "How goes the day?"

Melkor's eyes swept the anxious faces of the assembled Council. "Badly," he said simply. "The attack has been repulsed but with much loss of life on both sides."

"How many?"

"The reckoning is still to be completed, but I believe we have lost half our fighting force."

The faces darkened with anxiety. "Will they attack again?" said Druthin.

"Yes, and soon."

"Can we withstand them again?"

"No. They still outnumber us five to one, and they are trained and experienced warrior-priests, whereas we are scholar-priests with no experience of arms or battle."

There was a deep silence. Many had crowded forward to hear the words of the Council. At the outer circle a line of blue-robed members of the Bardic Degree strained their ears to catch the words. Melkor looked for the boy, Zelta, but could not see him. In front of the Bards and to the right was a cluster of Second Degree initiates, the green-robed Ovates, and in amongst them he could see several with green headdresses denoting their seniority in the Ovate Degree, the Third Degree initiates, the Ovate Druids. Behind the Council had gathered the Fourth Degree initiates, the Druids, white-robed as himself. It was strange to see them all robed at a time like this. Normally only the Fourth Degree Druids wore their white robes at all times. The three lower degrees only wore their robes at ritual assemblies, the gorsedds. It was Druthin himself who had ordered all degrees to wear their robes during battle. "Some will undoubtedly die," he had said. "If so, then it is fitting that they die wearing the insignia of their rank."

One of the Council stepped forward to face the Arch-Mage, and Melkor's eyes narrowed. What poison was Vordin about to inject? The senior Council member was a small, thin, stooped man with a hawked nose that dominated his sharp face. His eyes were almost black, fierce and glittering, the eyes of a fanatic. He leaned forward, his hand caressing the symbol of his Council rank, the serpent entwined on a pillar of rock. Involuntarily, Melkor's hand moved to touch the identical symbol that hung around his own neck. Druthin's eyes flickered to Vordin, and darkened. There were some who felt that Druthin regretted Vordin's appointment to the Council and would dearly love to take back the Serpent Symbol, but Vordin trod warily, always giving cause for concern but never enough to warrant his expulsion from the Council. Vordin was a scholar of undoubted repute. He was a clever man but one whose studies had not taught him courtesy or compassion, a man of much knowledge but little wisdom.

"And what does Vordin say?" said Druthin coldly.

"No more than I said three months ago when this foolishness was first mooted, and no more than Melkor is saying now." Vordin swept his arm around to indicate the entire assembly. "We are scholar-priests, not warrior-priests. We have been scholar-priests for a thousand years, since Druidry first began, with one learned man and three pupils at the Grove at Glaeston, centuries before we were even called 'Druids.' Never throughout that time have we ever interfered in the national life. It was the Wessex priests who were the priest-administrators of the realm, not Druids. It was the Wessex priests who were the warrior-priests who defended the land from marauders from the sea, not Druids. It was the Wessex priests who built Cor Gaur here and the great circle at Abiri, and the thousands of other stone ritual circles throughout the land, not Druids. It was the Wessex priests who built the trackways and leas in accordance with the ancient wisdom, and it was they who erected the standing stones and built the barrows, mounds, and dolmens, not Druids—and it is the Wessex priests who are responsible for the administration of the national religious life!"

"And it is the Wessex priests," thundered Druthin suddenly, "who have betrayed their trust, not Druids. It is the Wessex priests who have introduced foul rites here at Cor Gaur and at Abiri, not Druids. It is the Wessex priests who have instilled fear throughout the land so that even the King keeps to his castle at Caelon-on-Usk and dares not venture too far abroad.

It is the Wessex priests who drag women and children screaming from their homes and torture and abuse them in obscene rites here at Cor Gaur—here at the very sacred heart of our race—and it is the Wessex priests who are calling down evil forces from the Void to contaminate the land! It is the Wessex priests who are guilty of these monstrous things, not Druids!" The old man had risen to his feet to give his answer, his eyes flashing. He pointed at Vordin. "All that you say of history is true. For two thousand years and more the Wessex priests have discharged their spiritual responsibilities with great honor, but now they have degenerated into foulness and obscenity and the time has come when they must be driven out!"

"But not by Druids!" Vordin drew himself up and pointed straight back at the Arch-Mage. Whatever Vordin lacked as a priest and a man, there was no question of his courage. "I say again, we are scholar-priests, not warriors. Over the centuries we have built a reputation for learning. Our main college at Glaeston is known and respected throughout the civilized world. Must we now appear to the world as butchers? I tell you, Druthin, Servant of the Truth, that we have stained the good name of Druidry by our actions today, and there is a stain on the soul of every Druid priest who has today shed human blood!"

Again there was a deep silence. An over-dramatization, thought Melkor, typical of Vordin. He looked at the old man and his heart moved within him. Never in the history of Druidry had there been a greater leader than Druthin, and never before was a great leader more needed than now.

Druthin spoke quietly, almost in a whisper. "You are quite right, Vordin. There is always a stain on the soul of any man who takes a human life, regardless of his motive, and that debt to the life spirit has to be repaid, either in this life or in lives to come. But I tell you this, Vordin, of my own knowledge, that there is a greater stain on the soul of a man who sees evil and does nothing about it. Such men are called 'The Permitters of Destruction' and they are abhorred in the sight of the Great Ones, for to ignore evil is to encourage its growth. I would sooner accept the debt of having taken the life of an evil one than that of having allowed him to continue in his evil, and as the Arch-Mage of Druidry, I make that decision for the whole of Druidry as well as for myself!"

Vordin threw up his hands in exasperation. "I do not disagree with the principle, Druthin. All I have said over and over again is that the Druids should not have taken arms in this matter. I agree that we should not have ignored the situation, but to each their own particular function. The Druids should have remained at their studies and their meditation. We should have sought the help of Egypt to drive out the Wessex priests!"

"And pass the responsibility of shedding human life to another? Never! Not while I am Arch-Mage of all Druidry."

"The Egyptian priesthood send their finest each year to exchange ideas with us," said Vordin patiently, "and have done so for centuries. They are well aware of the worsening situation here and would have undoubtedly sent the Egyptian army against the Wessex if we had but asked. The sacred center of the entire world is the Great Pyramid in Egypt, and the priests of Re are concerned with spiritual matters everywhere. They would have helped had we asked."

Druthin shook his head. "I have the greatest respect and reverence for the Egyptian priesthood, but I would not want the Egyptian army rampaging through our realm. No, Vordin, it is our problem and we have to solve it. We cannot and must not abrogate that responsibility. The time has come for the Wessex priests to be driven out, and we their successors must do the driving at whatever cost!"

Vordin snorted. "At the moment it is they who are doing the driving."

"Enough of this opposition!" snapped Druthin.

"The time has also come for you to decide where your loyalties lay. If you remain with us, then you must do so willingly and with good heart. If you cannot do that, then you can no longer remain a member of this Council and I will have to demand the return of the Serpent Symbol and order you to Glaeston, to bury yourself in your studies and leave the future to us. Choose now, Vordin!"

There was a quick indrawing of breath from several of the Council members, and a ripple ran through the assembly. The sun had now cleared the horizon and threw long shadows from the giant stones. Melkor held his breath at this sudden confrontation. But Vordin was not to be stampeded into a hasty answer. If he was stripped of his rank and returned to Glaeston in disgrace, he could expect to exercise little influence in the future. "In the final analysis," he said slowly and finally, "I owe my allegiance to you, Druthin, as Arch-Mage." He paused for a moment and fingered the Serpent Symbol. "We have been encouraged by you to speak our minds in open council. I have spoken my mind and will not raise the subject again. Nor will I desert my companions in such times as these. With your permission I will remain with you."

"Very well. We are committed to this path we have taken. Let us tread it as best we can." The old man turned to the battle-commander. "Melkor, we came to Cor Gaur three weeks ago and drove out the Wessex priests in utter rout without the loss of a single life, due obviously to the element of surprise. Now we find ourselves unable to hold what we have taken."

Melkor nodded. "The final success of the venture always depended on our being able to capture Mog Agorn, the High Priest, and his seven foul sons, and bring them all to ritual trial here at Cor Gaur. Without him and his brood the Wessex priests would have run hither and thither like a bird without its head. We could have taken Abiri and rounded them up one by one." Melkor shrugged. "But he and his sons escaped."

"Aye, the first to flee the field."

"And now they are ready and we cannot hold. To remain is to risk a slaughter to the last man."

The old man sighed. "We have little alternative. Very well, we must abandon Cor Gaur and withdraw to Glaeston. Our time will come again."

Vordin spoke up again. "Mog Agorn may not let us withdraw in peace. He could follow and cut us down one by one long before we reach Glaeston."

Melkor nodded. "Vordin is right."

"If he follows, yes," said Druthin. "But if I know Mog Agorn he will be so flushed with triumph at having retaken Cor Gaur he will remain here to celebrate in the usual Wessex style."

At that moment a shaft of light glinted from a sword blade on top of the earthworks. "The signal!" said Melkor sharply. "They come again. Your instructions, Druthin, quickly!"

"Hold the top as long as you can and then withdraw through Cor Gaur to the south." He turned to Vordin. "You and Cludin, gather the Council and the younger Bards and retire to the south until it is safe to turn to the west. We will meet on the road to Glaeston. Go!"

Melkor turned and ran for the earthworks, tugging his sword clear, and several of the white-robed Druids ran with him. The inner surface of the earthworks was a long, sloping turf run to the top, and already he was breathing heavily.

"Vordin was right about one thing," one of the others panted. "We are no warriors, we Druids!"

And I, thought Melkor, am a Priest of the Sun, and no battle-commander for any real army. "Save your breath," he grunted.

"We should have pursued Mog Agorn during that rout three weeks ago," the man said. "We may have captured him and broken the power of the Wessex there and then."

"Possibly," said Melkor briefly.

"And failing that," the priest gasped, "we should have sent for reinforcements!"

Another priest, scrambling behind them, called

out: "We should have withdrawn to Glaeston days ago when we knew the Wessex were regrouping and knew their numbers."

"Aye," said another, "and those who died today would still be living!"

"Let alone those still to die!" panted the first priest.

They came to the top in a rush and Melkor stood panting heavily, surveying the scene across the plain to the north. "What you say may or may not be true," he growled. "All three of you were present at the open council meetings that we have held every day since arriving at Cor Gaur, and not once did I hear any one of you voicing these ideas. Any man can be wise after the event." His eyes scanned the earthworks. The Druid forces, such that they were, had taken their positions and were as ready as they would ever be. "As for those who died," he said, "at least Mog Agorn knows now that Druids are prepared to lay down their lives to oppose him, and the people will come to know as the word spreads and take heart from the news. That will count for much in the days to come." He pointed with his sword across the plain. "Let us not waste words on what might have been. *That* is the reality we have to face!"

Below and in front of them, across the northern plain, the Wessex priests in lines abreast were steadily approaching the outer earthworks of Cor Gaur.

"There must be five hundred of them!" breathed one of the priests to Melkor's left.

"Six hundred, more like it!" said another.

"And what do we have—ninety, a hundred?"

In the center of the Wessex line, and slightly in front of it, was Mog Agorn, a seminaked giant of a priest, his hair and beard streaming behind him in the wind, his feet and massive thighs braced against the front guard-rail of his chariot. In line abreast on either side of him were the seven chariots of his seven sons.

"Where did he get those horses?" asked one of the Druids suddenly. "If they *are* horses!"

The sixteen mares of Mog Agorn, two each to the

eight chariots, were not the heavy, lumbering beasts that the Druids knew as horses. These were smaller, lighter, and faster animals. Melkor had heard of them, but this was the first time that he had actually seen them. "They are horses all right," he said briefly. "From the lands near Egypt. I had heard that such animals could not survive the sea crossing, but obviously they can. Ignore them. They would be good in warfare on the plains, but they will not be able to haul those chariots up the face of these or any other earthworks. He has them for effect, to impress his followers. They need not worry us."

The lines of Wessex priests were now close to the outer face of the earthworks, and Mog Agorn raised his arm aloft and the whole line came to a halt. The Wessex High Priest urged his chariot forward a little. "Who commands the Druids?" he bellowed, and despite the wind his voice rang loud and clear.

Melkor glanced behind him. He could see Vordin and Cludin, and the more elderly of the Council, and a crowd of the younger blue-robed Bards, already hurrying away from Cor Gaur to the south. Fifteen or twenty minutes would see them clear. He stepped forward. "I do!" he called.

"Name yourself, priest!"

"I am Melkor of the Inner Council, battle-commander of the Druids!"

"Do you recognize me, Druid?"

Melkor folded his arms across his chest. "I can recognize evil when I see it!" he shouted. "You are Mog Agorn and your name is cursed throughout this land!" He flung out his arm suddenly and pointed down to the other chariots. "And I also recognize those seven obscenities you call your sons!"

The Wessex High Priest turned to his sons. Suddenly he threw back his head and roared with laughter. "Obscenities, he calls you!" The horses reared at the sound. "The seven obscenities of Mog Agorn! You are well named, you pigs!"

Not one of the seven uttered a single word, but all

eyed their father coldly, with hatred. Melkor had heard that Mog Agorn drove his sons as he would a pack of wild dogs, and that each dog was more inhuman, more foul than he who sired him. Rumor had it also that Mog Agorn's personal bodyguard looked more to the sons than to anyone else as a possible threat to their father's life.

The High Priest turned back to face Melkor. "Enough of these childish insults!" he bellowed. "Do you intend to stand against us, or do you yield?"

Melkor raised his sword and pointed. "Look about you at the Wessex dead that litter the field!" he roared. "Druids yield to no one!"

"Then you will die, Druid," bellowed Mog Agorn in sudden fury, "and all who stand with you!" He leaped from the chariot and handed the reins to a bearer, and the seven sons did likewise. He raised his battle-ax above his head and pointed forward and upward, and the whole Wessex line burst into shrieks of fury and rolled toward the Druid line.

"To your positions!" Melkor said sharply to the other priests with him. "Hold the flanks as long as you can. When your position becomes desperate, order your front rank to withdraw through Cor Gaur to the south and hence to Glaeston, and then let your rear rank take the brunt, and in the final moment get as many as you can of those away as well!" He stared hard at them and held their eyes. "We want courage but not suicide," he said quietly but tensely. "Do not leave your orders to withdraw too long, or else every Druid here will die! Go!" And the priests hurried away along the top of the earthworks to their positions.

He turned to face the attack. The Wessex priests were already halfway up the steep turf bank—a few minutes only would see the first to die. In the earlier encounter at dawn, Mog Agorn had remained in the rear, not willing to risk himself until the Druid mettle had been tested, but now he led the line, proof of his confidence in the outcome. Melkor edged to the left a few yards so that he was immediately above the climbing High Priest, and drew his forces a little more closely to the center. This was where the main battle would be.

Along the edge of the earthworks were several piles of boulders gathered since the earlier attack. He gave a quiet command and the Druid priests picked up as many as they could carry. "They will not kill," he said loudly, "but we may knock over a few and lessen the odds." He closed his eyes for a moment. "And may the Great Ones be with you," he whispered. He opened his eyes and risked a glance behind him, and to his sudden, shocked surprise saw Druthin still at the King Stone, alone, knelt in prayer. He was supposed to have left with the other elders. There was nothing he could do now. He would have to try to get him away on the next withdrawal. He turned back and saw Mog Agorn and the leading Wessex priests only a few feet below. "Now!" he commanded, and a rain of boulders swept the Wessex line. A few dropped unconscious, and a few more were bowled off their feet and slid down the steep face of the earthworks, but the majority came on, screaming abuse, a frenzied horde of mad dogs intent on death. The Druids snatched their swords as the giant Mog Agorn himself came bellowing over the top and plunged into their midst.

The seminaked giant whirled his battle-axe as though it weighed a feather, and in those first furious seconds one, two, and then a third Druid fell, their bodies gushing blood. Melkor saw the brains spill from a shattered skull, and saw the other Druids draw back. He leaped to the front, his sword forward. "Cut him down!" he roared. "He is no immortal!" And he lunged under the swinging axe and buried his sword in Mog Agorn's arm. The giant roared and plucked the blade away and fell back a pace as more Wessex priests came scrambling over the top— and the battle merged into a furious melee in which there was barely room to swing a sword.

At first it went badly for the Druids, six dead against three of the enemy, but the Wessex priests

could not move forward off the edge of the earthworks, and so prevented those following from joining them, and those in the forefront of the fight found
themselves outnumbered. The Druids took heart and
lunged forward, and the Wessex priests began to die.
The melee was so cramped that Mog Agorn found
himself as much hampered by his own men as by
the Druid defenders. Time and again he bellowed
forward, but he could not swing his axe, and each
time he was driven back to the edge. There was a
moment when it seemed that the Wessex would be
driven back off the edge, and Melkor knew that if
that happened the whole horde would turn tail and
run, Mog Agorn or no Mog Agorn. But the High
Priest's sons, more cunning than their father, had
ignored the center and had climbed the earthworks to
the right and to the left and so gained the top with
little opposition, and turned inward to join the melee.

Melkor's heart sank. He had begun with forty
Druids to defend the center—nearly half his remaining force—and already ten lay dead, and the battle
was barely minutes old. With the sons driving in on
either side, he knew he could not hold. He stepped
back, looked to his flanks, and saw that both were as
sorely pressed as he. Indeed the right flank had
already begun to withdraw some of its men who
were racing down the inner face of the earthworks to
safety. He barked an order and half his men drew
back and began to stream to the rear. The remainder
drew together and began to back away, shoulder to
shoulder, swords up, stumbling as they fought backward down the slope. The Wessex line howled in triumph and poured over the top to join the victory.

Melkor suddenly remembered the old man. "The
Arch-Mage!" he called out. "Get Druthin away!" At
that moment Mog Agorn plunged forward and downward, swinging the massive battle-axe clear, and Melkor saw the blade too late. He ducked the first swing,
but stumbled. And the weapon swung back and Melkor was smashed to the earth. "Get Druthin away," he
said, but his voice was a whisper. "Get him away . . ."

But the blackness welled up in him and his mind fled the scene.

The graceful ship, with its single mainsail furled, moved slowly up the River Parrett under the sweep of oars, toward the ancient stone landing jetties at Ponter's Ball. The late afternoon sun was still strong and the oiled bodies of the rowers were beaded with perspiration. Rows of shields ran along the ship's sides from bow to stern, each shield bearing the symbol of Horus such that it seemed as though a hundred giant eyes stared out across the water. The ship-master stood at the bow eying the decreasing distance warily, ready to bark a command to the rowing-master. Behind him the twelve strong bodyguard to Menahotep, the Priest of Re, stood drawn up in ranks ready to disembark. Their swords were drawn and their shields held in readiness, but this was more from custom than necessity, for the Druids at Glaeston were friendly to Egypt and had been for centuries, and the ship was expected. At the stern stood the aged but upright figure of Menahotep himself, and by his side was the young initiate, Ramin.

"Is it as you expected?" said the old man.

The boy shook his head in wonderment. "It's so *green!*" He spread his hands, trying to find the right words. "I've heard you describe it a dozen times and still I did not imagine so much green. And water—there's water everywhere—almost more water than land."

"True," said the old man. "We in Egypt wait for the Nile to flood once a year, and pray each year for it to happen. Here they pray for the river *not* to flood."

The boy pulled his robe more closely around him. "And it's colder than I expected, too."

The older priest grunted. "This is the height of their summer. This is as hot as it ever gets here. Once, many years ago, our ship was driven ashore in the wild sea near the Pillars of Heracles, as the Hellenes call it, and it took us several months to complete the repairs. We should have turned back, but foolishly we chose to continue and so arrived here in the depths of winter, and no words of mine can convey the horror of this land then." He swept his arm around in a full circle. "As far as the eye could see in any direction, the land was covered with snow and ice to a depth of a cubit and more, and there was no trace of green anywhere, believe me."

The ship-master signaled with his hand and the rowing-master barked a command, and the double bank of oars were stilled, poised, like the wings of a gliding bird. Another command, and with a deafening rattle the oars were withdrawn into the sides, and the ship glided on silently to the waiting jetty and came to rest perfectly in position, the twisted vine-ropes flung and secured by the waiting harbor-men in perfect timing. The ship-master came aft. "The Druids are no men of the sea," he growled, "but they always know how to berth a vessel."

"They do indeed," said Menahotep, "and you are no novice yourself, ship-master. Once more I thank you for a safe voyage. We will go ashore at once. I see they are waiting for us."

Ramin was staring curiously at the crowded jetty. It was an honor that so large a crowd had gathered to see them arrive. The group with headdresses and white robes must be the Druid priests, the first he had ever seen. It was strange that their headdresses were similar to his own in style, though not in color. Another example, presumably, of the far-flung influence of Egypt. The remainder were obviously the ordinary people. The men, for the most part, were stripped to the waist, with a curious lower garment made of some animal fur. The women were clothed to the neck with not a single bared breast anywhere that he could see. Their skins were white like dead fish, and rough, presumably from the rigors of their climate. "They are a hideous lot." He laughed.

Menahotep glanced at his young companion. "Does the olive laugh at a fig simply because it is not an olive? You have much to learn, obviously."

The boy cut short his laugh. "I'm sorry. I spoke in haste. It's just that they're so different to us."

"So said the olive. Come, let us go and meet the figs—unless you consider them unworthy of your presence?"

Ramin grimaced. "Enough, my teacher. I stand rebuked."

The gangplank was ready and the two priests, with their bodyguard at their back, went down to meet their hosts. The leading Druid priest, an older man and obviously of senior rank, gave the Druid salute and then embraced Menahotep as an old friend. They exchanged the warmest greetings and then Menahotep turned and beckoned Ramin. "May I present Ramin, my pupil, a Priest of Re. Ramin, pay homage to Hakin, Deputy Arch-Mage of all Druidry."

Ramin knelt and kissed the ring on the Druid's hand. He had previously thought that a deep bow would suffice, but his earlier churlish remark warranted a deeper obeisance as penance. "May the Great Ones smile on you," he murmured.

Hakin lifted an eyebrow. "A courteous youth, Menahotep. Obviously a great credit to you."

"He has been known to err," said the old man drily. "But he may yet become a worthy priest." Ramin stepped back, blushing furiously, but the two elder men turned to other matters. "I am surprised," said Menahotep, "that Druthin is not here to greet us."

"He is at Cor Gaur. Much has happened since you were last here. I will give you the news as we travel." He clapped his hands and a litter was brought forward. The two older men climbed in and the procession moved off, Ramin walking behind. A girl, no older than himself, came to walk at his side. "I am Thetan," she said simply. "Hakin commanded me to keep you company and answer your questions."

Her sudden appearance had startled him. He glanced covertly at her. She was almost as tall as he. Her hair was as black as that of Egyptian women, but it cascaded to her waist and blew in the wind. She wore no headband, nor any form of adornment that he could see. Her eyes were dark and alive. She seemed as fresh and naive as an early breeze, not at all like the heavily oiled, perfumed, and bedecked women that he was used to in Egypt. "Thank you," he said, "but if that's the case then you will be busy, for I have a thousand questions unanswered in my mind." Her stride matched his, boldly, freely—obviously a girl who spent more time in the wind than curled in her chambers. "My name is Ramin," he said.

"I know. I heard. And what are your questions, Ramin from Egypt?"

He laughed and threw up his hands. "Which of so many to put first?" She laughed with him, and suddenly, quite naturally, took his hand as they walked, and he blushed again. "Very well," he said, "first question. Where are we going?"

"To the Druid College at Glaeston. It is only a short walk."

"Much too short," he said, and instantly regretted his words.

She was suddenly shy, but then looked up at him and laughed. "That's the third time you've blushed since you landed!" He looked away from her, but she impulsively squeezed his hand. "I agree," she said solemnly, "much too short for so many questions."

They walked in silence for a little, but then he said: "Is your father a Druid priest?"

"No, both my parents are dead."

"Are you a servant-girl then?" he hazarded.

Her laughter pealed like bells and all heads turned in their direction. "No, Ramin from Egypt with a thousand questions. I am Thetan, a Priestess of the Sun, Pythoness in the Order of Theutates." She turned to him. "But you are right. I serve the Great Ones and as such I am indeed a servant-girl."

His mouth hung agape with astonishment, but then he shut it with a snap. Twice now he had made a fool of himself. "I am sorry," he stammered. "I had no idea!"

"How could you know?" she laughed. "I know I do

not look like anything that an Egyptian would recognize as a priestess, but nevertheless that's what I
am—a Sun-Priestess. In Egypt you call the sun Re,
or Ra, or sometimes Baal, and the Greeks call him
Apollo. Here we call him Og Ock in our tongue."

It was only then that he suddenly realized that
Hakin and the girl had spoken in the Egyptian
tongue. He shook his head. Menahotep was right.
He had much to learn. Clearly these people were no
primitive barbarians. "And Theutates?" he said.

"Theutates is our name for he whom Egypt calls
Thoth, and whom the Greeks call Hermes." At that
moment the procession rounded a bend and again
Ramin's eyes widened with astonishment. The famed
Druid College at Glaeston, a vast stone building, at
least a hundred chambers or more, the entire complex
surrounded by a massive stone wall into which was
set an enormous timbered door with a great iron
circular handle. Even as they approached, the great
door was swinging ponderously open to receive
them "As you can see, we are here," said Thetan, "and
I must leave you to attend my duties. Farewell for the
moment, Ramin, Priest of Re. I pray that we meet
again."

He drew himself up and saluted her, as one priest
to another. "Farewell, Thetan, Priestess of the Sun. I
have been honored by your company." She smiled
and walked on ahead of the procession and through
the gate.

Once in the great courtyard, Menahotep climbed
from the litter and came over to him. He was about
to say something but stopped short. He saw the look
in Ramin's eyes and noted the high color in his
cheeks, and turned and caught a glimpse of the girl
disappearing through a side-door to the main building. "Yes, they are a hideous lot," he said drily.

"She is beautiful," he breathed. "And a priestess!"

The old man smiled. "So the olive finds the fig not
too displeasing, after all? A lesson well learnt, I
think." He took Ramin's arm and led him toward
the building. "Go with the servants. They will show

you to your chamber and bring you food. You will have to dine alone tonight. I have grave matters still to discuss with Hakin, and I will not be able to see you again tonight. Sleep early, for we leave at dawn for Cor Gaur." He held up his hand. "No questions now. I will explain tomorrow. Go now."

The chamber was small but the couch comfortable, and in deference to his warmer blood the servants had placed a brazier in the center of the room, and the heat from it was welcome. The food was simple, a dish of roasted meats, a form of unleavened bread, and a jar of a hideously strong local brew—primitive by Egyptian standards but good enough to more than satisfy his hunger. He made his private obeisance as the sun went down and retired early to his couch to dream of Thetan, servant-girl to the gods.

They woke him while the sky was still black. He breakfasted frugally and speedily, and even before first light he and Menahotep, and the twelve soldiers of their bodyguard, were climbing onto the rough peasant saddles of the great ponderous beasts that the Druids called horses. There was no sign of Thetan and he cursed himself for a fool for hoping that she would come to see him off. Hakin waved them farewell and they turned the horses through the gate towards the east and Cor Gaur. They rode in silence for an hour, for it was obvious that Menahotep was deep in thought, but when the sun rose Ramin could contain his questions no longer. "What grave matters keep you so silent, my teacher?" he said softly.

"There is trouble here." He spoke of the Wessex priesthood and their former honor and all that they had accomplished, but then his face clouded as he described the depths to which they had sunk and of how Druthin had driven Mog Agorn out of Cor Gaur. "But that was three weeks ago. Druthin has simply remained at Cor Gaur with never a sight of the Wessex again, but I'll wager Mog Agorn has not spent these weeks in idleness."

Ramin was silent for a moment and then said: "But why build all these stone circles at all, thousands of them all over the country, and why all the trackways that join them if you say that many of them are rarely used by travelers? And what is so special about Cor Gaur, and why call it by such a strange name? There is no meaning to it, no purpose."

"To the ignorant," said Menahotep impatiently, "there is no purpose to anything except where it relates to their bellies or their loins! Let us see if we can at least clear away some of your ignorance while we ride."

The great horses plodded ponderously on, and Menahotep settled himself more comfortably in the saddle. "As to the name, Cor Gaur, it simply means a 'great circle.' It's inner name, the one that is used in ritual, is Cor Awr, the Circle of Time. The Gaels to the north call it Cathoir Ghall, the Great Choir, from the sound of the inner music that floods a man's spirit when he meditates within its sphere. In the ancient tongue in use when work on it first began, it was called Tyrru Cludair Cyfrangon—from Tyrru meaning a 'cluster,' from Cludair, meaning 'stone,' and from Cyfrangon, meaning a 'compilation by willing cooperation.' A great stone cluster built by willing cooperation."

"A great many names," said Ramin.

"And the marauders from the northlands over the sea," said Menahotep, ignoring the interruption, "call it the Hanging Stones. In their tongue, Stonehenge."

"But why build it at all?"

"To fuse the Solar Force with Cosmic Force and so generate a Life Force that sustains the land and everything on it, minerals, vegetables, animals, and Man himself." He cocked an eye at Ramin. "But that will mean little to you for, without understanding, they are merely words. We in Egypt," he went on, "speak often of the Earth Spirit, as indeed do the Druids here. The Greeks call it Magnes, and this entire world is imbued with this magnetic force, this Earth Spirit." Again he looked at the boy, but he was not getting through. He gave a command and the party came to a halt. "We will rest a while here."

The soldiers drew a little apart, and Menahotep and Ramin sat themselves at the side of the track. The old man took a twig and began drawing lines in the dust. "These magnetic forces cover the entire world in a complex pattern. This pattern expresses itself in lines and spirals—thus."

"The lines are either positive or negative, and spirals either righthanded or lefthanded. In Egypt the land is so flat that there are few spirals, and the lines run for hundreds of miles without deviation. There is only one great spiral in all Egypt, and that's where we built the Great Pyramid. But here in Hyperborea this pattern is so complex and crowded that any given hide of land would have at least two or three lines and at least one spiral. All life is affected by the movement of magnetic forces along these lines and spirals. In the mineral kingdom the magnetic forces cause resonance and oscillation, and in the vegetable and animal kingdoms they cause wave motions in the very structure of the body itself."

"But where did this Earth Spirit come from?"

"From Re himself," said the old man. "This entire world was born as a cloud of fearsome heat from the belly of the Sun and took with it a portion of the Sun's own spirit. We call it the Earth Spirit because it lives in the Earth, but truly it is the very Sun Spirit itself. But away from the Sun the cloud began to cool and solidify, even as a jar of hot wax solidifies when removed from the fire, and as it cooled it did so in accordance with the lines of magnetic force, the Earth Spirit, such that the lines became fixed and no longer fluidic—and remain fixed and unchanging unless an upheaval disturbs them."

"And the trackways follow the lines of the Earth Spirit?"

"Exactly."

"And the stone circles mark the spirals?"

"Not all, but certainly the major ones. When the lines run close together, or when they form a spiral, then the magnetic force is intensified, and it is these points of intensification that have become the points of contact with the Earth Spirit. The greater the intensification, the greater the religious significance, and the point of greater intensification of all in a land is naturally, therefore, the sacred center of that land."

"As at Cor Gaur?"

"Precisely."

The boy was silent for some time, digesting this, and then he said: "You spoke of the lines remaining fixed unless disturbed. You mean disturbed by Man?"

"No, I meant disturbances in Nature—earthquakes and other upheavals. If the structure of the earth changes, then the lines change and adopt new positions. In ancient times, in Lemuria, the sacred center of the entire world was at Shamballa in the east. It was an island in the middle of an inland sea, but a great underground upheaval drained away the entire sea leaving it a trackless waste, a vast desert that the Mongolians today call the Gobi. The Earth Spirit was so disrupted and changed that a new world sacred center had to be established elsewhere, and the great ones chose the continent of Atlantis in the west. That, too, was subsequently destroyed by natural upheaval and again the sacred center had to be moved, this time to Egypt where it now remains."

"Yes, I knew of Shamballa and Atlantis from our own Temple writings. You spoke of the Druids using Cor Gaur to fuse Solar and Cosmic forces. What does that mean?"

The old man eyed his pupil. "Curiosity," he observed, "has an insatiable thirst. Very well. All life, everything that exists, follows the same pattern. The human body contains a complex pattern of lines of force that our healers call the nervous system. The planet of Earth itself has this same pattern. The spirals in the Earth Spirit correspond to the nerve points in the human body, and the magnetic lines of force in the Earth which join the spirals one to another correspond to the nerve paths in the human body. The Great Cosmos itself, of which Earth is but a tiny part, is created in a similar pattern. The stars that you see in the sky correspond to the spirals in the Earth Spirit, and correspond to the nerve points in the human body, and in the same way that the nerve points in the human body are joined by nerve paths, and the magnetic spirals in the Earth are joined by magnetic lines, so too are the great stars of the Cosmos joined by lines of force."

Ramin sat up suddenly. "The great axiom that is written on the Emerald Tablet of Hermes Trismegistus!"

The old man smiled. "The light shines in the darkness—and what does that axiom say?"

The boy quoted from the teaching. "As above, so below, but after another fashion." He looked at his teacher. "But that axiom teaches that physical matter was created in accordance with spiritual nature. As in the spirit, so in matter."

"True, but it also applies to differing levels and degrees of physical matter. However, to continue. The forces that flow along the nervous system of the human body would soon be exhausted if there was insufficient contact with the Earth Spirit, and the magnetic forces of Earth would also become exhausted if there was no contact with Cosmic forces. Each level is sustained by the one above."

"But the Cosmic forces differ?"

"Indeed they do. The type of Cosmic force impinging on this planet at any one time, and its intensity, depends on several factors. Firstly the position of Earth in respect to the Sun. This is why the magnetic intensity on the Earth's surface varies according to the time of day."

"The greatest intensity is at dawn and at dusk?"

the boy hazarded. "Which is why the two main daily rituals are conducted at those times?"

"Precisely. The second important factor is the position of the Sun in relation to the other great stars in the Cosmos, and to the other planets in our Solar Universe."

"Which is why our rituals to the Moon, to the Sun, and to other great beings take place at set times during the year."

"Precisely. The ordinary man is instinctively aware of these forces but does not understand their true nature. We therefore refer to the great Cosmic forces as Set, Osiris, Horus, Thoth, and others—and to the various points of magnetic intensity in the Earth Spirit as godlings, elves, fairies of pools, rocks, and glades." The old man took the boy's arm. "But let me give you a warning, Ramin, lest you go astray in your thinking and your attitude. Just because we now refer to Horus, for example, as a Cosmic force, do *not* make the mistake of assuming that he is not a living being. Continue to invoke him and you will continue to feel his presence as a very real and very powerful living being of Cosmic power!" He let go of the boy's arm and stood up. "The great Cosmic and Solar powers are invoked at Cor Gaur, and the resultant Life Force is caused to flow throughout the land along the trackways, reinforced in each area by the stone circles that mark the spirals of the Earth Spirit. This system of energy transmission is vital in order to enhance the quality of life of the planet itself, of the mineral and vegetable kingdoms, and the quality of life of Man himself both as a species and as individuals. It is essential to both his spiritual and physical welfare. Any danger that threatens Cor Gaur therefore threatens the entire land, and any evil use of Cor Gaur can cause the most dreadful harm to the spiritual life of the nation!"

Ramin's face was clouded with intense thought. "But Menahotep, if. . . ."

The old man held up his hand. "Enough! The lesson is ended. I have sown the seed. It is up to you to cultivate it." He turned and gave a quiet command to the soldiers and then walked to the horses. "I have much to think on. Take two soldiers and ride on ahead to Cor Gaur and announce my coming. No argument, Ramin. Ride on ahead—and take care!"

Ramin knew better than to protest further, and he climbed into the great saddle and rode on, the two soldiers by his side, and soon they had left the old priest far behind. His brain was a whirl of thoughts, but one thing was clear. If the Wessex had been misusing Cor Gaur, then no wonder the Druids had taken arms, and no wonder Menahotep was so worried.

They rode on all morning and at noon they breasted the hill that overlooked Cor Gaur, and as they did so Ramin gasped with the magnificence of what he saw. The double circle of Bluestones and the great Sarsen Trilithons were even more gigantic than his imagination had conjured, but then his gasp of wonder changed to one of horror as he realized the significance of the human figures that crowded the great stone circle.

The dead littered the earthworks by the score. To the south could be seen the distant figures of the remnants of the Druid force making their way to safety and already turning westward to head for Glaeston, and in the center of Cor Gaur itself a group of Druid priests lay bound by thick ropes, guarded by a contingent of priests whom Ramin assumed must be the Wessex. The boy's sharp eyes could see that one of the captives was an old man—might even be Druthin himself, and if so then it was imperative that he be rescued.

Without thinking further, Ramin made as if to urge his horse forward and down the hill, but one of the soldiers grabbed the reins. "Death lies that way, master," he said shortly. "We cannot hope to change things down there with just three of us."

"You are right. I was not thinking clearly." He pondered a moment but could see no solution. "You are warriors," he said. "Advise me."

"We must carry the news, master. We must warn Menahotep and the Druids at Glaeston."

He did not like it, but it was the only sensible course. "Very well, but we will observe for a while. Come."

They moved the horses back a few yards down out of sight and tethered them, and then crept back up to the brow of the hill. Even in that short absence the scene had changed. The older Druid captive, and one other, had been taken to one side, and as they watched they saw the sickening sight of the remaining captives being put to the sword one by one until all lay dead. "By Horus!" whispered Ramin savagely. "These Wessex are no true priests!"

During the next hour the scene was one of bustling activity, as the wounded were tended and the dead dragged to a growing heap outside the earthworks. Then the giant leader of the Wessex, presumably Mog Agorn himself, gathered a party of some fifty or so, including the two surviving captives, and led them out of Cor Gaur toward the north, leaving the major part of his force to guard the great stone circle. The Egyptians watched a while as the party headed north across the plain, but then he saw them turn to the west toward Glaeston.

"On that road," said one of the soldiers, "they will encounter Menahotep."

"Right," said Ramin. "It's time to carry the news. Let's see how fast these lumbering beasts can go!"

Chapter Two

"He is not to be disturbed."

"Who says so?"

"I say so!"

The seven sons were gathered before Mog Agorn's tent. The elder son, Fangorn, was in an evil mood. "Uncle," he said viciously, "you and our father were once two of seven sons of our grandfather, with our father being the seventh and youngest. But five lie dead and only you and he remain." He fingered his knife and glared at the older man barring his way. "How long must we seven sons of a seventh son wait before we take control and command the Wessex?"

Sleg Agorn kept his hand near his sword-hilt. "You will wait the proper time until your father's natural death!"

One of the other sons stepped forward a pace to Fangorn's side. "We saved his life today, the bungling fool!"

Fangorn nodded grimly. "Aye, my brother speaks the truth. If we had not gone to his aid, he would not only have died there on the earthworks at Cor Gaur, he would have lost us the day as well!"

"I commanded the right," said Sleg Agorn, "and so did not observe the center. The truth lies between you and Mog Agorn himself."

"It is the truth."

"Perhaps it is, and perhaps not, but even if you do speak truly you can hardly expect him to reward you by handing over command of the Wessex. He is the High Priest and will remain so until the day of his natural death."

"But that could take forever!" said one of the others.

"No!" The voice was sharp and commanded an instant silence. Awrgon, the youngest son—truly the seventh son of a seventh son—stepped forward. "His time draws near," he said softly and ominously.

Sleg Agorn felt a momentary touch of ice in his heart. All knew that Awrgon had the gift of prophecy, and if Mog Agorn's death drew near, then so did his own. "Then you will not have long to wait," he said calmly.

"Perhaps his time is now," said Fangorn, and drew his knife, and instantly the guard at Sleg Agorn's back snapped to an instant alert.

A horse appeared through the gathering dusk, and a figure slid from the saddle. "Put up your blade, Fangorn," she commanded. "This is no time to squabble amongst ourselves." She was a tall, harsh-featured girl whose eyes glittered like a snake's. Her body glistened with oil, and even at this distance the sons were aware of the heavy musk perfume that their sister always wore.

Fangorn felt his loins stir as they always did at the sight of his twin sister. No other woman could command his lust so easily as she. Time and again he had ridden that wild body of hers, and time and again he had vowed that he would never mount her again, but always her body beckoned, and always his loins responded and commanded his will. It was not good that a man could be so easily swayed. She had lain many times with each of his brothers, even with Awrgon the youngest, but not one of them was so besotted as he, and this knowledge did not sweeten his perpetual anger. "What are you doing here, Asher?" he said harshly. "You were commanded to remain at Abiri."

"No one commands the High Priestess save the High Priest himself," she snapped. "I come and go

where I please." She strode up to him and took the
knife from his hand and thrust it back in his belt.
"And certainly I am not commanded by you!" She
leaned forward and whispered in his ear so that the
others could not hear. "Except at certain times . . ."
she breathed. "Was I to remain in an empty bed at
Abiri, Fangorn, while you were here? My body cannot remain too long away from yours!"

Her breasts pressed against his chest and he could
feel himself growing stronger against her. "Or is it
Mog Agorn himself you want again?" he whispered
harshly. She never denied that she had lain with his
brothers, nor with many another. Rumor had it that
she lay often with their father, with Mog Agorn himself, but this she would neither confirm nor deny.

She smiled at him. "Do not be so foolishly jealous,
my brother," she whispered. "Especially of one so
old as our father. It is you who commands my bed.
The others are merely the dalliance of an idle hour."

His hand tightened on her upper arm, and he
cursed himself for his need of her. They had lain together in their mother's womb and so established a
habit of a lifetime, but even then he had fought to
get away and had torn himself out into the world prematurely, leaving the healers to rescue the tiny Asher
from the bowels of their already dead mother.

She laughed at the expression in his dark face, and
moved away from him and turned to Sleg Agorn.
"Remove the guard, my uncle. I wish to see my father."

Sleg Agorn hesitated. "He commanded that none
may disturb his meditation, Asher," he said.

She moved close to him, her eyes glittering dangerously. "Very well. I will not speak of uncles and
daughters and fathers, Sleg Agorn, but will put it another way. I, Asher, High Priestess of the Wessex,
seek audience with the High Priest and command
you to clear the way. Do you disobey?"

He bowed and muttered a command to the guard,
and they moved to one side. Asher drew herself up
imperiously and strode into the tent.

Mog Agorn lay on a couch deep in meditation. He lay on his back, his arms straight by his sides. His chest barely moved, and when she lay her hand on his breast she could feel that his heart beat at half its normal pace. She moved her hand to his forehead, tapped once lightly with her middle finger, murmured a ritual phrase, and then drew back to wait. Soon his chest began to move with normal breathing, and a few seconds later his eyes opened and he sat up. "Asher! What are you doing here?" he growled. "I commanded you to remain at Abiri."

"And so I did, my father, until I saw certain events that caused me to come here at speed to speak of them."

"Events? What events?"

She fingered the sigil of the High Priestess that hung on a cord between her breasts. "At the fire ritual at Abiri this morning, I saw in the flames your capture of Cor Gaur."

"So?"

"Once I knew of your success, I was about to close the ritual when I saw strangers in the flames. An Egyptian priest and two soldiers were observing you from the hilltop. They waited until you drove off and then returned to the road to Glaeston."

"Egyptians!"

"And that is not all, my father. As I watched the flames I saw them meet up with another Egyptian priest and ten more soldiers. They conferred a while, and then took to the forest to avoid you. They hid themselves and watched you ride by. They then went deeper into the forest and picked up the trackway that leads to Glaeston, the long way around. I could delay no longer. I closed the ritual and rode here to warn you."

Mog Agorn's face grew dark with anger. "Egyptians! How dare they come uninvited!"

"Invited by the Druids, obviously," she said calmly.

"Two priests and twelve soldiers, but how many more at Glaeston?"

"I do not know."

He fumed a while and then said: "You did right to come. Did you see the priests clearly enough in the flames to describe them?"

"One is young in years," she said, "and by his aura he is young in spirit also. I got the impression that his dedication to the priesthood began in this present life of his, and that there was no thought of the priesthood in his earlier lives."

"And the other?"

"An older man, aged even, though he bears himself well. His aura is a brilliant white with flashes of vivid blue like the lightning. He has been a priest for many lives."

"Menahotep!" said Mog Agorn suddenly. "It can be no other. You don't know him. When he was last here you were away to the north, and you were still a child at the time of his earlier visit. His presence here bodes no good for the Wessex. He was always friend to the Druids!" The High Priest paced the tent in thought. "I have already thrown an astral fog over Glaeston," he said suddenly. "They can chant their rituals as much as they like and they will not be able to observe us. As for Menahotep, when the moon rides high we will send a few dark forces to keep him busy. Meanwhile, we will see what our captives have to say." He strode to the tent opening and called a guard. "Bring Druthin here, the old one." The guard saluted and withdrew. Mog Agorn turned back to his daughter. "While Druthin is here, go and visit Melkor. See what effect that body of yours has on his priestly vows. Learn all you can from him."

She frowned. "Are you sending me to another man's bed, Mog Agorn?"

"Why not? There is nothing that so befuddles a man's brain as the warm body of a willing woman."

"Perhaps. But I choose my own men!"

"Then choose this one for me. You may learn something of the Druid plans." He smiled and drew his daughter to her feet. "You will not find it an odious task. The Druid is young and strong, and more fair of face than Fangorn."

She felt herself grow suddenly warm at the prospect. "Very well. I will do it. But only because the High Priest commands it."

"And partly because your own loins command it," he said shrewdly.

She laughed. "You know me well." She moved to the tent opening. "Shall I report to you later tonight?" she said archly.

She stood in the tent opening, provocatively, her legs apart, her breasts glistening in the torchlight, all but naked. The musk perfume was heavy in the air. "Yes," he said thickly, "and do not leave it too long. We must stir things for Menahotep before the moon rises. Go now."

She chuckled low in her throat and left the tent. Mog Agorn was sweating heavily. He sat on the couch and wiped his brow. He looked up as Sleg Agorn came silently into the tent. "What manner of daughter have I sired?" He ran his hands along his thighs. "She is the Dark One herself! Half the Wessex are besotted by her!"

"Including even her own brothers," said Sleg Agorn. "Particularly Fangorn. He would fight half the world for one night in her bed." He looked at his brother cautiously. "And her own father is not blind to her charms either."

"Not blind, but not besotted either!"

Sleg Agorn moved closer to his younger brother. "What if Asher whelps a son? Have you thought of that?"

"If so, then I will claim the child as mine and honor it."

"Fangorn, your son, will undoubtedly wish to do the same. Will you fight your son as to who is the father of your daughter's son?" Mog Agorn did not reply. "And I tell you this, my brother, only a Dark One from the Void could be whelped from such an unholy union."

"Enough!" growled the High Priest. "You go too far. The child might even be yours."

"No, not mine. I am one of the few who remain a

stranger to her arms. If she whelps, then it will be between you and Fangorn, and believe me Fangorn could not ask for a better excuse to force a showdown with you. His burning ambition is to someday command the Wessex."

"That he will never do!"

"Who is to stop him if you die?"

"But I am not ready to die yet. Awrgon, my youngest, will be High Priest after me. Already he is more of a priest than Fangorn will ever be."

Sleg Agorn shook his head. "He would not be able to control Fangorn. The struggle between them would tear the Wessex apart!"

"If he were to succeed me now, then yes I agree. But the time will come when Awrgon will be able to command Fangorn with the flick of an eyebrow. When that time comes, then I will withdraw in favor of Awrgon." Mog Agorn turned to his brother. "But Awrgon himself will only command for a little while. I tell you now, my brother, that there will rise a leader the like of whom the Wessex has never seen. Awrgon's task will be merely to hold the Wessex together until his coming."

Sleg Agorn frowned. "Who is this great one? I do not know of any such as you describe."

"Do not press me further. I have already said more than I should. All I can say is that Fangorn, Awrgon, and even myself, are but children compared with he who is coming to lead the Wessex as High Priest." They both heard the sounds of the guard returning. "Go now and say nothing of this to anyone. If you utter even a single syllable of this matter, you will die a death so foul that men will speak of it for centuries to come, and I would not be able to lift a finger to stop it. Be warned!"

Sleg Agorn left the tent and stood aside as the old Druid was led in to the High Priest. The guard took up their positions again and Sleg Agorn moved away. His brother's words had struck an ominous note. There was obviously some evil that he was planning.

The seven sons were seated by the fire but he did not give them greeting. The most ominous note of all was the fear that he had heard in Mog Agorn's voice, for his brother had never feared anything or anyone. As he passed the tent where the captives were held, he saw Asher inside just closing the tent flaps behind her. Whatever it was in Mog Agorn's mind, it had to do with Asher; but it was doubtful if the girl knew of it as yet. He paused and looked up at the darkening sky. A few of the stars were out already but it would be at least an hour to moonrise. He shrugged and moved on to his own tent. Whatever it was, it would be revealed in good time, and until then it would indeed be wise not to speak of it to anyone.

Inside the captives' tent Asher stood and looked down at Melkor. "I am Asher, High Priestess of the Wessex," she said softly. She moved the torchlight a little closer. "I have come to keep you company." Mog Agorn had indeed spoken truly; he was fairer by far than Fangorn. "It grieves me that so noble a priest and scholar is bound by thongs like a peasant criminal."

"Then free me," he said quietly.

She sat on the couch by his side. "That I cannot do." Her naked thigh pressed close to his, and she could feel the warmth between them. "I would like to, certainly, so that I could come to know you better, Melkor." She leaned over and put her hand on his forehead. As she did so her tunic gaped, as she knew it would, and her warm breasts hung naked before his eyes. "You are perspiring a little," she murmured. "Is it hot in here?"

"It is the nearness of the torch," he said.

She laughed a little and drew back, and as she did so she allowed her hand, as if by accident, to rest upon his groin. She pretended not to be aware of where it lay, and she drummed her fingers thoughtfully. "You are a problem to us, Melkor, you and Druthin." She could feel him beneath her hand, but he did not stir. "What are we to do with you?" Her hand moved slightly, again as if by accident, but still he did not stir.

"Asher," he said calmly, "my body is under my control. When I command it to rise, it rises. When I command it to lie still, it obeys. I am not Fangorn, to be stirred by the fingers of a whore!"

She snatched her hand away and stood up. Her eyes blazed with anger. "You will die for that insult, you Druid dog!"

"Perhaps," he said quietly. "But I would sooner die than add my name to the long list of men who have marched between your thighs."

"Then you are a fool!" she spat. She lifted her hand and smashed her open palm across his face. The rings on her fingers cut deep into his flesh, and the blood ran down his cheeks. His eyes were quite blue, a rare sight in either Druid or Wessex, and their expression did not change one iota. A silence grew between them as she struggled to control her temper. "Let us not quarrel, Melkor," she said at last. "I came here to be friendly, to seek a settlement of the differences between Wessex and Druid. There is no call for you to insult me." She sat down on the couch again and leaned over him. Her breasts fell clear and pressed their softness against his chest. Her perfume was heavy in the air. Her eyes were liquid with desire. Her tongue trailed across his cheek and her hand slid between his thighs. Never before had she been refused by any man, and this new experience inflamed her. "Melkor," she whispered, "be friendly to me!"

He lay quite still, but the revulsion was growing in him more and more strongly. "Asher!" he whispered in her ear.

She had him! She knew it by the hoarseness of his voice. "Yes, my love," she murmured.

"Asher, you are wasting your time," he whispered. "You will have to return to Mog Agorn and tell him that you have failed. You will learn nothing from me."

He felt her stiffen, her hands clenching cruelly. "And you are really not even a very good whore."

She sprang from his side and snatched the dagger from her belt. For a moment she towered above him—her arm upraised, the dagger glinting in the torchlight, her eyes ablaze with fury—and then she turned and ran from the tent.

Fangorn leaped up from the fire and raced to her side. "What is it, Sister?"

"Nothing," she snapped.

"You don't get that expression from nothing. And why the dagger?"

She thrust it back into her belt. "Mog Agorn told me to lie with the Druid to get information, but I couldn't. He is too revolting."

He smiled in the darkness. "Then come with me, sister. You have never found me too revolting." He put his arm around her but she pushed him away.

"Get away from me, you oaf, lest you wish to feel my knife yourself."

He was startled, and fell back a pace. "What is the matter with you?" he snapped.

"Get away from me!" she screamed in fury. "I am not your whore, that I must come whenever you snap your fingers! Leave me alone tonight or you will regret it!" And she turned and ran toward Mog Agorn's tent.

The High Priest came to his feet, startled, as his daughter burst in through the flaps. Her face was a mask of absolute fury. "What is it, Daughter?" he said, though he knew full well. There was no mistaking that particular type of woman's rage.

"These Druids are vile and revolting creatures!" she exploded. "Would that I could wipe every one of them from the face of the earth!"

Mog Agorn turned to look at Druthin. "This old one is not being cooperative either," he said mildly. "Very well, then they must go to their fate." He moved closer to the old man. "Tomorrow at first light we move to the gates at Glaeston and call upon

Hakin to surrender the entire Druid force. If he re-
fuses, then you and Melkor will die the ritual death
on the first ray of the Sun. He will choose wisely,
I think."

The old man did not move. "Hakin will not surrender," he said quietly.

"Then you will die."

"So be it."

Mog Agorn drummed his fingers impatiently.
"You are stubborn, you Druids."

"More stubborn than you realize, Mog Agorn." The
old Druid rose to his feet. "For centuries the Wessex
and the Druids have lived in peace, each fulfilling
their priestly responsibilities with honor. But then
your cursed grandfather, and your equally cursed father after him, began to lead the Wessex on the
paths of evil. And you, Mog Agorn, are intent on
leading the priesthood and the people down to utter
destruction amongst the Dark Ones." His eyes flashed
a blue fire as he faced his opposite number. "You
have not yet begun to realize, cursed one, that every
single Druid in the land is willing to lay down his
life to stop you treading further the foul path that
you have chosen."

"Then let every single Druid die!" said Asher viciously.

"As for you, spawn of filth," he thundered, "there
is a special curse upon your soul, and upon your body,
and in particular upon your vile womb! You above
all others are a particular vessel of obscene evil.
Doubly cursed are you, Asher, for your soul is des-
tined for utter annihilation for what you will seek to
do."

Mog Agorn was silent with shock. It was not possible that the Druid could know of his plans for Asher. He had spoken of them to no one, not even to
Asher herself. He pulled himself together and strode
to the tent opening. "Guard!" he bellowed. "Take this
thing away." And the guards laid hands on the old
man and dragged him into the night. Mog Agorn

flung himself on his couch. His hands were clammy with sweat.

Asher came to stand in front of him. "What did he mean?" she hissed.

"Nothing. The ramblings of an old man."

"What did he mean, Father? That was no rambling curse."

He was silent for a moment. "It is not fit for you to know as yet," he said finally.

"Not fit? I am the one he doubly cursed, not you. I demand to know."

He sprang to his feet in sudden fury and grabbed his daughter by the throat. "You *demand?* Who are you to make demands of me? You will be told when I am ready to tell you, and not before." He flung her to the ground. "Now go and prepare yourself. We have other work to do. The Moon will rise soon and we have Menahotep to deal with. Go!"

Asher glared up at her father. She was filled with a trembling urge to fling herself upon him and strip the flesh from his bones with her hands and teeth, but the fear of him kept her still. "Very well," she spat. "But we will speak of this again, believe me." And she turned and followed Druthin into the night.

For a time they were able to follow the Sun toward the west, but soon it sank from sight and the forest grew darker and darker until they could barely follow the trackway. Before long they were forced to dismount and lead the horses by hand.

"I do hope we find the place soon," said Menahotep. "I am too old to tramp the woods all night."

Ramin looked anxiously at his mentor. "Soon, my teacher, soon," he said softly.

An hour back, when the light was still good, they had seen a small stone circle on a hilltop across the valley. It had seemed the ideal place to head for, to eat their evening meal and camp for the night, but now the sky was so dark and the forest so dense that they were not even certain they were on the

right trackway. But at last the ground began to rise
and the trees began to thin, and one of the soldiers
called back to them that the circle was just ahead.

It was a small circle, no more than a dozen
stones, each the height of a man, with a central flat
stone that Ramin presumed was used as an altar. It
was too dark for closer observation, for the Moon
had not yet risen, and in truth Ramin was too busy
during those first few minutes to spare more than a
cursory glance around him. Since they had expected
to be entertained by Druthin at Cor Gaur, they had
not brought with them any special provisions for a
night under the stars. But they had plenty of furs for
bedding and enough water and dried meats to stave
off thirst and hunger. Ramin made the old man comfortable on a pile of skins while the soldiers foraged
for dry wood for the fire. When this was done, the
Captain came up to Menahotep. "As you can see,
my Lord, we have concealed the fire between stones.
I have been below and it cannot be observed."

"Good. We do not wish to advertize our presence."

"Indeed, my Lord. I will of course be posting a
guard all night."

"Of course."

"And at first light, with your permission, my men
will hunt for game."

The old man sighed. "Fresh game would be welcome, Captain, but we must not delay too long.
You can have from first light to sunrise to kill, to
cook, and to eat, but we travel at sunrise. Understood?"

"Yes, my Lord, it will be done."

Ramin had gone to the edge of the circle to peer
down at the black forest below. He rested a hand
against one of the standing stones and then leaped
back with a startled oath. He had felt a small but
distinct shock in his hand, a tingling in his fingers.
He stared at the stone and saw that its entire surface
emitted a very faint bluish light. He stared again but
the light was so faint that he could not be really sure
that it was there at all. He put out his hand cautious-

ly to touch the stone again, but to his disappointment he felt nothing.

The old man chuckled when the boy told him. "I should have warned you. The stones have life of their own and should be treated with respect."

"But what was it?"

"The light, the tingling? Energy—a solar force—the Earth Spirit—call it what you will. Stone is a crystalline substance and as such it is ideal for the storage and transmission of energy. I told you this morning that the entire network of trackways and circles is used as a form of energy transmission throughout the land. You have felt a little of it, that's all."

"Can you see the light, Menahotep?"

"Not with these old eyes of my body, no, but with the eyes of my spirit I see it as clearly as I can see moonlight or starshine." The old man looked fondly at the boy. "The young miss so much through inexperience, but the beauty of youth is that the wonder of revelation is all before them. If you were more practiced in leaving your body, you would be able to rise up in your spirit and look down and see the network of trackways and circles as a silver web over all the land, pulsing with energy. It is a vision of beauty, a vision of splendor, an insight into the very machinery of the universe itself."

"A silver web!" said Ramin in wonderment.

"At least, that's how it should be," said the old man. "But in truth, since the Wessex took to evil ways the silver has changed to blood-red, and the web pulses with the forces of the Dark Ones, and Cor Gaur is the center of that web, and Mog Agorn the foul spider that feeds on the very life-force of the people and the land itself. Mog Agorn has much to answer for to the Great Ones."

The boy was thoughtful for a moment. "Do you think that Thetan can rise from her body easily?"

The old man shook his head and sighed. In response to a tale of incredible evil, all the boy could think about was a girl. But why not? He was a youth and was reacting accordingly. Only a fool would chide the rain for being wet, or punish a leaf for being green. He chuckled aloud. "Undoubtedly! She is, after all, a Priestess of the White, of the Druid grade, and I believe she also holds high office in the Order of Theutates." His eyes twinkled in the darkness. "Too high for the mating aspirations of a mere junior Priest of Re."

Ramin could feel himself blushing yet again and was thankful of the darkness to conceal it. "You misunderstand me, Menahotep. Curiosity prompted my question, nothing more."

The old man suddenly frowned. "A Priest of Re is a servant of the Truth. Or should be." He looked up at the boy. "Curiosity only?"

Ramin was silent for a moment and then said: "In truth I do not know myself. I am drawn to her. I have never known a woman like her, and that is as honest as I can be."

"It is enough. Sleep now. We have an early start in the morning."

Ramin smiled, made the obeisance, and retired to his own pallet of furs. The soldiers were busy for a few more minutes and then they too retired one by one, until only the single guard was left. The boy lay for some time blinking drowsily at the fire. It was hard being a junior priest. Every word he uttered and every movement he made was automatically weighed against the teachings, and usually found wanting. But then it was no simple matter to be a teacher either, to have to be constantly on the alert for even the tiniest of errors from the juniors. It was no easy life in the priesthood at any level.

He lay and thought of Thetan at Glaeston. He tried to picture the Druid College as he had last seen it that morning, but failed completely. All he could see was a thick black pall of fog. He knew the college was in the fog, but try as he might he could not clear the scene. This was strange, for his imagination was usually strong enough to conjure any scene he wished. Perhaps he was more tired than he knew. He opened his eyes momentarily and saw that the fire was beginning to die down and that the moon had just risen. He closed his eyes again and thought of what Menahotep had said about astral travel. It must be wonderful to be able to rise at will at any time and go anywhere. He knew the theory of it well enough. You imagined yourself floating a little way above your body, looking down on yourself. At that stage it was pure imagination, but then there was a shift of consciousness and you were indeed outside of yourself in reality. That peculiar shift of consciousness could not really be explained, or taught. The student could only be told about it, could only be told that it would happen. And then it was up to him to practice the art until suddenly one day the shift occurred. The first success, however, did not guarantee an easy repetition, for even those skilled in the art still did not know how it happened. The elder priests had said that it had required years of practice before they were able to shift at will at any time. Ramin himself had achieved the shift only twice before, in controlled conditions during his Temple training in Egypt. He had always felt that he would progress more quickly if he could practice on his own, but junior priests were forbidden to practice without the presence of a teacher. It was a cardinal rule and disobedience brought instant punishment. It seemed a harsh rule to Ramin, an unnecessary curb on progress. One tiny practice could hardly cause any harm to anyone. Drowsily, almost without thinking, he pictured himself floating above and looking down at the stone circle, at Menahotep, at the sleeping soldiers, at the single guard sitting hunched and alert by the dying fire, and at himself lying on his pile of skins —and instantly, unbelievably, the shift occurred.

For a brief instant he was filled with elation, but then suddenly the scene below blotted out under a cloud of that black fog that he had seen earlier. Alarmed, he plunged downward towards his body, but the fog began to swirl, faster and faster, building up into a gigantic black vortex. He felt himself caught up in its grip, spinning around and around in the maelstrom, being inexorably sucked down to the eye of the vortex. He struggled and thrashed about in panic, but the grip was too strong, and with a despairing cry he plummeted down into the heart of the vortex and was engulfed utterly. He could still feel himself being whirled around but, totally disoriented, he had lost all sense of direction. Gradually the spinning slowed and came to a stop, but the fog was still around him, and he could see and feel absolutely nothing.

Gradually the fog began to thin, and he became aware of a pulsing red light and waves of almost intolerable heat. As the last of the fog rolled away, he realized that he was in a small underground cave, no more than a dozen yards across. The red light, though of a somber hue, was intense and hurt his eyes. It was pulsing in a manner that he knew to be obscene though there was no rational reason for its obscenity. The stench was appalling, a musty, disgusting smell. The rocks under his hand were wet, not with water but a sticky revolting slime. He felt as though he was in the lair of some foul and loathsome creature of the half-world.

As that thought entered his mind, he saw that the tiny entrance to the cave was blocked by a monstrous spider web, and there in the center of the web was the spider itself, a huge, bloated monster as big as himself. In that instant he knew a fear that he would not have believed possible. Wave after wave of pure terror bubbled up in his throat, and shriek after shriek of near insane screams echoed and reechoed throughout the tiny cavern, and as he screamed the spider moved slightly on its web, and those gigantic eyes turned in his direction. Ramin knew that he was doomed.

His screams reverberated throughout the half-world, and echoes of them disturbed the planes with their ripples of abject terror. So intense and piercing was the call that the last wave, now almost undetectable, even reached Menahotep in his far-off place. The elder priest had traveled in his sleep to an older time, to be with a companion of his spirit who was not currently in incarnation. The two had exchanged greetings and had then fallen into that silent companionship that needs no words. They had created for themselves a scene of tranquillity in which to rest, a gentle river, a grassy bank. But then, suddenly, the scene shimmered slightly as though from a far-off tremor. The two of them were instantly alert. "It is a call," said his companion, "and it is for you, my friend."

"Yes, and an urgent one," said Menahotep. "I must go. Farewell."

"May the Great Ones guard you," said his friend. The scene disappeared and Menahotep woke in his own body. He sprang to his feet and glanced about, but all seemed quiet. The moon was high, the scene tranquil, and the soldiers were peacefully asleep. "Has anything happened?" he said sharply to the guard.

"No, my Lord, nothing. All is quiet."

Menahotep strode over to the boy and peered down at him, and knew instantly that Ramin was in deep trouble somewhere. The boy's face was mottled and almost black, as though something was throttling him. He grabbed the ice-cold hands and sent call after call echoing through the half-world, but after a few minutes of intense effort he knew that he was not getting through. He needed the power of a full ritual to break through and he could not do that here. The only chance of success lay at Glaeston. The full Druid ritual might just be enough to reach the boy.

He strode to the sleeping captain and woke him. "The boy is stricken, Captain," he said tersely. "To horse! We must reach Glaeston without delay."

The captain did not waste time in futile questions. Though no priest himself, he had served with priests of power on many a foreign voyage, and had been involved in many a strange adventure. His function was to defend the priests from physical harm and to leave priestly matters to the priests. He woke the soldiers and within a few minutes they were away, Ramin's inert body thrown across the saddle of the largest horse.

They followed the trackway along the valley. Now that the moon was high their way was reasonably clear, but Menahotep fretted at the slow pace. Suddenly one of the soldiers gave a startled cry, and then the captain and two soldiers plunged into the forest. There were sounds of a scuffle and then they returned, dragging a peasant-girl.

"Who are you, girl?" said Menahotep sharply.

The girl struggled but the captain clipped her ear. "Brisis!" she said angrily.

An arrow whistled out of the darkness and narrowly missed the captain. Then another—obviously from a single bow. The captain barked a command, and three of the soldiers plunged back into the forest. Again there was a struggle, this time more violent, and then the panting soldiers returned dragging a man, an angry and violently struggling man in peasant's clothing. "Spawn of hell!" the man was screaming. "Filth! Scum! Get your hands off my daughter! I will kill her myself before I let you drag her to Mog Agorn's evil rites. You filth!"

Menahotep's eyes narrowed. "I am no friend to Mog Agorn," he said firmly.

"Liar!"

The old man climbed down from his horse and went over to where the man was still struggling in the grip of two soldiers. "Look at me," he commanded. "Do I look like a Wessex priest? We are Egyptians."

The man stopped struggling and glared at him. He looked from the priest to the soldiers and back again, and gradually the anger died from his face. "It could be a trick," he said suspiciously.

"It is no trick. Release him," he commanded, "and the girl." The man, freed, grabbed his daughter. Menahotep turned back to his horse. "Farewell, my friend. We are in a hurry and cannot delay. We must reach Glaeston with all speed."

The man watched him climb back onto the great horse. "Wait," he said. "I know you." He came up to the horse and peered up. "I saw you some years ago. You were with the Arch-Mage. You are . . ." and as recognition dawned on him he dropped to his knee. "You are Menahotep, the Egyptian. Forgive an ignorant woodsman, my Lord. I did not know."

"It is nothing. Forget it."

The man rose to his feet. "Wait, my Lord, please. You can help us."

"I would like to, but we have no time."

"You must. Mog Agorn's camp lies nearby and he has Druthin and Melkor held captive. I crept to a tent and listened. They are going to kill them at dawn! Brisis and I are going to rescue them, and if you are any friend to the Druids you must help us."

The captain grunted. "Just you against fifty? How?"

"We have a way."

Menahotep paused. "What is your name, my friend," he said softly. "And what is your grievance against the Wessex?"

"I am Cyffru, my Lord. I am only a woodsman. I collect wood for the Druids at Glaeston, and Brisis there collects herbs for them."

"And your grievance?"

The man snorted angrily. "Once I had a wife and three daughters, my Lord. Brisis is the only one left to me. The Wessex came and dragged them away to be used in the filthy rites at Cor Gaur. They would have had Brisis, too, if she had not hidden herself in the woods."

"And the others?"

"Murdered!" said Cyffru bitterly. "Murdered when their usefulness was done."

The girl had drawn back in awe at the knowledge of strange Egyptians in the night who spoke the Druid tongue, but now she came forward. She was about the same age as Ramin. Her hair was as black and shining as a raven's wing and her skin was as white as pure cream in a bowl. She was beautiful, with little of the peasant roughness that Menahotep could see. "My Lord," she said urgently, "we do have a way of rescuing the Arch-Mage. We really do, but we must hurry!"

"How?"

The girl hesitated. "By luring away the guard."

The captain smiled. "And how will you do that, wench? Put a spell on them?"

"There is only the one guard, and I will lure him as any woman would lure a man—how else?" she snapped. "I could do it to any man, though I wouldn't bother with a dolt like you."

The captain began to berate the girl, but Menahotep said sharply: "Be quiet, all of you. Let me ponder." He had a problem, a choice of two priorities. If he delayed any further, Ramin might die. But if Druthin were to die, then the Druid cause would collapse. Hakin was a good man and a good priest, but he could not wear Druthin's mantle. He glanced at the boy. His face was still dark and his breathing still labored, but at least he was no worse—as yet. But in the final analysis it would be worth one Egyptian life if it would help destroy the Wessex, even if it was indeed the life of the one he loved as a son. "Very well. We will help you."

After a brief discussion they left the horses and Ramin in the care of six of the soldiers, and Cyffru led the remainder off the trackway and through the dense forest. Soon Menahotep was panting heavily even though he was being helped along by the captain. "Not far, my Lord," Cyffru whispered. "But we must be quiet."

A few minutes later they crept to the edge of the forest and there before them was the highway between Glaeston and Cor Gaur, and at the side of the highway were the tents of Mog Agorn's band. All was still and quiet. Only one of the tents showed a light. "That is where Mog Agorn is," whispered Cyffru, "and that hell-cat, Asher. I saw them go in earlier."

"And that," thought Menahotep, "is where they set the trap for Ramin."

"And that tent there," the woodsman whispered, "is where they are holding the Arch-Mage."

"And only one guard, as the girl said," the captain said.

"Brisis," whispered her father, "go ahead. We do not have much time."

Now that they were here, the plan seemed ridiculous. "Are you sure this is going to work?" said Menahotep.

"Be assured, my Lord," the man whispered. "You do not know the Wessex as I do."

The girl stood up and moved out of the forest toward the tents. As she moved, she began to untie her waist-cord so that her dress fell back. She was completely naked beneath the gown. Her bare feet made no sound on the turf. The guard-priest was so drowsy that he did not see her until she was almost on him. He snapped to the alert, startled, and leveled his spear. He could hardly believe his eyes. He peered suspiciously at the forest beyond, but not a leaf stirred. He knew he should call out, to summon the other guards, but he could barely take his eyes off the vision he was seeing. "Who is it?" he whispered. Surely none of his fellow priests could summon an astral like this. Unbelievable though it was, she had to be real.

She came up to him. "Just a girl of the woods," she said demurely, "out collecting herbs by moonlight."

"Naked?"

She tossed her head. "Fine priest you are if you do not know that love-herbs must be collected naked! You are a priest, aren't you?"

"Yes," he said. He licked his lips and stared greedily at the girl's body. "And also a man."

"Oh, a man are you? I would not have known." She used her dress to hide her body. "You don't look like any real man to me."

"Man enough for you," he said roughly and reached for her, but she slipped away.

"Poor specimen you are," she retorted. "You cannot

even catch a slip of a girl like me!" She let loose the dress again and her breasts shone in the moonlight. "I cannot waste my time with you." She tossed her head and moved away toward the forest.

"Wait," he commanded, but she did not stop. He took a few paces after her and then looked back. The guard would not change for another hour—time enough to collect a few herbs.

She heard him coming and gave a low laugh and ran for the forest, her dress streaming behind her, her breasts bouncing. He came flying after her and never saw the spear that tore into his throat, killing him instantly.

Menahotep shook his head. So simple! Lust could indeed be a costly vice. "Fetch Druthin," he commanded, "and the other. Hurry!"

The captain and two of the soldiers ran silently to the tent. The captain called softly, and a minute later they returned with the two Druid prisoners. Menahotep stepped forward to greet his old friend. "From the majesty of Sesostris III, King of Upper and Lower Egypt, may he live forever," he said softly. "To you, Druthin, Arch-Mage of all Druidry, I bring greetings!"

Druthin stepped forward, hardly able to believe his eyes. "Menahotep! What manner of miracle is this?"

"A miracle of a people's love for their true leader, Druthin." He turned and drew his two new friends forward. "To Cyffru, your woodcutter, and to Brisis, your collector of herbs, you owe not only your life but possibly also the salvation of all Druidry. It was their plan and it was they who carried it out."

Both of them knelt before the old Druid, but Druthin raised them up. "Words are too inadequate to express so large a debt," he said quietly. "The Great Ones will not forget, and nor will I."

Melkor came forward. "And I, too, will remember you for the rest of the life you have given me."

Druthin turned to the Egyptian. "And what of the other miracle? How came you to this hour, Menahotep? Is life too dull for you in Egypt?"

The old man chuckled. "It will seem so after this. But we must make haste. There is another who has been taken by the Dark Ones, though in a different manner. I will explain as we go."

Cyffru and Brisis led the way. Ramin was still as they had left him, for which Menahotep was truly thankful. They turned the horses to the West and pressed on as fast as they could, and as they went the two older priests, one Druid and one Egyptian, spoke of all that had happened. "Dark days indeed," said Menahotep.

"And will grow darker yet before the Light shines again," said Druthin. "But shine again it will, of that I am confident."

They cleared the forest just on first light—half a mile only to Glaeston. Suddenly the captain knelt and put his ear to the ground. "Horses," he said sharply. "And coming quickly. We are discovered!"

Their own great, lumbering horses could go no faster than a clumsy trot. One of the horses carried Menahotep and the unconscious Ramin, and the other bore Druthin. The captain and all twelve soldiers took the rear. Melkor ran by the horses' side. Cyffru and Brisis ran on ahead to alert Glaeston.

Five hundred yards . . . three hundred . . . Cyffru and Brisis were within earshot of the great gates. "The gates," he yelled. "Open the gates! The Arch-Mage Druthin is rescued! Open the gates!"

Behind them, from over the brow of the hill, came the chariots of Mog Agorn and his seven sons, but the rest of his band were far behind. The Egyptian captain smiled. "Keep calm," he said to his men. "Twelve Egyptians against eight Wessex is hardly a contest."

Ponderously the great gates of Glaeston College moved slowly open. Cyffru and Brisis were through. Mog Agorn came roaring down upon them, but too late. The two great Druid horses lumbered in through the gates. A flight of arrows rained from the battlements. The Egyptian guard fell back steadily and calmly. Mog Agorn, with only himself and his seven sons, hesitated, and in that moment the Egyptians withdrew into the courtyard and the great gates thundered shut.

Hakin came rushing out of the main building. "Druthin! Druthin! We had given you up for lost." There were tears in his eyes. "They have thrown a fog over Glaeston. We could not find you."

The two Druids embraced warmly. "I am well, Hakin. But make haste. There is one here who needs our help. Open the Hall of Ritual, get Thetan, and come yourself. Hurry!"

Some younger priests appeared and bore Ramin into the main college, along a series of flag-stoned corridors, and into a vast stone-walled chamber that must have been at the very heart of Glaeston. All others withdrew leaving only Druthin, Hakin, Mena-hotep, and the priestess Thetan who had arrived at a run. Menahotep stared curiously at the great chamber. Around them rose a grove of black pillars, polished, symmetrical. The floor was of black and white paving. At the center stood the altar of the double cube with a Light upon it. Around it were the high seats of the Magi. Druthin had been ex-plaining quickly to Thetan. Now he said: "I will take the East. You in the West, Menahotep, Thetan in the South, and Hakin in the North. When we are ready, you, Menahotep and Thetan, will go out after him. Hakin and I will guard the Temple and keep clear the way for your return."

They placed the inert body of Ramin by the altar and took their positions. When they were seated, Druthin began to intone the opening phrases of the ages-old ritual, and already Menahotep could feel the forces gathering. With the seals firmly set on the cardinal points, and the lines of force drawn, Druthin drew himself up. "East and West, South and North!" he thundered. His voice rang with power and rever-berated down the planes. "Seek and find, ye of other evolutions—seek and find! And thou, great lords of the manifested universe, thou Lords of Flame, and Form, and Mind, and thou great Lords of Humanity who are as yet unborn—draw near, ye mighty ones, and give succor to we, thy servants, who stumble in darkness and who are beset by the Dark Ones! Command thy servants of other evolutions in the name of the Most High that they may guide us truly in the worlds below! Seek and find, ye brethren of other evolutions—seek and find!"

With a great crashing roar, the inner doors sprang open and a mighty wind swept to the four points of the heavens, and the earth, and the dark places beneath the earth, and Menahotep, the Egyptian priest, and Thetan, the Druid priestess, slipped from their bodies and allowed themselves to be rushed within the wind, borne up by unearthly hands, carried by the servants of the Most High, beings of evolutions other than earthly humanity. Faster and faster they whirled, and down and down they plunged to the Dark Regions below, down into the pulsing blood-red depths of foulness and obscenity, until at last they were brought to a rushing halt, floating, borne up by many hands, and there below them was a cave, a monstrous web sealing its entrance, a bloated spider dancing with loathsome anticipation—and through the web, within the pulsing cave, they could see Ramin, his back to the far wall.

"Ramin," thundered Menahotep. "Ramin, Priest of Re! Gather thy courage and come forth."

From within the cave Ramin could see his friends outside and heard his teacher's command. He stepped forward joyfully, but the spider danced on the web and he drew back in terror.

"Ramin," came the thunder of his mentor's voice. "Come forth!" But still he could not move.

Menahotep knew that spiders, even the tiniest of the species, were the one thing that the boy feared above all else. Mog Agorn must have drawn that fact from the boy's mind.

At a command Thetan was lowered to the ground. She walked forward toward the cave. The spider turned at her coming.

"Go back," shouted Ramin. "Go back!"

She held out her hands toward him. "Come to me, Ramin," she called, and her voice was clear, without a trace of fear.

"I cannot. I cannot!"

"You must or you will be lost! The spider does not exist! It is not there! It is a projection of your own terror! Come to me before it is too late! If you delay too long, the spider will draw more and more force from your depths until it achieves an independent life of its own, and then it will be able to destroy you! Come out, Ramin. Just walk through it. You will not be harmed!"

A projection of his own mind? It could not be. It simply could not be! The sight, the smell of it, the loathsome creature's evil eyes . . . The web . . . It could not be!

"Ramin," thundered Menahotep. "She speaks the truth. Command your fear to be still and walk out. You will not be harmed!"

He took a step forward, and then another. He faltered. "Have faith in my words," cried Menahotep.

Thetan stepped closer until she was almost touching that monstrous web. "It does not exist, Ramin! Walk toward me. Keep your eyes on me. Do not look at it. Stretch out for my hand. Do not falter—step by step!"

He took another pace—another—now he was so close he could see the individual hairs on the monster's legs.

"Look at me," Thetan cried. "Keep your eyes to mine. Keep coming. Keep coming!"

Another step and he brushed the web, and in that instant the great, loathsome, obscene creature leaped upon him, its fangs close to his face, its revolting hairy legs wrapped around his body. He started to panic anew.

"Don't fight it," thundered Menahotep. "Keep walking!"

"Come to me," Thetan called. "One more step. One more, Ramin. Ignore the creature!"

A great bubbling terror welled up within him. He

tried to remain still, not to fight, but the creature was all over him, its fat glistening body pressed against his mouth. He could stand it no longer. A scream of abject terror was bursting his throat.

"One more pace and you will touch my hand," Thetan cried. "One more pace!"

The very soul of him was bursting with terror, but he took one more stumbling pace and felt the coolness of Thetan's hands, and in that instant the spider, the web, the cave, the pulsing and obscenely revolting red light all disappeared and he came shrieking back into his own body in the ritual chamber at Glaeston, vomiting, crying, scrabbling in profound terror at the floor—but safe!

Chapter Three

"Trouble indeed, my Lord," said the ship-master, "but I do not like the idea of abandoning you."

The Egyptian vessel still lay berthed at Ponter's Ball. Menahotep stood at the head of the gangway. "I am not asking you to abandon me. I say again: At the very first sign of danger you will immediately take the ship downriver and, if necessary, you will put to sea. But you are to remain close to shore. I will find a way to get a message to you as to where to pick us up." He eyed the ship-master sternly. "Your first priority is the safety of this vessel, otherwise none of us will see Egypt again for a very long time. Do you understand?"

"Yes, my Lord."

"Very well. Frankly, I am surprised that Mog Agorn did not try to take the ship this morning. We can be thankful that he must have had other things on his mind." He looked down at the crowded jetty. "Warn your men not to stray too far. If the Wessex come down on you, it will be sudden and swift. You will not even have time to untie the warps. Just cut and run, even if you have to leave some of your men behind. I cannot stress too strongly the importance of keeping this vessel safe!"

"You need have no fear of that, my Lord. I will keep her safe and do as you say." He grinned suddenly. "But I tell you this, my Lord, Wessex or no Wessex, trouble or no trouble, this vessel brought you from Egypt, and it will take you back again—that I promise you!"

Menahotep smiled. "I hope you are right." A sudden thought crossed his mind. "But how are your provisions?"

"Already taken care of. Normally I would leave the water-casks till last, but in view of what happened this morning I have already begun to take on a certain amount, enough anyway for an emergency. And I have taken the liberty of purchasing three bullocks, my Lord, from one of the local peasants. If we do have to leave in a hurry, we will have enough provisions for at least a week, and we still have plenty of corn. If necessary we can always put a landing party ashore to hunt for game and get more water. We will not starve."

"Good. You obviously have everything in hand." He paused for a moment. "And the local peasants —no problems?"

"None. They seem to like us well enough, and they certainly like the sight of the gold I paid for the bullocks."

"Good. Then I will leave you to your tasks. If you need me I will be at Glaeston."

He stepped ashore and passed along the crowded jetty. Some of the men nodded and smiled at him, and he returned their greetings gravely. One burly fellow stood in his path. He was naked to the waist, a short, squat, ugly man with great knotted muscles. "Some of us have heard," he growled, "that you helped rescue the old Druid." His accent was thick, and Menahotep had difficulty understanding him.

The Egyptian paused, his way barred, and others began to crowd around. "My part was small," he said carefully, "but I was certainly there." There were no Egyptians nearby, nor any of the Druid priesthood. By the look of him this fellow could snap a man's neck with his bare hands.

"The Druid healers once saved my child," he said.

"And mine," said another.

A smaller man pushed his way to the front. "Once, last winter, the hunting was poor. The Druids performed their magic and told us where to go, and the game was there even as they had said!"

Menahotep smiled, suddenly relieved. "They are fine priests," he agreed. "But what of the Wessex priesthood?"

One of the other men spat on the ground. "They are servants of the Dark Ones."

"They took my two daughters," said another, "and I have not seen them since."

"I have heard," said another, "that there are strange signs in the sky when the Wessex meet, and on the following day there is blood on the giant stones!"

They were all silent for a moment, and the Egyptian could see the fear in most of their eyes. The first man, the burly squat fellow, grunted angrily. "I know nothing of signs, or of blood," he growled. "Nor do I know aught of the Dark Ones. But you tell the old Druid this: If the Wessex come, many of us will fight alongside the Druids. You tell him."

Menahotep looked around the small crowd. "All of you?" he said softly.

"All that you see here, yes. But others have too much fear in their bellies and will run when the Wessex come."

The Egyptian stared thoughtfully at the man. "What is your name, my friend, that I may convey your message?"

The man flexed his muscles. "He knows me. I am Gargan, the stonecutter."

"Why have you not told him yourself?"

"We did," said one of the others, "but he fears for our safety, since we do not have stone walls and a great gate to guard us like the Druids."

"We are not children to be shielded from danger," said another.

"We can fight if we have to!"

"It is our wives and daughters who are carried off."

"Aye, and our homes burned to the ground!"

"We have a right to fight!"

Gargan raised his arm for silence. "And there is the

truth of it, Egyptian," he growled. "We have the right to fight. You tell the old Druid."

Menahotep nodded. "I will tell him, my friend, and thank you." He moved on and the crowd parted to let him go.

Once at the College, he sought out Druthin and told him what Gargan had said. The Arch-Mage was silent for a moment and then said: "Menahotep, there are those within the Druid ranks—Vordin foremost amongst them—who feel that the Druid priesthood should not oppose the Wessex, but should seek the help of Egypt. In my opinion this would be an abrogation of our responsibility." Druthin's private chamber was in the eastern quarter—a small, sparsely furnished, stone-walled room with a brazier, a couch, a rough-wood table, benches, and a great carved chair. "This situation is a clash between two types of priesthood—the Dark and the Light, if you like—and as such the struggle must be resolved by the priesthood itself." He drew the wineskin toward him and filled two beakers, pushing one toward the Egyptian. "I will not seek the aid of the Egyptian army, nor will I endanger the lives of the people by involving them in our struggle."

Menahotep nodded. "The principle is correct. Indeed, you must not abrogate your responsibility by handing over the problem to a layman army, Egyptian or any other. But the situation with regard to the people is different." He sipped the wine and took a piece of the rough Druid bread. "By accepting help from them, you are still keeping your responsibility. Indeed, I believe you are further fulfilling it." He broke the bread into small pieces and began to eat slowly. "I am not saying that you should go out and arouse the countryside to war. That is perhaps premature, though it may come to that yet. But I have spoken to several peasants who, through their own inner states, have recognized the difference between the two types of priesthood, have made their choice between them, and who now wish to activate that choice by direct physical-plane action. Such are entitled to the opportunity desired. By so doing they will be serving the Great Ones. It is a form of initiation for them, if you like, and I believe that you are abrogating your responsibility as a priest by denying them this opportunity."

"But they may die if they fight!"

"As Gargan says, they have a right to fight. And he is correct. After all, Druthin, it is their women who are dragged off to obscenity, torture, and death, and it is their homes that are burned. As for dying, each incarnation comes to an end sooner or later. If by actively opposing Mog Agorn they forfeit their lives, then their deaths will be with honor. And anyway, I have the feeling that Gargan and his friends are going to fight whether you approve or not, and it would be better if they fought under Druid guidance rather than rush off on independent action."

The Druid sighed. "Yes, that certainly is true. The thought of Gargan and his friends rushing off in all directions has caused me many a sleepless night." He offered the wine again but the Egyptian refused. Druthin poured a little for himself and sipped it thoughtfully. "There are certainly many ways in which they could be useful to us."

"Indeed, yes."

"They could, for example, keep watch for us at Cor Gaur and at Abiri, and give warning should the Wessex move in force toward Glaeston."

Menahotep nodded encouragingly. "And if the Wessex moved in force, they could harry them at night." He remembered the arrows that had come whistling out of the blackness of the night forest. "When the Wessex make camp at night, our friends could burn their tents by using fire-arrows, and then vanish into the forest."

"True. They certainly know the forest better than either Wessex or Druid." He glanced at Menahotep and smiled. "I feel better already," he confessed.

The Egyptian laughed. "A problem shared always

sits more lightly on the shoulders." He rose to his
feet. "You have more than enough on your shoulders
with other matters. Leave me to organize the peasants. And I will place my captain and his soldiers
under Melkor's command. The captain is a wily bird
in the ways of war. Melkor will find his advice invaluable."

Druthin also rose. "Thank you, my friend," he said
softly. "You bring a little light into darkness."

"To add to your own. Together we may yet dispel
the darkness that is Mog Agorn and his brood. And
now I must visit my foolish young pupil to see how
he fares."

"He is awake and well, and wiser for his experience, I think," Druthin said. "Thetan is with him
now."

"Ah yes, Thetan. Ramin's heart beats more soundly
when she is near."

"And hers, too, though she hides it well."

Menahotep paused by the door. "Truly?" He was
thoughtful for a moment and then smiled suddenly.
"A marriage between Egyptian and Druidic Mysteries would be no bad thing."

"He would be welcome among us as a priest. We
will, of course, offer him initiation into Druid rites, as
is our custom for visiting initiates of the Egyptian
priesthood—as you yourself were initiated many
years ago—but now our offer may perhaps have special significance."

"It may indeed. Have they met before?"

"Not as far as I can judge. Thetan has not incarnated since Atlantean days—she was a priestess there
also—and this incarnation is Ramin's first in the priesthood. Their paths have not crossed before."

"A new beginning for them. I will look upon
them with different eyes than hitherto."

Ramin's chamber was in the northern quarter, and
the carved oak door was slightly ajar. Menahotep entered silently and smiled to himself as Ramin hastily
moved away from Thetan. The boy's face was flushed,

though Thetan remained calm. "Greetings, Menahotep," she said gravely in almost perfect Egyptian.
"Ramin has recovered well, as you can see."

"Greetings, priestess," he said. "His stupidity and
disobedience hardly warranted so easy an escape. He
may not be so lucky if such a thing occurs again." He
turned to his pupil. "Your incredible folly not only
endangered your life," he said harshly, "but put your
very soul in danger! Not only that, but others had
to risk their lives in order to rescue you. You deliberately disobeyed a cardinal rule. When we return
to Egypt you will be summoned before the Council
of Priests to give account. It would not surprise me
if you were expelled from the priesthood. What
have you to say?"

Ramin stood up to face his teacher. His cheeks
were burning. "I recognize my folly," he said tautly.
"I can only bow to the authority of the Council,
thank those who aided me, and give my solemn oath
that it will not occur again." He struggled to find the
right words. "I cannot adequately express how deeply
sorry I am that I let you down."

It was handsomely said, but Menahotep merely
grunted. "Because of your folly I had to leave our
refuge and bring you to Glaeston, and so put in
jeopardy our entire party!"

"By leaving your refuge," said Thetan coolly, "you
were able to meet Cyffru and Brisis, and so were able
to effect the rescue of the Arch-Mage. Were it not for
that fact, Druthin would probably now be dead, and
without Druthin the Druid cause is lost, and if the
Druid cause is lost, then this land will be plunged
into utter darkness for many centuries, perhaps forever."

"Cyffru and Brisis would have rescued Druthin
without our help."

"Perhaps—perhaps not. We will never know."

"Are you saying that Ramin was guided by the
inner planes that night to leave his body?"

"Why not? It is possible. The events were hazardous, true, but the result could not have been better. We are all here safe at Glaeston. That you cannot deny."

Ramin held his breath. There were not many who would even dare argue with Menahotep at all, let alone so commandingly.

The older priest sniffed and turned his attention again to Ramin. "And while you were in that cave in the half-world, I commanded you on several occasions to come forth, but fear kept you rooted. Such fear is not expected in a Priest of Re."

Ramin made as if to speak, but Thetan interrupted. "All of us have known fear, Menahotep," she said fiercely. "There is no shame in that. But the test of a human is whether he can rise above that fear, and Ramin certainly did that."

"Only by an extreme effort."

"But nevertheless he did it!" She was not quite so cool now. Her face was as flushed as Ramin's. "We in the priesthood come to know and experience the half-world gradually, under careful guidance. And again it is only gradually that we are brought to face the dark reaches of our inner selves. Ramin was brought face to face with both, suddenly and without warning, and without anyone to guide or help in those first moments. Most would have succumbed almost immediately. Frankly, I was surprised to find him still unconquered when we arrived—few at his level could have survived that long—and when he commanded his fear, and walked out with that loathsome thing clinging to his face and body, it was the finest act of bravery that I have ever seen in my life—and if the Egyptian priesthood is so stupid as to punish such valor, then it is you and those like you who should be brought to account, not Ramin!"

Ramin closed his eyes and offered up a silent prayer. Never had he heard anyone speak to Menahotep like that, but at the same time his heart leaped at what Thetan had said of him.

Menahotep's expression did not alter. "Ramin," he

said calmly, "you and I will speak of this again when this tigress is not around to defend you." He turned and walked across the room and paused by the door. "And as for you, priestess, by all means leap to his defense against his enemies, but do make some effort to find out who his enemies are before you rush into battle!" His eyes were twinkling as he left the chamber. Druthin was right about Thetan's feelings. It had been worth being harsh with the boy to have brought that truth to the surface.

When he had gone, Ramin let out his breath in a sudden gasp. "By all the powers of Re, you Druids do like living dangerously!"

"Pompous fool," she said sharply. "He must be blind!"

He shook his head. "He sees more clearly than any other I have known—and he was right. It was curiosity and impatience that led me to disobediently experiment, not the inner planes. You spoke yourself of learning under careful guidance. We were lucky that it turned out as it did."

"Perhaps so, but he had no right to speak to you as he did."

"But he had, Thetan. He not only had the right, he also had the duty as my teacher to comment sternly on my failings. Have you never been rebuked by Druthin?"

She was quiet for a moment. "Yes, once," she said, and suddenly smiled, "and he was just as harsh and pompous as your Menahotep."

He moved closer to her. "There you are, then." He took her hand. "What you were saying about me makes me think that . . ."

Before he could finish, she disengaged herself and moved slightly away from him. "I know the direction in which your thoughts are moving, Ramin." She looked at him directly, and her dark eyes were warm. "But it is too soon for such thoughts. Later, if you are of the same mind, we will speak of such things, but not now."

"But . . ."

"Later, Ramin, later." She rose and moved to the embrasure in the northern wall. "Before Menahotep arrived, I was telling you the meaning of the word 'Glaeston.' In our ancient tongue the word 'glas,' or 'glaes,' meant 'green,' and the word 'ton' meant 'hill.' Glaeston therefore means the Green Hill—and as you observed when you landed and walked up to the college, we are indeed situated on a green hill. The village by Ponter's Ball where you landed is a community in its own right and as such is a 'biri' in the old tongue, now corrupted to 'boro' or 'borough' or 'bury.' Its true name is therefore Pontersbury Ball. But because it is situated so close to the hill, it is often referred to as the Borough of the Green Hill, or Glastonbury."

Ramin shrugged his shoulders and grimaced to himself. It was lesson-time again, obviously. Later he would speak of more important things. "Very well," he said resignedly. "I accept. Glaeston means Green Hill, but this college is not on the hill, but at its base, and I noticed that there is a stone circle on the summit, and within the circle something that looks like a tower."

"Yes, Glastonbury Tor. In the ancient tongue, 'tor' did indeed mean 'tower'—the 'tor' on the 'ton,' the tower on the hill. Glastonbury Tor therefore means, in the ancient tongue, the Borough of the Green Hill on which stands the Tower, but we call it Glaeston for short." She came back to the couch. "And you were going to show me a parchment that shows the plan of your Great Pyramid."

"Yes, I have it here." He unfolded a piece of parchment and spread it out. "It is only a rough drawing. The original is kept in our Temple, but each student is required to make his own drawing from the original, and this is mine."

She looked at it carefully. "It doesn't mean a thing to me. I'm afraid I don't know the Greek science of geometria, or even the Greek runes, alpha, beta,

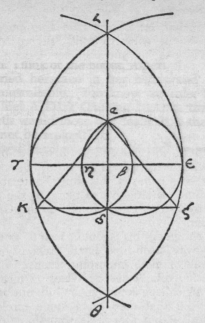

and the rest—though I recognize them when I see them."

"It doesn't really matter. Look at the drawing. The two small circles are the same size. Each has a diameter of 555½ of your Druid feet. You can see that the diameter of each passes through the center of the other."

"Yes."

"Good. Now, using epsilon and gamma as centers, you draw those two large arcs so that they intersect each other at top and bottom. You then join the two intersecting points by that vertical line there. Now at that point there, delta, on the base of the vesica, you draw a line parallel to epsilon/gamma. You then draw two lines from alpha to the two points where that line intersects the two outer arcs. The resultant triangle is the basic figure of our Great Pyramid. The height is 480½ feet, or 280 Egyptian cubits. Each side is 755 feet, or 440 cubits. And the perimeter is 3,020 feet, or 1,760 cubits." He looked at her anxiously. "And the whole thing is called a tetrahedron and has a base angle of 51 degrees 51 minutes." She did not say anything at all—just looked at him. "If it is not clear, I can express it in some other runic characters if you like."

"No," she said hastily. "It is as clear as it will ever be."

"Good. Now the original measurement of 555½ feet for the first circle is very important—it must be exact—because a circle with that diameter has a circumference of 1,746 feet, and the basic spiritual equation is $1,080 + 666 = 1,746$. All life is created by the fusion of two principles, the positive dynamic and the negative receptive, represented symbolically by sulphur and mercury. And in the other science of gematria, the science of numbers, sulphur is 1,080 and mercury is 666. Also, 666 is the number of the Sun, of Re himself. And the tip of solid gold that sits on top of the Great Pyramid is itself a tiny pyramid whose number is again 1,746, which is also the number of the mystical Grain of Mustard Seed. At our Great Pyramid is thus achieved the marriage of heaven and earth, the union between the Earth Spirit, the magnetic current within the Pyramid, and the divine spark of Solar Force which is derived from the ether of the gold tip. And thus the Great Pyramid is one giant generator of Cosmic Force!"

She smiled at him gently. "You are quite learned, as well as brave," she said softly.

"I can explain it some more if you like."

"No, not now. Let me borrow your parchment and meditate on what you have told me. Later I may have some questions for you. In the meantime I also have a parchment to show you." She pulled a roll from her robe and spread it out. "You mentioned the science of gematria. We, too, know something of that, though we express it in terms of the magic squares. Look at that and tell me what you think."

4	9	2
3	5	7
8	1	6

SATURN
15(10)×3=45

4	14	15	1
9	7	6	12
5	11	10	8
16	2	3	13

JUPITER
34(17)×4=136

11	24	7	20	3
4	12	25	8	16
17	5	13	21	9
10	18	1	14	22
23	6	19	2	15

MARS
65(26)×5=325

6	32	4	3	35	1
31	5	33	34	2	36
30	8	28	27	11	25
7	29	9	10	26	12
24	14	22	21	17	19
13	23	15	16	20	18

SUN
111(37)×6=666

22	47	16	41	10	35	4
5	23	48	17	42	11	29
30	6	24	49	18	36	12
13	31	7	25	43	19	37
38	14	32	1	26	44	20
21	39	8	33	2	27	45
46	15	40	9	34	3	28

VENUS
175(50)×7=1225

8	58	59	5	4	62	63	1
49	15	14	52	53	11	10	56
41	23	22	44	45	19	18	48
32	34	35	29	28	38	39	25
40	26	27	37	36	30	31	33
17	47	46	20	21	43	42	24
9	55	54	12	13	51	50	16
64	2	3	61	60	6	7	57

MERCURY
260(65)×8=2080

37	78	29	70	21	62	13	54	5
6	38	79	30	71	22	63	14	46
47	7	39	80	31	72	23	55	15
16	48	8	40	81	32	64	24	56
57	17	49	9	41	73	33	65	25
26	58	18	50	1	42	74	34	66
67	27	59	10	51	2	43	75	35
36	68	19	60	11	52	3	44	76
77	28	69	20	61	12	53	4	45

MOON
369(82)×9=3321

He studied the chart for a moment and then shook his head. "I don't see how the glyphs are derived from the squares."

"All right, take the simplest one, Saturn." She bent over the parchment. "There are nine numbers from 1 to 9. You simply write them out in order in a perfect square—1, 2, 3 on the top line, 4, 5, 6 on the second line, and 7, 8, 9 on the third line—and use a dot to mark the position of each number—like this."

$$1. \quad 2. \quad 3.$$
$$4. \quad 5. \quad 6.$$
$$7. \quad 8. \quad 9.$$

"You must make sure that the dots form a perfect square though. You then refer to the magic square and join the dots in the order stated. For Saturn you begin by joining dot 4 to dot 9, then dot 9 to dot 2, then dot 2 to dot 3, then dot 3 to dot 5, and so on. For Saturn you will see that each vertical line and each horizontal line adds to 15. There are three lines, and $15 \times 3 = 45$, which is the sum total of all the numbers in the square. The number of Saturn is therefore 3, and 45 its inner secret—and the glyph is the symbol of it."

"Fascinating."

"You can do the same for each of the magic squares, and you will arrive at those glyphs there. On each of the squares, bar one, you will find that each horizontal line, each vertical line, and each diagonal line all add up to the same number. You multiply that number by the number of lines to arrive at the basic number, which is 45 for Saturn, 136 for Jupiter, 325 for Mars, 666 for the Sun, 1,225 for Venus, 2,080 for Mercury, and 3,321 for the Moon."

"All bar one, you said."

"Yes. The Sun is a special case. The horizontal lines do not add up to 111, nor do the opposite corners add to 37. Each vertical line adds to 111. And not only that, but each pair in each vertical line adds to 37. On each of the horizontal lines throughout the square, the two triplets on each line add to either 38 or 36, and if you read the pairs downward, the figures 38 and 36 alternate on each line. This is one of the prime secrets of the magic square of the Sun, not known to many, that the principle number of 37 is repeated over and over again, either pure or plus or minus one. Each vertical adds to 111 and there are six lines, and $111 \times 6 = 666$, the number of the Sun. Some priest-mathematicians have been completely unable to solve the glyph of the Sun. They produce a magic square whose opposite corners do indeed add to 37, and where both vertical and horizontal lines add to 111, but the glyph that is produced from that square is nonsense." She stabbed a finger at the parchment. "*That* is the correct way to form the square of the Sun. All other so-called Sun Squares are incorrect."

He laughed in admiration. "All this is very clever," he admitted, "but to what use is this knowledge put?"

"We build our stone circles according to those glyphs," she said simply.

He looked at her doubtfully. "How?"

She bent over the chart again. "All right, I'll show you how Cor Gaur was built. It was required that Cor Gaur be dedicated to the Sun, and therefore it was built in accordance with the glyph from the magic square of the Sun. You can see that the glyph throws up two centers. Using each center in turn, you draw a series of arcs from the top points to the bottom points, and where the arcs cross each of the points, that is where the major stones are located. And if you would care to pace around the perimeter of Cor Gaur, you will find that the measurement is 370, and 370 is the sum total of the numbers around the outer edge of the magic square of the Sun—37 the principal number again."

He studied the glyph, and then the building plan. "That's incredible!"

"Thank you, but the Druids did not build Cor

Gaur. It was the Wessex who erected the giant stones. They were once a very fine people indeed."

"They must have been." He frowned. "But they are not true circles."

She smiled. "Indeed, they are ellipses. When you travel around our land, have a closer look at our so-called circles. They are all ellipses."

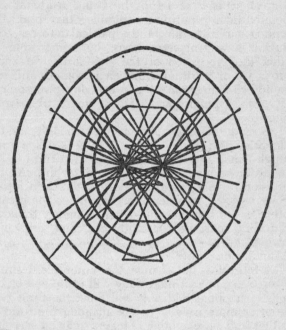

He straightened up. "And can you really call down the power of the Sun at Cor Gaur?"

"Of course, and not only call it down but radiate it throughout the land along the trackways, reinforced and relayed on by every stone circle, cairn, dolmen, and mound throughout the entire kingdom."

He smiled in admiration. "That really is quite remarkable."

"Oh, and that's not all. At Cor Gaur we can predict

every eclipse of the Moon, every eclipse of the Sun, and the movement of every single star in the heavens for the next thousand years. On a short-term basis, for day-to-day ritual purposes, we are vitally concerned with the relative positions of the heavenly bodies, because by knowing in advance which cosmic forces are going to be focussed on us, we can help the great scheme of things by being ready at the appointed time to perform a suitable ritual to aid the reception and radiation of the particular forces concerned. On a long-term basis, by being able to predict the Procession of the Equinoxes, we know what phase of spiritual evolution is coming and can so guide the direction of our evolving philosophy."

"Evolving philosophy? Does your philosophy change then?"

"The mode of expression changes, though not the basic principles. Every spiritual force seeks a form through which to express itself, and that form is human attitude, human thinking, and feeling. As the expression of that force deepens, so the form has to change, to grow, in order to accommodate the greater expression, and so human attitude, human thinking. and feeling must be constantly changing, constantly evolving."

"And if it does not?"

"If a form does not change, the inexorable desire of the force to manifest more fully will cause one of two things to happen: Either it will burst the form from within; or more usually it will abandon the form altogether and seek another. Many a religion has died because it refused to change. The indwelling force is withdrawn, leaving the religion as an empty cult whose rituals are meaningless and without life." She gathered her parchments together and rose to her feet. "And that is what happened to the Wessex. At one time they were a fit vessel for the indwelling force. But having built Cor Gaur and the other great circles, and having laid out the network of trackways, they were vain enough to think that they had reached the peak of their evolution and so resisted any urge to change, and thus they ceased to grow. The force was withdrawn to seek new expression, which is how the Druid cult arose. The empty vessel of the Wessex, however, did not remain empty for long. The Light having been withdrawn; the Darkness entered, and instead of evolving upward toward ultimate life and creation, they are now plunging downward toward ultimate death and destruction."

"And we Egyptians?"

She shrugged. "If you continue to evolve, then fine. But if ever your philosophy ceases to grow, then inevitably the time will come when your priesthood will have been forgotten, a time when even your Great Pyramid will have become a plaything for children, a curiosity for the ignorant to gape at."

He felt the shiver of an impending doom. She spoke the truth. He had heard Menahotep say much the same thing. Indeed, the old man was more worried than he showed, for he said that there were already signs within the Egyptian priesthood of a philosophy that had become stagnant. There was already an attitude that sought to maintain the existing scheme of things simply because it had been that way for a thousand years and more.

"And now I must go," she said. "I have to prepare for this evening's ritual."

He took her arm. "When can we speak of other things?" he said quietly.

Her eyes softened. "Later, Ramin, later. The time is not right."

"I accept that. But when?"

She hesitated and then said: "When the Wessex are destroyed, and when the Druids stand at Cor Gaur in all their ritual strength, when the power of the Serpent rules the land, *then* I will speak to you. Be content until then." And she turned and left the chamber.

He remembered the symbol that hung at Druthin's neck: A serpent entwined about a pillar of rock—the Power of the Serpent, the sign of the Druid. Very well. He would wait.

He sought out Menahotep and told him all that had passed between Thetan and himself—or most of it. "She is no child," Menahotep agreed. "Do not be fooled by her youthfulness. In terms of the priesthood, she is of a higher grade than you. She was already a priestess in ancient times in Atlantis, whereas this is your first life as an initiate of the Mysteries."

"So I am beginning to realize," he said feelingly. "It is a bit disconcerting to find a chit of a barbarian wench turning out to be a priestess of an advanced grade."

"Does it worry you?"

"A bit, but she is also a woman, and her spiritual powers have to be expressed as a woman. She may not realize it, but a time will come when her womanhood will seek to fulfill itself."

"Ah, the beginnings of wisdom! And you will be waiting, no doubt."

He smiled. "Perhaps. We will see." He looked thoughtfully at his teacher. "You have never told me much about Atlantis," he said.

"Nor will I. Atlantis is the source from which both Egyptian and Druid have sprung. Knowledge of Atlantis is something that you have to seek yourself."

"How?"

"By remembering."

He frowned. "I do not understand."

The old priest smiled. "The waters at the mouth of the Nile remember the source from whence they came—for one very obvious reason. Do thou likewise." Ramin made as if to speak, but Menahotep raised his hand. "Enough! This is something that you must do yourself. There is the Beginning, the Ending, and the Way Inbetween for all things. The Way Inbetween can seem so long and winding that only faith can believe in the truth of the Ending, and only memory can link to the Beginning. But from another viewpoint, there is no ending, and no beginning, and no way inbetween, for all are three facets of the same jewel. To link the past with the present, and with that which is to be such that all is One, is the work of the priesthood. What you have been, you are now. What you will be, you are now. It is a question of latent potential or activated functioning. Go and meditate on these things and seek your own answers."

The old man rose and walked over to the embrasure and looked out on the courtyard. "Ah, I thought I heard sounds. The Druids are gathering for their ritual. Come, we had better join them."

They walked down to the courtyard together. "I have been trying to find out what this ritual is all about," said Ramin.

Menahotep smiled. "To make the flowers grow."

"As simple as that?"

"Not really, but it is as good a way of describing it as any." The flag-stoned corridor was quite cold on their feet. "The Druid calendar is remarkably similar to our own. In Egypt our year is divided into three seasons, each season having four months of thirty days each. Our year begins with the heliacal rising of the star Sothis in the eastern horizon just before dawn."

"Osiris," quoted Ramin softly, "it is Sothis, thy daughter, thy beloved, who has made thy year offerings. Years are reckoned from her shining forth."

"Precisely. That event we call the 'Opener of the Year.' Our months are named after the most important feasts that occur in them. Name again for me those feast months."

Ramin cleared his throat. "The four months of the first season, *Bahte*, are: Thoth, Phaophi, Athyr, and Choiak. Of the second season, *Apurte*: Tybi, Mechir, Phamenoth, and Pharmathi. Of the third and last season, *Somewa*: Pachons, Payni, Epiphi, and Mesore."

"Correct. Twelve months of 30 days each making 360 days—plus the five epagomenal days after the twelfth month making a year of 365 days." They arrived at the Great Door and stepped out into the courtyard. "The Druid year is also 365 days, but they divide it into eight parts of 45 days each, with the same five days left over as we. Their 'months'—if we can call them that—are named after the ritual that commences each period. Their year begins with the Vernal Equinox. Then comes Beltane, the Summer Solstice, Lammas or Lughnasadh, the Autumnal Equinox, Sowen or Samhuinn—sometimes called All Hallows, then the Winter Solstice, and finally Candlemass, the Festival of Brighid at which they perform an incredibly awe-inspiring ritual called Washing the Earth's Face at Imbolc."

"Each year is 365 days," said Ramin, "but they begin theirs at a different point to ours."

"Indeed. Our 1 *Bahte* 1—or *Tipy Renupet*—the rising of Sothis occurs somewhere between their Summer Solstice and Lammas."

"And today is Beltane."

"Yes. The spring sowing took place at the Vernal Equinox 45 days ago, and today the Ritual of Beltane is to encourage the sturdy growth of the new shoots. It also helps the growth of the newly born animals, the fledgling birds, and indeed everything that lives."

They fell silent as the assembled priesthood began a low-keyed chant. The courtyard was beginning to fill up. Along the outside walls were assembled the ranks of the Bardic Grade, their blue robes dazzling against the whiteness of the stone walls. By the Great Gates were assembled the green-robed Ovates and Ovate Druids. Before the door of the main building were gathered the white-robed senior Druids, Melkor and Vordin amongst them. Each grade had its sprinkling of seeresses and priestesses, though the male priests outnumbered them four to one. It was the priestesses who had begun the chant, low, soft, and hauntingly beautiful. Ramin tried to catch the words but they eluded his ear. They were probably in the ancient tongue.

Melkor came over to them and bowed. "When we move off," he said softly, "our guests will be welcome amongst the Druid grade."

Menahotep bowed in return. "We will be honored."

At that moment Druthin, the Arch-Mage of all

Druidry, and Thetan, Pythoness, to the Order of Theutates, appeared in the doorway. Instantly the chant rose a key, and the deeper voices of the priests joined those of their sisters.

Druthin and Thetan moved across the courtyard, between the ranks of the priests and priestesses, toward the Great Gates, and as they did so the Ovate Druids removed the bars and the gates swung ponderously open.

Druthin carried a great carven staff, the Serpent entwined on a Pillar of Rock—the sacred emblem of Druidry—and as he moved through the priesthood each one bowed and made the deep obeisance.

Ramin could hardly take his eyes from Thetan. She wore a full-length silver robe that was almost transparent. Her movements were so graceful that she seemed to glide, to flow, rather than walk. Her black hair cascaded to her waist and stirred in the evening breeze, and her body rippled like silver water in moonlight as she moved.

As Druthin passed, the white-robed Druids fell in behind, Menahotep and Ramin amongst them. The Ovates, Ovate Druids, and Bards followed in line, and the whole procession, with Druthin and Thetan at its head, passed out of the great College and began to move up Green Hill toward the Tor.

The route they followed was helicular, slowly moving around the hill, gradually moving upward with each circuit. The path they followed was well trodden. The local peasantry lined the path from top to bottom, and as the procession wound its way upward they fell in behind as the line passed. Ramin spotted Cyffru, the woodcutter, and his daughter, Brisis. He tried to catch their attention as he passed, but they did not see him.

The chant did not cease; indeed its tone deepened, and as they moved slowly upward, more and more of the column began to sway to its rhythm as they walked. The effect of the deep, resonant chant and the swaying bodies was almost hypnotic, and despite himself Ramin began to sway with the others, and as he did so, he stopped trying to analyze what was happening, stopped being merely an observer, and became part of the magic of the ritual, receptive to its mood and influence.

The procession became a serpent, coiled around the hill, gradually moving upward. Druthin and Thetan at its head were its two eyes, the column its body, the serpent gliding upward toward its ritual destiny, its mating with the Moon-force that would descend to fuse with this ritual offering.

The stone circle on the summit radiated a faint blue light, and pulsed with seeming anticipation. Druthin and Thetan, the serpent's eyes, guided the way into the circle and then stopped, the serpent's body gradually entwining itself throughout the shimmering stones until the whole snake lay coiled on the summit, waiting.

The Tower was in the western quadrant, a giant needle of a stone, thrusting to the evening sky. At its base was a flat stone. Druthin and Thetan moved to the West, and Thetan laid herself on her back full-length on the flat stone, her arms and legs spread-eagled, her raven's hair spilling in a cloud across the stone. Druthin took up his position behind the stone, facing the center of the circle, and raised his arms to the rapidly darkening sky. As he did so the chant rose a tone, and deepened its intensity, waiting.

Druthin began to chant in the ancient tongue, intoning the words sonorously and vibrantly, pointing his serpent's staff at the distant horizon. The tableau poised, vibrant, expectant, waiting, pulsing, and then the Moon, the Queen herself, rose as if bidden by the Druid command, and the first ray of her power lanced between two stones and fell on the flat stone at the base of the Tower, bathing the waiting High Priestess, the Pythoness, in a pool of vibrant silver. As the moonlight flooded over her, Thetan moved and undulated, still in time to the rhythm of the chant, swaying her body, inviting the intercourse with the Moon, drawing it into herself and holding it until her body pulsed with the power of it.

Druthin pointed with his staff again, this time at the senior Druids, and one by one the procession moved slowly past the writhing priestess, each one placing his hand on her brow and drawing into himself the power that she radiated.

As Ramin reached the stone, he saw her face, radiant as the moon itself, her very skin a shimmering silver, and as he put his hand on her brow, he felt the inrush of power and his heart leaped and his whole being quivered with the force of it. He moved on, following the procession, coiling in and out of the radiating silver stones, and back down the hill. As he swayed and moved and danced to the now joyous chant that welled up over Glaeston Tor, he saw the incredible sight of the silver power spreading out ahead of them, racing down the hill, splitting into dancing threads of glittering light that flowed along the trackways, across the plain, through the forest, bursting into silver fire as it reached each of the stone circles, racing on to the distant hills, a glittering silver web throughout the land—and he saw the Earth stir and absorb the life-force, and he felt the burst of new life. His heart uplifted, and his soul sang of joy and beauty and the wonder of all that is.

Chapter Four

Hakin, the Deputy Arch-Mage of all Druidry, walked slowly along the banks of the River Parrett lost in thought. After a nighttime moon ritual he always felt the need to walk on grass in the sunlight, to be with the trees and the flowers, to hear the birds, to feel the rush of daytime life. He was never at his best in moon rituals, they always disturbed him too much. He was much more at home in the sun rituals.

He was more pleased than he cared to admit that Druthin was safe and back with them again. Naturally he was pleased for Druthin's sake, but his pleasure was more than a little tinged with pure relief. The possibility of him having to lead the Druids was a terrifying one. He had no illusions as to his position as Deputy Arch-Mage. He owed his position to his scholarly ability and his ritual prowess. He loved nothing more than to escape the everyday world through the inner aspects of a good ritual, or to escape into the realm of his academic studies, and his love of such pursuits made him good at them. He simply would not have been able to cope as the leader of Druidry, particularly in times of war. He could make ritual decisions, and could make academic decisions, but he could never make decisions involving human relations, particularly where human life or human destiny was in danger. He would be too easily swayed by the opinions of others instead of following the commands of his own inner knowledge and inner contacts. He was in many ways a coward, and had said as much to Druthin on more than one occasion. Druthin had said that "cowardice" was too strong a word, but Hakin knew in his heart that the word was accurate. He needed the experience of having to make decisions that involved others, but such experience was rare, for all matters were automatically referred to Druthin. He sighed as he walked. He was obviously not ready for such command; perhaps in the next life he would be given his chance.

He rounded a bend and came across a young Bard stretched asleep on the bank. He prodded the form with his staff and the boy sprang to his feet, startled, terrified almost. "Thought I was Mog Agorn, did you, boy," he said gruffly. He never really knew how to deal with children. In many ways they frightened him more than adults. "It would have served you right if I had been. Where are your senses, sleeping out here in these troubled times?"

The boy rubbed his eyes. "I . . . I'm sorry . . . I'm sorry, my Lord." He looked around him. "It was still dark when I came. I didn't mean to fall asleep."

"You attended the ritual?"

"Yes, my Lord."

"Then you should have followed the Serpent home, not gone off on your own." He looked more closely at the boy. "You're Zelta, aren't you?"

"Yes, my Lord."

"Melkor mentioned you to me. Cludin is your master, is he not?"

"Yes, my Lord."

"Then you had better report to him immediately. He will be worried about you." He eyed the boy sternly. "And tell Cludin from me that you are then to report to Vordin for corrective measures to curb your disobedience."

The boy's heart sank. Vordin was a dour, ill-humored man. Amongst other duties he was also responsible for the fulfillment of the principle known as the Admonition of the Magus. Breaches of discipline were always referred to him for corrective measures, and his admonitions were well-known for their dispassionate sternness, and the willow wand that he wielded was noted for the sting of its bite. Zelta hesitated. "I will do as you command, my Lord Hakin," he said, "but Vordin is not at Glaeston." He looked up at the disbelieving expression on the older man's face. "I saw him ride off—truly I did!"

"When was this?"

"This morning, my Lord. It was still dark. The ritual was barely over when I left the Serpent to come here, and as I came to the river I saw my Lord Vordin leading one of the great horses toward the road to Cor Gaur."

Toward Cor Gaur? What was Vordin doing in that direction? And in the secrecy of darkness? "Was he carrying his staff?" he said to the boy.

"Yes, my Lord. And he wore his traveling cloak."

Cloak and staff! Obviously no restless jaunt but a genuine journey of some length, and there were only two places of significance on that road, Cor Gaur itself and the Great Circle at Abiri, both held by Mog Agorn. What mischief was Vordin up to now? Something of no good, to judge by the secret departure. Vordin must be stopped, must be recalled to Glaeston for explanation. He looked down at the young Bard. "What time was this?"

"About an hour before dawn."

"And it is now about an hour after dawn—a two-hour start." Hakin knew that Vordin hated horses and would walk most of the way. He would only ride occasionally to rest his legs, and anyway, the great horses could not travel faster than a man's fast walk. But it would take another two hours to return to Glaeston and organize a pursuit, giving Vordin a four-hour lead. Too much. If Vordin was to be stopped the pursuit had to begin now. He took the boy's face into his hands and stared hard into the young gray eyes. "I hear that you are something of a runner."

"Yes, my Lord."

"Could you overtake Vordin for me, before he reaches Cor Gaur, and give him a message?"

The boy's eyes widened excitedly. "I could try, my Lord!" he said eagerly.

"Very well." He took the great ring from his right hand. "Give him this as proof of your message. Tell him that it is my command that he return to Glaeston at once—at once! Have you got that?" Zelta repeated the message. "Good. Off you go then."

The boy sped away to the east, to the road to Cor Gaur, and Hakin hurried as best he could to Glaeston. Once there, he roused the council members and the two Egyptian priests to an urgent meeting in the Hall of Learning. They had been up all night at the Ritual of Beltane and were not pleased to be routed at so early an hour, and as such they were perhaps more testy than they would have been in other circumstances. Cludin in particular was terse indeed. "Do I understand you correctly, Hakin, that you have sent an eleven-year-old boy on foot and unprotected to Cor Gaur, right into Mog Agorn's hands?"

"Not to Cor Gaur, Cludin—to catch up with Vordin."

"With a two-hour start he will be at Cor Gaur by the time the boy reaches him! You may very well have sent him to his death!"

Hakin's manner was glacial. "You are over-dramatizing, Cludin. The important thing was to stop Vordin."

"Why?"

The question hung in the air, and Hakin was taken aback. "That is obvious," he said testily, but the others could see that he was suddenly unsure of himself.

"No, it is not obvious," said Cludin sharply. "Explain it to me."

Hakin drew himself up stiffly. "I do not have to explain myself to you, Cludin."

"I think you do!"

Hakin tried to gather his resolve together. "It should be obvious even to you, Cludin, that one of the possibilities is that Vordin has gone to Mog Agorn to betray us."

"So what?" Cludin's eyes were sharp. "What could he betray? We have made no specific plans, and therefore there are none to reveal." He stepped forward a pace. "We are not sure that he has gone to Mog Agorn at all. He might be absent for any one of a dozen different reasons. And yet in the face of all these unanswered questions, you have taken it upon yourself to send a mere boy into danger, and if he comes to harm on this foolish errand then you, Hakin, will have much to answer for!"

Druthin rose and stepped forward. "Enough of this squabbling! Your words are ungracious, Cludin, even though they are born of your love and anxiety for your pupil." He looked around grimly at the assembled council. "Hakin is right in one thing. It is certainly possible that Vordin has gone to betray us, to weave his destiny with that of the Wessex."

"If so," said Cludin acidly, "then I for one can face his absence from our ranks with considerable equanimity!"

"Again your words are ungracious," said Druthin.

"Perhaps so, but they are spoken from the heart. Vordin has no stomach for this struggle. If he has gone to Mog Agorn, then I say good riddance!"

Several of the council members nodded. Vordin was not popular amongst them. "Very well," said Druthin, "your feelings are noted, Cludin. If, however, Vordin returns and it is proved that he has not betrayed us, then you will make full obeisance to him in the gorsedd before all Druidry here at Glaeston."

"That I will do, and gladly."

"So be it. The matter rests there."

Cludin shook his head. "With all the respect I can command, Druthin, how *can* the matter rest there? Whether Vordin is traitorous or not, it still leaves the boy, Zelta, in considerable danger."

"What would you have me do?"

Cludin wrung his hands in desperation. "Something, at least! Can we not go after him? We cannot just sit here and wait."

Druthin turned to Melkor. "Is there any means at all whereby we could overtake the boy?"

Melkor shook his head. "None at all. There are few enough adults here at Glaeston who could outrun the boy even with an equal start, let alone with an hour's difference."

Druthin turned to Menahotep and Ramin. "Is there anything the Egyptians could do to help us in this matter?"

Menahotep also shook his head. "Regretfully, no. For the same reasons."

"Then we will wait." He looked at Cludin and his eyes softened. "I am sorry, Cludin," he said gently, "but there is no other decision that we can take. We can only wait—and pray."

He dismissed the meeting but motioned for Hakin to remain. When they were quite alone, Hakin said: "I know what you are going to say, Druthin—that my decision to send the boy was ill-considered."

"Does your opinion differ?" he asked softly.

"No, I agree. Now that I have had time to think, I can see that the decision was a rash one. If Vordin is indeed going to join Mog Agorn, then no command of mine through Zelta would bring him back."

"And if Vordin is *not* going to join Mog Agorn, then there was no reason to send anyone after him."

"I see that now, but at the time it seemed the right thing to do. I can only pray for the boy's welfare."

"And I for your's," said Druthin gently.

Fangorn stood on the hill overlooking Cor Gaur. His face was dark with long-suppressed fury. "I called you up here alone," he said fiercely, "so that the others would not see us at variance with each other."

Mog Agorn grunted derisively. "The difference between us is already well known!"

"But so far we have never quarreled openly, in public."

The older man nodded grudgingly. "True enough," he growled. "Very well, Fangorn, speak what is on your mind."

The elder son fingered his knife. "Just one question, Father: Why don't we go in and finish off the Druids once and for all?"

Mog Agorn stared in disbelief for a second and then bellowed with laughter. "Fangorn, you never cease to amaze me! You're no good as a priest, and you're no good as a warrior! How I ever came to sire a son such as you is beyond me."

Fangorn's hand trembled with rage. "Don't underestimate me, Father," he hissed. "I may yet be the cause of your downfall. In the meantime, answer the question."

Mog Agorn shook his head despairingly. "Look, boy, the Druid College at Glaeston is no village hovel. Its outer walls are of solid stone eighteen feet thick, and their outer face is as smooth as ice and thus unscaleable. There is only one break in those walls, and that is where the gates are situated, and those Great Gates are made of specially treated hardened wood six feet thick and impervious to fire. It is said that seven great trees that had stood for a thousand years went into the making of those gates. Oak trees, boy, the Druids own sacred tree, constructed no doubt under special ritual conditions. They have their own chalybeate well in the courtyard that never runs dry, and so they would never lack for water. I know for a fact that they have enough provisions stored within those walls to withstand a siege of a year or more. A hundred ordinary men could withstand an army of thousands, and the Druids are no ordinary men. On top of all this, they are masters of ritual magic. Believe me, boy, there is no way for us to take Glaeston!"

Fangorn shook his head. "Are you saying that we cannot defeat the Druids?"

Mog Agorn grinned. "No. I am saying that we cannot take Glaeston. But the beauty of it is, we don't have to." He eyed his son mockingly. "You don't understand, do you, boy? Look, we hold Cor Gaur and Abiri, and thus control the land. To defeat us the Druids have to leave Glaeston and come to us. The last time they tried that it cost them dearly. Next time it will cost them all they have. When I have finished with them there will not be a Druid left alive to defend their precious college. Glaeston will lie empty, its Great Gates open, and we will walk in unopposed. Don't talk of taking Glaeston by force, boy—we don't have to!"

At that moment they both noticed a single chariot leave Cor Gaur and come racing toward them. The horses were a beautiful sight—slim, fast—nothing like them had ever been seen before on these hills. Awrgon, his youngest son, reined the chariot and pointed to the west. "A Druid—alone—walking—leading a horse," he shouted. "Coming this way. I have sent the guard to bring him in."

Down below, Mog Agorn could see twelve of the guard leaving Cor Gaur at a trot, their sword-blades glinting in the sun. "Go with them," he shouted. "You may have to run him down. Bring him to the King Stone." He turned to Fangorn. "As I said, boy—they have to come to us!"

"One lone Druid is no victory," sneered his son.

"It is a start. Come, let us go down."

Half an hour later, Awrgon and the guard returned, and with them was a disheveled, dusty figure, his cloak awry, and blood on his face. "He was too pompous for my taste," said Awrgon, "so I roped and dragged him behind the chariot to teach him some manners!"

Mog Agorn grinned. "Who is he?"

"He says his name is Vordin of the Druid inner council, but he doesn't look like any senior priest to me."

Vordin stepped forward. His eyes were blazing with anger. "I am who I say I am," he said roughly. "You have no right to treat me like this."

"No right?" said Mog Agorn softly. "We are at war, Druid—remember that. And when you speak of rights, remember also that it was the Druids who started this war, not the Wessex!"

"Be that as it may," said Vordin. "I have come to seek a settlement of our differences so that this war may cease. Too much blood has been shed already— blood that either of us can ill afford!"

"That certainly is true," said Mog Agorn. He eyed the Druid thoughtfully. "So Druthin seeks a truce, does he?"

Vordin shook his head. "He seeks a settlement, certainly, but he does not know that I have come here today, nor does Hakin, nor indeed do any at Glaeston. We conducted the Rite of Beltane last night, and I slipped away at dawn. Most at Glaeston will sleep the day through. Providing I am back at Glaeston by late afternoon, none need know that I have been here to Cor Gaur."

"A secret mission—and without authority."

Vordin looked around at the assembled Wessex. "As to authority, Mog Agorn, a settlement that preserves the honor of both Wessex and Druid will be authority enough, surely."

Suddenly a sword-blade glinted from a hilltop to the west. Once, twice, three times it flashed. "We will wait," said Mog Agorn. "The guard have found something."

"Hear me out, Mog Agorn!" cried Vordin.

The High Priest of the Wessex glanced up at the hills and then back to the Druid. "You are suddenly anxious," he said suspiciously. "Have the guard found something that you know about?"

"How do I know what your wretched guard have found?" he said angrily. "It has nothing to do with what I have to say."

Mog Agorn frowned. "There is something here I do not like," he said suddenly. "We will wait. If you utter one more word without my permission, I will have you thrashed! Keep your tongue still, Druid." Vordin threw up his hands in exasperation, but wisely kept his mouth shut. Mog Agorn was suddenly in a vicious mood. "Keep him here," he growled. "I will go and meet the guard." He climbed the great outer earthworks and waited on the summit. The guard came down from the hill and threw a figure at his feet—a boy, robed in blue, a neophyte of the Bardic Degree. "Who is this?" he said gruffly.

"He says his name is Zelta," said one of the guard.

Mog Agor knelt by the figure. "Zelta, is it?" The boy was obviously terrified. "Do you know who I am, Zelta?" The boy nodded but did not speak. He was trembling quite badly. "Say my name, boy," said Mog Agorn gently. "Say it."

"You . . . you are Mog Agorn?" Zelta whispered.

"Yes, and I see that you know the name well." He put his hand on the boy's shoulder. "If you answer my questions truthfully, you will not be harmed," he said softly, "but if you lie to me, then you will die slowly and painfully. Do you understand?" The boy nodded, but again he did not speak. "Good. Then here are the questions. Why have you come to Cor Gaur?"

Zelta looked about him desperately, but there was no escape. But now that he had failed, there seemed no harm in answering. "I was commanded by Hakin to give a message to Vordin before he reached Cor Gaur," he whispered. "I ran as fast as I could but I could not reach him in time."

Mog Agorn nodded. "What was the message?"

"It was Hakin's command that Vordin return to Glaeston at once."

"So Hakin knew that Vordin was on his way here."

"Yes."

Mog Agorn reached into the boy's pouch. "Yes, this is Hakin's ring—I recognize it—to be given to Vordin as proof of the message, no doubt." He patted the boy on the shoulder. "You have spoken the truth, and that was wise." He rose to his feet. "Take him to Asher's tent. See that he is fed, and do not harm him. I will speak with him later." He turned and strode back down into the great circle and confronted Vordin. "So . . . you lie, Druid!"

Vordin felt the sudden chill of danger. "I have told you the truth!" he said stubbornly.

"You told me that none at Glaeston know you are here. That was a lie."

"It was the truth!" Suddenly he spotted Zelta being led away, and his heart sank. "I must have been seen leaving Glaeston," he said desperately, but Mog Agorn's expression did not change. "I saw the boy coming after me and was waiting for him to catch up when your men swooped down on me." He stepped forward. "I truly believed that I had left Glaeston unnoticed. I swear it."

Mog Agorn pursed his lips. "It is possible," he said slowly, "but I prefer to believe that Druthin and Hakin sent you here to lie to me—to set up a trap for me, no doubt—but that something has happened to change their plans, and they sent the boy to bring you back."

"It is not true. I swear it!" Vordin could feel the touch of death in his heart. "You have my word."

"Which has already proved to be false. *Silence!*" He beckoned the captain of the guard and whispered to him. Vordin's eyes snapped from one to the other but he could discern nothing from their expressions. Mog Agorn nodded. "Take him, then, and do as I command." And he turned and strode away. Vordin was bundled roughly away, still protesting.

Three hours later two chariots came roaring down on Glaeston and came to a halt a hundred yards from the Great Gates. A figure was unceremoniously thrown to the ground.

Druthin and Menahotep happened to be at the eastern embrasure. "It is Vordin," said Druthin suddenly.

The figure picked itself up and began to stagger toward the gates. The Wessex captain cynically allowed Vordin to cover a dozen yards, and then he drew back his arm and sent his spear thudding into his back. The two chariots wheeled about and roared away, back from where they had come.

The Great Gates swung ponderously open, and the Druids streamed out toward their stricken priest. Druthin and Menahotep hurried as fast as they could down the great stone stairway, across the courtyard, and out through the gates. As they approached the group, a healer-priest rose and shook his head. "He is still alive," he said softly, "but it is only a matter of minutes, perhaps even seconds. There is nothing we can do."

Cludin was kneeling by the figure. "Where is Zelta?" he was saying fiercely.

Vordin groaned, a trickle of blood at the corner of his mouth. The Wessex spear had been thrown so hard that it had rammed right through the body, its point protruding from Vordin's stomach. "He is alive," Vordin whispered, "but Mog Agorn has him." Cludin would have said more but Hakin motioned him to silence. Vordin's eyes met with Druthin's. "Why did you send after me?" he whispered. "Why?"

Druthin knelt by his stricken friend. He had known Vordin all his life. They had been boys together, had joined the Bardic Degree together, and had taken the Initiation of the White at the same ceremony. "There were some here," he said gently, "who thought you had gone to Mog Agorn to betray us."

"Betray?" he whispered. "How could I do that? I have been a Druid all my life. I have given my unreserved dedication to the Great Ones, and it was accepted. No priest could betray his calling once that vow has been given." He groaned again, his hand clutching the spear-point. "No, no!" he said violently. "I know that I was unpopular amongst my fellow priests, but I had not even guessed that they thought me capable of betrayal!"

Druthin took his friend's hand. "Why then did you go?" he said softly.

"To arrange a meeting—to get Mog Agorn to agree to meet with the Druids. Perhaps we could have settled our differences. Too much blood, too much violence—it is not the priestly way."

"Did you succeed?"

"I did not have a chance to speak of it. I told Mog Agorn that none at Glaeston knew of my visit, and then Zelta arrived, so seeming to prove me a liar. The rest you know." Tears sprang into his eyes. He struggled up and clutched at Druthin's sleeve. "I would not betray the Druids. I swear it, Druthin—I could not! I could not."

"I know," said Druthin gently.

"Ask the Great Ones. They know." He sat bolt upright, his eyes staring. "I did not betray!" he called out in a terrible voice. "I did not betray!" A great gush of blood spurted from his mouth, and his eyes glazed. His body shuddered once and then was still.

Druthin stood up. "Let all know," he said harshly, "that Vordin will be honored at the full Ritual of the Dead as befitting so loyal a servant of Druidry. Let what has happened here be set down so that those priests as yet unborn will know the truth of Vordin. That is my command."

He looked at the group surrounding the body. "There is a lesson here for all of us. Vordin has paid for that lesson with his life. See to it that the lesson is well learned." And he turned and strode away back to Glaeston.

Ramin turned to Menahotep. "Why did he say all that to Vordin about betrayal?" he whispered fiercely. "Why darken the man's last seconds before death?"

"Vordin had a right to know why he was dying, and the truth had to be made known to those who are left. It was a harsh decision, but a right one." He pointed. "Look there!"

Some of the priests had begun to lift the body. "Leave it," said Hakin harshly. "He is dead because of me. I will tend him personally. Let no other come near." The old man took hold of the haft of the spear and savagely tore it from Vordin's body, broke it across his knee and hurled the splintered halves away. He knelt by the body and began to wipe the face gently with his own robe, and they could see great tears streaming down his cheeks.

Mog Agorn held up his hand. "Before you utter one single word, I must warn you that this is a command from the High Priest of the Wessex, and I will brook no argument whatsoever!" He stared hard at his brother. "Do you understand?"

Sleg Agorn looked at Asher, but the girl kept her eyes lowered. "I had no intention of offering any argument," he said quietly, "but Fangorn will not like it."

"Fangorn has no say in this matter." The long shadows of late afternoon had already darkened the entrance to Mog Agorn's tent. "I say again: Before nightfall you will withdraw the entire Wessex force, except Asher and myself, out of Cor Gaur and make camp one mile to the west. Under no circumstances are any of you to return until tomorrow's dawn. You will post a double guard around your camp with specific orders to kill anyone who attempts to leave during the night. And I mean *anyone!*"

"Including Fangorn?"

"Particularly Fangorn."

"What about the prisoner?"

"The boy remains with us."

Sleg Agorn pursed his lips. "And you cannot tell me what this is about?"

The High Priest hesitated. "All I am permitted to say is that Asher and I have a particular ritual to perform tonight, and if that ritual is disturbed it will bring untold disaster down on all our heads."

"Very well. I can command all the Wessex as you require, except Fangorn. He will require the command to come from you personally. Otherwise, guard or no guard, you will have trouble with him tonight."

Mog Agorn grunted. "You are probably right." He flung up his hands in exasperation. "That boy has been nothing but trouble since the day of his birth!" He rose and picked up his knife-belt and strapped it around his waist. "Very well. Let us go see Fangorn."

Asher remained in the tent. All day she had felt an impending omen hovering over her. It was a curious feeling and one that she had not experienced before. She had mentioned it to Mog Agorn, but he had smiled knowingly and said nothing. She had tried to question him about this special ritual but he had refused pointblank to discuss the matter.

Outside she could hear Fangorn's strident voice raised in anger and Mog Agorn's bellowing answer. She knew that sooner or later one of those two had to die by the other's hand. Fangorn was a fool. He was no match for his father and never would be. She rose and went to the entrance. Again she felt that intense portent, like a cloud hovering over her, waiting to descend and envelop her. It gave her a curious feeling in the stomach, as though her guts were tied in great knots—a feeling she would have called fear had she not known herself better. She had never feared anyone or anything in her life, and she was not going to start now. She dismissed the matter from her mind and stepped outside.

Mog Agorn and Fangorn—father and son—faced each other like two angry bulls. The guard stood in readiness at Mog Agorn's back. "For the last time, Fangorn, you will do as I command or face the consequences."

"Not without some explanation," shouted Fangorn defiantly, "and my curse on your wretched consequences!"

Mog Agorn shook his head. "Very well. You leave me no choice." He stepped aside and motioned to the guard. "Seize him!"

The Wessex priests looked on in astonishment as the twelve-strong guard leapt on Fangorn. There was a short scuffle, and at the end of it Fangorn lay trussed with thongs, unable to move, a gag of leather stuffed in his mouth. Mog Agorn had noted the astonishment and doubt in some of the faces. He strode over to his son and raised his voice so that all could hear. "The Great Ones have commanded that I do not speak of the ritual that I must perform tonight. All I am permitted to say is that, if successful, then great glory, honor, and power will come to the Wessex." He glared around at the assembled priests. "And the Great Ones also commanded that if any man disturbs or interferes with that ritual, then that man must die." He looked down at Fangorn. "Even if it is you, my son."

Sleg Agorn stepped forward and raised his arms. "You have heard the words of the High Priest. Be warned by them!" he said ominously. "And know you that I am the instrument of discipline. It is I who am commanded by the Great Ones to kill any man who seeks to disturb the Great Work. Be warned, Priests of the Wessex!"

Mog Agorn grunted impatiently. "All right, all right! They've got the message. Get on with it." And he turned and strode back to his tent.

Two hours later, at dusk, Cor Gaur lay seemingly deserted, the great stones looming lonely against the evening sky. Mog Agorn and Asher were in the tent where the boy had been held prisoner for a week. The High Priest bent over the boy and raised an eyelid, and then nodded in satisfaction. "He sleeps soundly and will do so until the moment comes." He stepped back. "That is a potent brew of yours, Asher. It would put a mountain to sleep."

"Never mind that!" the girl said impatiently. "*Now* can you tell me what this is all about?"

He turned and looked at her thoughtfully. "Yes, the time has come. Follow me." He led her from the tent and to the very center of the ancient circle, to the King Stone itself. Around them the great Sarsen Trilithons towered blackly against the rapidly darkening sky. Beyond them the Holy Bluestone Circle stood like giant black sentinels, and at the northern point the great broad avenue of standing stones led out of Cor Gaur and swept majestically across open country, mile after mile, down to the River Avon itself.

Mog Agorn sat himself on the King Stone and motioned for Asher to sit at his feet. He waved his arm around at the stones. "This is Cor Gaur," he said somberly, "the spiritual and magical center of the land. He who controls Cor Gaur controls the destiny of the land and all who dwell in it. From this great circle the forces are caused to radiate throughout the land along the trackways that our ancestors built, and he who controls Cor Gaur is the one who determines which force shall permeate the land."

He looked at his daughter. "At the moment it is we, the Wessex, who control matters, but the Druids seek to overthrow our rule, and the Druids are formidable enemies." He stared hard at her. "Never," he said softly but sternly, "*never* make the mistake of underestimating the Druids. Never! They are priests of power in the fullest sense, and they have deep and powerful contacts with the inner planes." He took her hand and squeezed it, almost lovingly. "But while I am High Priest of the Wessex, the Druids shall never prevail against us and we shall continue to rule."

He sighed and sat back. "But who is there to follow me when I am gone? Fangorn?" He shook his head. "He is no priest, no warrior. His only talent lies in his loins, and no man can rule from between a woman's thighs. The Wessex would not last a year against the Druids if Fangorn ruled.

"Awrgon, the youngest?" he went on. "He at least is a priest, and in due course he will rise to power and lead the Wessex after me for a short while. His priestly powers will be so formidable that he will be able to keep the Druids at bay, at least for a few years. But in the long term he must eventually fail, and then the Wessex are finished.

"No, daughter mine," he said grimly, "there is no one in the Wessex ranks of sufficient stature to lead the Wessex. What we have to do, you and I, is to contact one who is yet unborn and bring him through into incarnation—one of such greatness that he will be able to destroy the Druid cult utterly, and so preserve the Wessex rule for thousands of years."

Asher frowned. "But even if that could be done, it would take twenty years and more before he was man enough to do these things."

"True, which is why Awrgon must rule after me to preserve the Wessex for his coming."

"But how do you bring such a one through?"

He smiled. "In the usual manner."

She sat bolt upright and stared at him. "You mean . . . you and I? The usual way?"

Mog Agorn bellowed with sudden laughter. "Don't look so astonished, my daughter. Incest is no stranger to your thoughts. You have lain with me before, and you have lain with each of your seven brothers, including Fangorn and Awrgon, the youngest." He raised his arm. "Don't bother to deny it. I know, and it is no matter to me. Indeed, I am pleased, for at least you have no fear of the ancient taboo to overcome."

Asher stood up suddenly. "Father, what you are proposing is highly dangerous. It is one thing for me to lay with my brothers, or with my father, with the juice of the Netzian berry to stop me being with child, but to deliberately commit incest with a view to bring through a child is quite another. You know as well as I that during an incestuous mating the joint psychic inner-plane vortex does not rise up as it should but, as it were, twists sideways and so can reach into the dark realms, and if that happens, who knows what entity we would bring through?"

"Precisely," said Mog Agorn calmly.

The knot of fear suddenly clutched her guts. "Oh, no. No . . ."

"Wait," he commanded. "Get hold of yourself. I thought you were a woman without fear."

"Ordinarily, yes. But this is something else!"

"You have no need to fear. This will be no blind probing in the dark realms. All the preparatory work has been done." He took her hand and pulled her gently down beside him. "What we need is no ordinary human soul." He hesitated, and then went on. "We are to be honored, Asher, honored as no parents have ever been honored before. One of the Dark Ones himself has agreed to incarnate through you, Asher. Think of it, one of the Dark Ones himself. With one of them made flesh of your flesh to lead the Wessex, how can those cursed Druids survive?"

"Oh, no. No . . . You *can't*, Father . . ."

"Don't worry. It is all arranged. There is nothing you have to do, beyond what you have done a hundred times before."

"You're lying, Father. I have read the ritual. You know what I must do. At the height of the mating, I have to leave my body, follow the vortex down into the dark realms, and there I have to join with the Dark One and lead him back to my womb!"

"It is nothing," he said gently. "You have been to

the dark realms before. It is nothing. As to the Dark One, he will not harm you. He needs you to incarnate. Think of the honor, Asher. You are to be the mother in earth of a Great One such as the world has never seen. Think of the honor, Asher!"

She buried her face in her hands and her body shook uncontrollably. "You know the rule, Father—a life for a life! A Dark One can be born through me, but its birth would mean my death. It is the old rule, and it cannot be broken!"

He stroked her hair gently. "Hush," he said softly. "There is no need to fear. I am not a priest of power for nothing. A rule such as that cannot be broken, I know, but there are more ways than one of satisfying such conditions."

She looked up at him. "How? A life for a life. How can you get around that?"

"But it doesn't say whose life." He smiled at her. "I have been dreaming of this moment for a long time. I knew that this was the most propitious year, but I did not know what month. Originally, I thought to conduct the rite at the first full moon after the Autumnal Equinox, six months from now, but then I received a sign." He looked at her. "The boy, Zelta—a virgin youth. What could be better—a Druid, a consecrated priest, albeit a junior one—and he came to us almost out of nowhere—a sign from the Dark Ones that the time is now, and tonight is the seventh day after the full moon of Beltane!"

"Zelta!"

Mog Agorn smiled grimly. "One life comes in, one life goes out. A life for a life. It is the rule, as you said."

She looked up at him. "How will you arrange it?"

"You leave that to me."

Asher stood up and stared around the silent circle. The cloud of her omen hovered nearer. "This is no small thing you ask of me, Father." Her hands were twitching slightly. "To carry a Dark One in my womb for all those months is a prospect that fills me with dread."

"Indeed, it is no small thing," he agreed. "It will be a stupendous, magnificent achievement. Think of it, Asher—a Dark One made flesh! And it will be born at the time of the Winter Solstice, during the Cleansing Tide, the Tide of Destruction during which the old is destroyed to make way for the new. What more appropriate time could we choose? And think, Asher, you will be its mother. The Dark One will owe you a great deal for having been the means by which it incarnated. Much honor and power will be yours, Asher. No High Priestess in the whole history of humanity will have wielded anywhere near the power that will come to you."

Asher smiled grimly, stirred by the prospect despite her fears. "Then let us hope I live to use it."

He rose and put his arm around her shoulders. "Go to your tent now and meditate. Try to contact the Dark One. Create a link between you. It will make it easier during the rite."

When she had gone, Mog Agorn climbed onto the King Stone and spread his arms to the sky. He wanted to shout with exultation, but did not dare for fear of alarming Asher. The culmination of his plans! It was hard to believe that the time was almost at hand. "Soon," he whispered to the sky, "soon you will be with us. I, Mog Agorn, High Priest of the Wessex, await your coming!"

For two hours Mog Agorn sat, a grim and lonely figure on the King Stone at Cor Gaur, waiting for the coming of the Moon. When he judged the rising to be near, he stirred and came down to Asher's tent. The girl lay flat on her back, her arms rigid by her side, her fists clenched, her face strained and set in a grimace of extreme tension. Mog Agorn nodded grimly to himself. She was with the Dark One—there was no mistaking that expression. Gently and carefully he removed her robe, stripped her tunic and other garments, and removed her rings and the heavy symbol of her position as High Priestess from around her neck, until she lay quite naked and unadorned. Carefully he put his arms beneath her and lifted her up. Slowly, cautiously, not wishing to disturb her contact, he carried her into the great circle and laid her on her back on the King Stone itself. He spread her legs and her arms and positioned the body at exactly the right angle so that it faced the archway of one of the great Sarsen Trilithons. Satisfied, he went to fetch the drugged boy and laid that smaller body at her head, arranging it so that the boy's hands lay across Asher's breasts. He then stood at their head, drew his knife, and waited, his eyes fixed intently on the distant horizon.

The sky was already lighter, more silvery, and then at last the Queen herself rose up, and the first ray of her power struck like a silver arrow through the archway of the Sarsen Trilithon and fell on the body of the naked High Priestess. As it did so, Mog Agorn uttered a great cry in the ancient tongue, reached for the boy's hands, and slashed the wrists. The blood spurted high, a twin fountain that cascaded redly across the girl's body.

Mog Agorn threw off his robe and stood as naked as they in the moonlight. Again the ancient tongue cried out and Mog Agorn, High Priest of the Wessex, threw himself across the body of his naked Pythoness, his loins to hers, holding himself, poised, waiting. Death and Life had to occur together. One life comes in, one life goes out—a life for a life. The blood still spurted, but not so powerfully, and the boy's body writhed feebly. Then at last the moment came: the boy's eyes glazed with death—and with a great cry of triumph, Mog Agorn plunged and plunged again to the climax of his ambition!

Chapter Five

"Tomorrow night," said Druthin, "is the seventh night after the full moon of Beltane. It would be an appropriate time for Ramin's initiation into Druidry."

Ramin's heart leapt at the words, and there was a curiously tight feeling in his stomach—not fear, though there was some apprehension in the feeling— more a sudden excitement. "I am ready," he said simply.

"I hope so," said Druthin sternly, "for if you are not truly ready, it can prove to be a nasty experience for you."

"The initiation will take the customary form, I presume," said Menahotep.

"Yes. The procedure has not changed since your day." He turned to Ramin. "You will spend tonight in prayer and meditation," he said. "An hour before dawn tomorrow morning, you will be conducted to a mound to the west of the Green Hill. With due ceremony you will be led deep within the mound to its central chamber beneath the earth, and as the first ray of dawn strikes the Tower, the attendants will leave you, sealing the entrance behind them and leaving you quite alone and in utter darkness. You will remain there for one full circle of the Sun. On the dawn of the following day, the attendants will return to release you. You will then be granted some hours in which to reflect on your experiences, and then at the zenith of the Sun you will be required to stand before the Council and recount all that happened to you. If the initiation is a success we will hear you speak of certain key experiences. If you do not mention them, we will know that the initiation has failed. Do you understand?"

"Yes," said Ramin. "Egyptian initiation ceremonies are similar."

"Indeed, yes. In the Egyptian Rite of Initiation, the Candidate is sealed within the Great Pyramid, and if he is ready to be given the opportunity for initiation, the jackal-headed god Anubis comes to him and leads him out of his body to undergo certain tests—which is why he is called the Opener of the Way. In Druidry the experience is similar, except that the being who comes for you we call Theutates."

Ramin nodded. "I presume I am allowed no food, no water, and no light."

"And no clothing either," said Druthin. "Naked you were when you came from the gods, and naked you must be when you stand before Theutates." He rose to his feet. "I suggest you retire to your chamber early."

Menahotep also rose and escorted Druthin to the door. "There is no news of Zelta, I presume."

The Arch-Mage frowned sadly. "No, I'm afraid not. It was a good plan of yours to send Cyffru and Brisis to spy out Cor Gaur by night, though they risked their lives by disobediently spying by day as well. Zelta is still held prisoner in that tent. Food is still being taken in twice a day, so obviously he is still alive. But what their plans for him are, we still do not know."

"You have no plans to move against the Wessex?"

Druthin shook his head. "No, not yet."

"Not even to rescue Zelta?" said Ramin.

"No, not even for that. When all argument is finished, we are still left with the fact that Zelta, albeit an eleven-year-old boy deserving of our protection, is still only one life, and I have all Druidry to consider. The Wessex are far superior to us in the arts of war and they still outnumber us five to one." He sighed heavily. "It is very tempting to launch at least some sort of action to attempt a rescue, but the result would be disastrous. Hard though it may seem, the wise course is to do nothing and simply wait for opportunity."

"And I will pray," said Menahotep gently, "that we have the wisdom to recognize that opportunity when it appears."

"And I will pray," said Ramin harshly, "that Zelta does not die while we wait."

"We all pray for that," said Druthin quietly, and he bowed slightly and left the chamber.

Menahotep put his hand on the boy's shoulder. "It is hard to accept, I know," he said gently. "But you must put this matter out of your mind and prepare for your initiation."

Ramin's soul was obviously deeply troubled. "I feel strongly for that boy," he said helplessly, "and I am not even of these people. A guest in their land! What must the Druids themselves be feeling? And what sort of desolation must fill Hakin's heart, since he is the cause of all this?"

"We may never know," said Menahotep. "But you must forget all this. You cannot go in to your initiation with a heart and mind so troubled."

Ramin sighed. "You are right." He looked up at his teacher and smiled. "At least I have all night to compose myself."

"Indeed, yes. And now I must leave you." He walked to the door. "One word of advice: Do not think Egyptian; think Druid. It is not Anubis who will come for you, but Theutates."

Ramin nodded. "I understand."

"Good. And this must be my farewell. You are not permitted to speak to anyone as from tonight, not even to those who will attend you tomorrow. You will not see me again until you stand before the Council to give account of your experiences."

"The day after tomorrow. Yes, I understand. Farewell then, my teacher. I will not disgrace you, or my calling."

"I know that." The older priest smiled encouragingly. "My thoughts will be with you," he said simply, and closed the door behind him.

Three young, blue-robed Bards, no older than Zelta, their eyes still heavy with sleep, came to his chamber a full hour before first light. Two of them carried between them an earthen cauldron of near-boiling water, and the third carried a casket containing phials of many different oils. They did not speak but motioned him to disrobe and lie on the couch. Carefully and meticulously they washed every part of his body and then anointed his skin with the most exquisitely fragrant oil that Ramin had ever known. They combed his hair and attended his hands, and then finally they dressed him in a coarse black robe, a white cord circling his waist. Still without speaking, they collected their equipment, bowed three times to him, and left.

A few minutes later a double rap sounded at the door, and a young seeress entered. She was robed in purest white of the Druid Degree, and on her dark hair she wore a circlet of blue denoting her function as Mistress of the Blue. She did not speak but laid a leather thong around his wrists, drawing them together in front of him. She looked deep into his eyes and, seemingly satisfied, she took his hands and led him from the chamber, down the flag-stoned corridor, and out into the courtyard.

Ramin had expected only a few to attend him, but he was astonished to find the entire Druid complement assembled in the courtyard waiting for his appearance. Druthin and Melkor and all those of the White were silently gathered in a three-deep phalanx immediately in front of the great steps. Behind them stood the serried ranks of the Green, and beyond them the lines of the Blue, and there, beside Hakin of the White, stood Menahotep, his teacher, no longer dressed in the yellow robe of his rank in the Egyptian priesthood, but robed in the White even as Druthin himself.

No sound as yet disturbed the scene—no whisper, no rustle of an errant robe. It was eerie, almost unnatu-

ral for so many to have gathered in so profound a
silence—a silence so deep that Ramin could hear the
beat of his own heart. The tableau froze thus for a single moment, and then the Mistress of the Blue raised
his bound wrists high above his head for all to see, and
as she did so Druthin raised the Serpent Staff and
rapped three times on the courtyard stone, and on the
third stroke the entire assembly began to sing softly,
slowly, a hauntingly beautiful chant from the Fourth
Degree, so full of hope, and love, and expectation, and
gentle encouragement that Ramin could feel the sudden tears spring to his eyes, and his heart leaped forward eagerly to join the companionship of such souls as
these.

Druthin turned and pointed the Serpent Staff at the
Great Gates. Obedient to his command the Bards
leapt to unbar the way, and the massive portal stood
open before their feet. Druthin led the way, slowly
and majestically, with Thetan, Pythoness to the Order of Theutates, at his side. Behind them came the
Council, with Menahotep granted much honor to be
permitted within their ranks, and behind them came
the seeress leading the Candidate toward his avowed
intent, and behind them came those of the Green, and
of the Blue, and the voices welled up joyously and
poured their hopes toward the pale predawn sky that
had already dressed herself in delicate hues in honor of
the coming of the Sun.

Slowly and majestically, Druthin of the White led
the procession around the base of the Green Hill toward the west, and there, no more than a spear-cast
from the base of the hill, was a long, low, turf-
covered mound, roughly a hundred feet long and
fifty feet wide. Since their arrival in this strange
land, Ramin had seen a score and more of these con-
structions dotted around Glaeston, and on the road
to Cor Gaur, and because he had heard the Druids
refer to them as "mounds," he had assumed that they
were burial mounds, but a discussion with his mentor
had revealed otherwise. Some of them, Menahotep
had said, had indeed been used for the burials of

High Priests and High Priestesses, but this was by no means their main function. They were, without exception, he had said, situated on spirals of magnetic intensity, and were constructed very carefully of differing layers of turf and soil, alternating each layer in a particular manner such that each mound was in effect an energy accumulator, and thus caused an in-guards on either side. The Priestess of the Mound, within the central chamber deep underground. Because of this intensification, the mounds were therefore especially suitable for certain types of ritual, particularly initiations.

The entrance to the West Mound at Green Hill was a solid oak door-frame with a massive oak lintel above it. The great door itself stood open in readiness, two guards on either side. The Priestess of the Mound, robed in the colors of Earth, a beautiful flowing robe of citrine and black, a shimmering russet and gold headdress and a cloak of rich olive green, waited to challenge those who would seek to enter.

As the procession came to a halt, the Priestess of the Mound stepped forward, and her voice rang across the morning dew. "Who is this who comes to the West Mound?" she challenged.

Thetan, High Priestess of the White, Pythoness to the Order of Theutates, motioned Ramin to step forward, and took him by his fastened wrists. "One who has expressed a need to be accepted by the Great Ones as a servant," she cried in a powerful voice, "and to be accepted by them as a seeker!"

"All who come thus with a pure and single heart," came the reply, "are entitled to the opportunity desired. Let him be placed within the mound to undergo the tests of his avowed intent."

Thetan turned and handed him back to the seeress who had first escorted him, and she led him forward toward the ominously dark cavern of the doorway to the mound. The Priestess of the Mound turned and led the way, lighting a waxen torch just beyond the entrance, and the two guards brought up the rear, their spears leveled at Ramin's back. The interior of the mound, as far as Ramin could judge from the flickering light of the crude torch, was surprisingly small compared to the outside measurements, and consisted of a single passageway sloping downward, with small cells cut out of the walls on either side as they descended.

Although it was difficult to judge, Ramin decided that they must have descended nearly twenty feet belowground when they came to a halt before a small oak door that barred the passageway. The Priestess of the Mound unbarred the door and stood to one side, her torch held aloft, and the two priest-guards escorted Ramin within the chamber.

It was much smaller than he had anticipated—no more than a dozen feet square—and at its center was a slab of bluestone six feet long by three feet wide, standing as high as a man's waist and covered by a bull's hide. The Priestess handed the torch to one of the guards and came over to Ramin. She untied the thongs from his wrists and slipped the robe from his shoulders. The guards took the robe and thongs, handed the torch back to the Priestess, and left the chamber to return to the surface. The Priestess of the Mound stood by the half-open chamber door, the torch held high, staring gravely and silently at the naked candidate—waiting.

Outside, the guards lay the robe and thongs at Thetan's feet and returned to their post on either side of the entrance to the mound. The assembled ranks of the Druids were still singing the initiation chant, but softly, muted, all eyes on the Pytheness—waiting.

Thetan stood calmly, quite still, staring up at the summit of the Green Hill from which rose the Tower at its western edge, standing out blackly against the morning sky. So perfect was the timing that the assembly had only to wait a few minutes before suddenly the topmost tip of the Tower burst into life from the first ray of the morning Sun, and the chant ended abruptly. Thetan turned to Druthin. "The Sun has arisen!" she cried in a powerful voice.

"Then let the trial commence," he commanded.

Thetan signaled to the guards, and one of them

turned and reentered the mound. Ramin heard him coming and his heart leapt with apprehension. This was the moment. The guard bowed to the Priestess of the Mound. "The Sun has arisen," he said softly. "Druthin, Arch-Mage of all Druidry, commands that the trial begin." He bowed again and withdrew.

The Priestess turned to Ramin. "If it is still your will to serve the Great Ones, raise your right hand in sign of assent." Ramin slowly raised his hand, and the Priestess bowed. "It *is* his will," she said gravely. "Then let it be done," and she stepped back into the passageway. The door thundered shut, and the great transverse bar dropped into its sockets, sealing the Candidate within the chamber in utter darkness and utter silence. Ramin stood stock-still until he heard the outer door above at the entrance to the mound also thunder shut, and he knew that he was utterly alone, at least for the time being.

He backed carefully until he touched the stone slab, and rested against it. He knew that his eyes were wide open—unnaturally so, straining—but the chamber was utterly without light. Few human beings, he knew, ever experienced the horror of a total absence of light. Even on the darkest winter night there was always at least some light, no matter how minute, but here the blackness was so profound that it felt as though it was pressing in on him, enveloping him, crushing him, filling his mouth and ears, pressing heavily against his staring eyeballs. The blackness was a living horror that evilly, insidiously, flowed in through the openings of his body, filling his skull, pouring throughout his frame until every atom of him was filled with loathsome blackness.

He shook his head and stamped his feet and pressed his naked skin against the cold stone to orientate himself again. His previous experience in similar Egyptian rites stood him in good stead. The utter blackness, the almost living, throbbing silence, the desolation of being totally alone, buried alive, were the first fears to overcome. Despite the rigorous Egyptian training and preparation, some did not even survive these first simple tests. Ramin himself had been present on one occasion when the chamber had been opened to find the Candidate dead, his fingers just bloody stumps from having insanely tried to claw his way through solid rock to get out. The healers had subsequently reported that, from the condition of the body, the Candidate must have died during the first hour, probably from pure terror.

The next test was always the thought of betrayal, or accident, or some event that would prevent the Candidate from being released, such that the initiation chamber was already the Candidate's burial tomb. Rather than allow these thoughts to creep up on him, Ramin deliberately invited them so as to dispose of them by clear thinking. Betrayal was out of the question. There was not only the honor of the priesthood in general to consider, and the honor of Menahotep in particular—plus the deep love that Menahotep and he had always shared. There was no motive for such betrayal. Indeed, there was a strong motive for Menahotep, and indeed Druthin, to hope and to pray that the Candidate would succeed, for such success always favorably reflected on the teacher, and failure was always held to be in part the responsibility of the teacher, for having failed to adequately prepare the Candidate.

As for accidents, Ramin knew better than to try to convince himself that no such things could happen, for indeed it was certainly possible. In his own case, it was just within the realms of possibility that Mog Agorn, for example, could launch a sudden attack on Glaeston and slaughter every Druid, every Egyptian, destroy the vessel, and put every peasant to the sword such that no one would be left who knew of the initiation or his own burial within the mound. However, having accepted the possibility, and knowing that there was nothing he could do about it, he was able to dismiss the matter from his mind.

He eased himself onto the slab of rock and pulled the bull's hide around him, and lay in the stygian darkness, his mind calm and expectant, his heart untroubled by fear. He thought of Egypt and saw himself in the Temple amidst the others of his grade, walking in procession. He saw himself that first time he had been entrusted with a ritual task, lighting the incense at the Feast of Min and circumambulating the Great Hall, swinging the thurible, smelling again the pungent smoke of Kyphi, the most sacred of all Egyptian incenses. He smiled as he saw again the benign figure of Menahotep nodding approvingly at his ritual bearing. His heart leapt at the sight of Menahotep—the wise and loving old man who was not only his priest-teacher and Master-in-Earth, but who also fulfilled for him the role of a father, since his own blood father had died before his birth. With that thought he saw again his mother, Pharenutep, named for the goddess, Beloved Child of Renutep. His father had been a Captain of the King's Guard, killed in a skirmish with a Nubian tribe at Egypt's southern border—but not before he had planted the seed that was Ramin in his mother's womb. Tradition had it that he was to be trained for the Army, as his father before him, and indeed he had undergone the preliminary training at the house of his father's brother, who had given shelter to the young widow with child. But his mother had wanted him for the priesthood and would not be swayed from that ambition by any family pressure. The argument had raged around her for a year or more but she had been obdurate, unbending in her plans for her first- and only-born, and at last his uncle had capitulated and given her permission to approach the Master of the Outer Court at the Temple of the Sun. This, of itself, was an incredible achievement for so demure and quiet a woman, for his uncle was a strong man not given to yielding to a woman's will. But how proud she had been that day when the great door to the initiation chamber had been unbarred and her son, Ramin, had walked forth to receive for the first time the yellow robe of the fully initiated priesthood. A great achievement it had been for her, but also a great sacrifice, for since that day she had seen him but little.

Ramin stirred on his couch of rock and pulled the

bull's hide more closely around him. Think Druid, Menahotep had said, not Egyptian. But thoughts of Druidry led him to thoughts to Thetan, and these he must dismiss or else they would fill his mind and heart to the exclusion of all else.

Instead he visualized with all the clarity of a trained priest the image of himself standing on the summit of the Green Hill, at the center of the circle of stones, facing the Tower in the west, alone, waiting for the one who would come for him. As he stood thus, the image of the Tower began to subtly change, to grow, to shimmer—a needle of rock that towered to the sky, the harshness of the stone softening, the lines of force racing upward, a stream of power, a rush of energy, a fountain of life gushing from the bowels of the Earth, streaming upward to the source from which they had sprung. He moved toward that pillar of force and entered the upward-rushing stream, and felt himself caught up, and whirled around, rushing upward, higher and higher, until his senses reeled and he lost all thought of time and place, until it was he himself who was the stream of force, his own god-self that poured upward in a living stream to find its own place in the deep heart of the timeless source from whence it had sprung that long, long ago before the beginning of all that was.

The headlong rush through inner space and time subtly changed. Suddenly it was he who remained still, and all else was rushing toward him and past him at incredible speed. Gradually—so gradually that the difference at first was barely perceptible—the speed began to diminish until at length it was as though he stood in swirling fog, the white wisps brushing past his face—a fog, a mist, swirling as if under a strong breeze, thinning gradually until at last he broke clear and looked down on the scene below.

He knew—though he did not know how he knew—that the Glaeston he saw below was the green hill as it had been ten thousand years ago. But he also knew that he was not looking at the reality of that time but rather, as it were, looking at a record of it, an impress, a memory, and he realized with awe that he had been privileged to view a part of that great inner plane Akhasic Record that stores the images of all that transpires during the course of human evolution, indeed the images and impressions of all evolution since the very creation of the Universe itself.

He recognized the green hill even though it was so different from his memory of it. The Tower itself was still there on the summit, and also the altar stone, but the other stones, the ring, had vanished utterly. A few hundred yards to the south of the hill was a crude structure of wattle that looked as though it might be some form of primitive temple, and he realized with a slight shock that it stood on the exact site of Glaeston College, but of that famed Druid seat of learning there was not a single trace. He looked to the west of the hill for the mound that contained his physical body, but that, too, had vanished. The River Parrett, as far as he could tell, ran much the same course, but the jetty at Ponter's Ball was now a primitive wooden affair of tree trunks lashed together, rather than the solid stone structure that he remembered. He willed himself to the east, following the road to Cor Gaur, though the road was now no more than a track, and when he arrived, he found absolutely nothing at all save rolling grassland and forest. The great stone circle at Cor Gaur had not yet been built, and for all he knew it had not even yet been conceived.

He willed himself to return to Glaeston, and rose a little higher so that he could see beyond the green hill, across the western marshlands to the sea. It was a nightmare coastline for any sailor. The whole area was one vast mass of islands, and the marshland was so extensive that it was difficult to tell where the marsh ended and the sea began. Here and there were patches of clear water, but the only unbroken line was the twisting route of the River Parrett itself, and even then it was hard to tell the precise location of its mouth.

Suddenly he realized that beyond the marsh, in the open sea, was a fleet of three vessels of a design and markings completely alien to him. They were like nothing that he had ever seen before. They were in line ahead, cautiously threading their way through the islands, and even as he watched he saw the leading vessel nose into the Parrett and begin the long haul up to Ponter's Ball.

He descended slowly and saw that the jetty at Ponter's Ball was crowded with short, squat, ugly men almost entirely covered in thick coarse hair, dressed in animal skins. But here and there in the crowd were tall, hawk-eyed men, black-robed and commanding, members of the ruling priesthood, without a doubt. Ramin descended still lower and drew near one of the priests and touched his mind to know his thoughts.

The priest was inwardly excited and, as such, his thoughts were too jumbled for immediate understanding, but soon it became clear that the strange vessels had been spotted two days before in the Temple mirrors. But the real excitement lay in the fact that the strangers too had seeresses on board, and their own mirrors—and furthermore the sails of the vessels were marked with a huge, five-pointed golden star, symbol of the Sun, and all knew that this was the emblem of old Atlantis, long since vanished beneath the sea. To speculate was useless—they could only wait for the actual arrival itself.

The sun was quite low when the first of the vessels nosed into the crude jetty and the mooring thongs made fast. The gangway was thrown down and the first of the strangers began to disembark. First came the guard, lining each side of the gangway, and then came a young man of commanding presence, robed in white. By his side was a priestess robed in the deepest blue. Behind them was one robed in black whose manner spoke of even greater authority.

The young man in white bowed low to the black-robed priests assembled on the jetty. "Greetings," he said calmly. "Are there any here who understand this tongue?"

A ripple of excitement stirred the assembly—the old tongue! It was the ancient tongue! One of the black-robed priests stepped forward. "I am Karadoc," he said slowly, "High Priest of these people. Nations have risen and fallen since last the old tongue was heard in normal usage. We of the priesthood use it in our rituals, but the people do not know of it. We saw in our mirrors that you come in peace. But who are you that you speak the sacred tongue?"

The white-robed younger man smiled. "As you saw in your mirrors, Karadoc, we have mirrors of our own. We saw that we were welcome and so came boldly in." He stepped forward a pace. "I am Helios, High Priest of the Sun, and this is Netziachos, the High Priestess." The girl bowed and smiled her acknowledgment. Helios beckoned the black-robed one of authority. "And this is one who stands higher than any of us. He is the voice of the inner on earth, our true and wise counselor, Melchadek."

Karadoc bowed low in return. "You are all truly welcome, as you already know. By your bearing and your tongue, we feel we already know from whence you have come, but would prefer to hear it from your own lips."

"I understand," said Helios. "We are from the Sun Temple of Atlantis, in the City of the Golden Gates, on the topmost plateau of the Sacred Mountain that straddles the mighty River Naradek, on the Island of Ruta to the far west of the world!" As he spoke, another buzz of excitement stirred the assembly. "We," said Helios proudly, "are from Atlantis!"

Karadoc smiled wryly. "So, too, are we," he said calmly.

Helios looked at him keenly, his brow suddenly furrowing. "How can that be?" he said sharply.

Melchadek stepped forward. "If you will permit me," he said quietly, "I think I can explain. Ten thousand years ago, the Third Great Age of Man began when the survivors from Lemuria founded the civilization that came to be known as Atlantis. Three times throughout the great history of Atlantis, the people fell on evil ways despite the guidance of the true priesthood, and three times a great cataclysm arose and brought death to those of evil intent. But before each cataclysm could fall, the true priesthood sent forth an emigration comprised of those of good heart—the seedbearers to the new age. But so great was the time gap between each emigration, the knowledge of the earlier emigrations had become but a legend to those Atlanteans of recent times." He paused for a moment and then said quietly: "You, Karadoc, I suspect are descended from those of the second emigration that left Atlantis ten thousand years ago. Whereas we are of the third emigration that fled from the final holocaust a few short months ago." He looked from the one to the other. "A womb can bring forth more than one seed," he said.

There was a deep silence, and then Helios shook his head in wonder. "And we were guided to this exact spot!" he said.

Karadoc nodded in agreement. "The ways of the Great Ones are beyond our understanding until it is time for us to know. The records handed down to us from our ancestors speak of the utter destruction of Atlantis. They could not have known that Atlantis had survived yet again."

"The second cataclysm ten thousand years ago was the greatest of all three," said Melchadek. "It destroyed an entire continent leaving only the islands of Ruta and Daiteya. Those that survived the terrible destruction built a new Temple and a new city, the City of the Golden Gates, and for ten thousand years the people flourished, thinking that they were the sole survivors of the Atlantean culture. But again evil found its way into the hearts of the people, and indeed into the hearts of the priesthood itself. The Dark Lords found their greatest channel through an evil one called Vardek, Lord Commander of the Army, who rose up against the Temple of the Sun. The resultant struggle brought down the third and final cataclysm which utterly destroyed both islands and everything and everyone on them."

"But Kumara," said Helios, "the High Priest of the Withdrawn Temple—perhaps the greatest High

Priest that Atlantis ever produced—had foreseen the possibility of these events and instructed Melchadek here to send forth the emigration." The memory of it saddened his eyes. "We escaped," he said simply, "at the very last moment, leaving Kumara to perish alongside the people he had loved."

"Seven long ships stood out from Ruta," said Melchadek, "and we saw the final destruction with our own eyes. The islands were destroyed by fire that rose up from the bowels of the earth. All night long the destruction raged, and when the Sun rose there was no longer a single shred of evidence that the islands had ever existed—just the empty sea.* Seven ships sailed thus from Ruta, and now there are only three!"

Netziachos stepped forward. "We are now wanderers, Karadoc," she said simply. "Wanderers without a home or land to call our own. But we are still seed-bearers, and we ask that we be allowed to make our home here with you and your people, to share with you the knowledge that we have brought with us. We ask this of you in the name of Atlantis, whose name must live on as a source of inspiration to all men—and we ask this of you as brothers, since we are both children of the same mother."

There was a long and deep silence. The sun was now almost below the horizon, and the last rays of the day lanced across the sea and threw the strange ships into stark silhouettes against the western sky. Finally Karadoc lifted his hand. "You bring a titanic tale of death and destruction, but also one, I suspect, containing deeds of great valor and honor. When you have rested after your long and dangerous journey, we will eagerly seek the details of your tale." He raised his voice so that all could hear. "I tell you this,

*Author's note. The bloody story of the immense and violent struggle between the corrupt priesthood and the power-hungry commander of the Army that brought about the utter destruction of Ruta—and the parts played by Helios, Netziachos, and Melchadek—can be read in the first novel of this trilogy, *The Seedbearers,* also published by Bantam Books.

you wanderers from Atlantis: I, Karadoc, High Priest of the Wessex, by the power vested in me in earth, bid you welcome as brothers, and grant you the freedom of this land in return for the wisdom you bring with you!"

The senior members of the visitors from across the sea all bowed low, and as they did so Ramin felt the tug of power, and already the scene was beginning to fade. The wisps of white fog began to swirl around him again, faster and faster, until again he was caught up in that stream of power, being rushed headlong into seeming nothingness. Again, just at the point when he felt he could bear it no longer, the speed began to diminish gradually until he again broke clear into the scene below.

He had expected to find himself either back in his body within the mound, or back to his visualization of himself on the summit of the Green Hill, and therefore it was a shock to find himself hovering over what could only be Cor Gaur in the very early days of its construction, and hence he had moved on to within two thousand years of his own real time.

But Cor Gaur was barely recognizable. The outer earthworks were there, but newer, the raw earth as yet not overgrown with turf. Of the great Sarsen Circle there was not a trace, nor the Holy Bluestones, nor the Altar Stone, nor the Hele Stone, and no trace either of the great broad avenue, lined with standing stones, that swept from Cor Gaur northward to Abiri and then to the River Avon. Indeed, throughout the entire site there was not one single stone, and he only knew that it *was* Cor Gaur by the surrounding landscape, particularly the hill from which he had watched Mog Agorn ride out that second day of his arrival in this land.

But although there were no stones, there was a curious arrangement of posts joined by ropes of some sort of creeper, like giant lengths of thongs, and the whole site gave the appearance of some giant geometric figure. And then suddenly he realized that he was looking at an enormous figure taken from the

magic square of the Sun—the self-same glyph that he
had seen on the parchment that Thetan had shown
him. The two larger posts there in the middle marked
the two centers, and the arrangement of ropes
marked the triangles and the double star. It was
obvious now how the circles, or ellipses, had been
created. It would be a simple matter to cut off a
length of rope to the exact measurement required,
fasten one end to a ring that would slip over one of
the center posts so that the ring could move freely,
and then fasten the other end to a wooden pointer—
and then simply walk around with the rope taut,
marking the ellipses that joined the points of the triangles. Once the ellipses were marked—and the
points of the triangles that fell on those ellipses—then
all the ropes, and extraneous posts, could be removed, leaving all the major post-holes marked ready
for the construction of the Sarsen Circle, the Holy
Bluestone Circle, and all the other stone locations. It
really was quite simple when you could see it laid out
like this.

Suddenly he felt himself urged away, the land
passing beneath him, picking up the River Avon,
moving swiftly to the north. The grasslands gave way
to thick forest, and the ground rose toward the hills
that jutted from the trees some fifteen miles from Cor
Gaur. He remembered the parchment that Menahotep had shown him, and looked to his left for the
great circle at Abiri. There, below, was certainly a
stone circle, but there were not above twenty stones
all told, and certainly no broad avenue that was supposed to link up with the one from Cor Gaur. Menahotep had said that Abiri was far older than Cor
Gaur. Parts of it were, obviously, but not all. The
Abiri that Menahotep knew had yet to reach its full
flowering.

But there, certainly, was Silbury, though as yet
there was no settlement to add the "bury" to the old
name of Sill Hill. And there was the great mound,
similar to the one at Glaeston, through larger, far
larger. What secret records were held impressed on

the Akhasic Record of the strange rites at Sill Hill Mound? No one knew how old it was. Druthin had said that it predated any Druidic records, and even the Wessex had no knowledge of who had built it—or why. It referred to the older time, to the days of the barbaric Elder Rites and, as such, was no longer used for modern rituals.

His speed decreased now as he reached the hills. That first one must be Kna-Put Hill, and the second one there must be Kennet. The one that was two or three miles further on must be the one they referred to by that curious name, the Wind on the Stone. Halfway between Kna-Put Hill and the Kennet, he saw a small cliff of naked rock, and as he dropped lower he saw a hive of activity. The cliff swarmed with peasants, and here and there a black-robbed Wessex priest supervised an individual party. Great slabs of Sarsen rock, some twelve to fifteen feet long, were already lying scattered at the base of the cliff, but he could not at first tell how these monstrous slabs had been quarried.

He dropped still lower and touched the mind of the senior priest who seemed to be in charge—and then he understood. The slabs were quarried at the point where a natural fault line ran across the face of the cliff, a great crack in the solid stone face of the cliff. The first operation was to drive a whole series of long, thin wooden pegs into the crack as deep as they would go, and then to pour a continuous stream of water into the crack, hour after hour, until the wooden pegs swelled and forced the crack open a little wider. Then, larger pegs would be driven in and the operation repeated, and then again with still larger pegs—day after day, on and on—until finally, unbelievably, a monstrous slab would move slightly, fractionally, and then great levers, like small trees, would be rammed in behind the stone, and gradually, fraction by fraction, the slab would be urged clear until its point of balance would be lost . . . And the great slab would slide ponderously over the edge and come crashing down to the valley floor below.

Some of the slabs would break up on impact, shattering into a thousand useless pieces of rock, wasting days of incredibly arduous work, but most remained intact, and these were prepared on the spot to cut them down to the size required before being hauled away to Abiri and to Cor Gaur to the south. One such slab, a monstrous fifty feet or more, was being broken into two equal lengths, and Ramin was fascinated by the method. He would not have believed it possible, and when he successfully searched the priest's mind as to how this was to be achieved, it still seemed quite fantastic. For two days now, one half of the length of the slab had been encased in a raging fire that had been continually fed hour by hour throughout the day and night until the solid rock was almost aglow, and now the time had come. Dozens of peasants were hastily pulling away the fire, shoveling the glowing, white-hot embers to one side. Nearby was a line of peasants to a tributary of the Avon close by, patiently waiting, gourds of water in their hands. At a signal, the first dozen men leapt to the glowing rock and hurled the water over that half of the slab, and then raced away to the river as the next dozen moved up. Over and over again, the maneuver was repeated, and so perfectly timed that the rock was being submitted to an almost continuous stream of water that boiled on impact, sending great clouds of steam to the sky.

At a point exactly halfway along the slab, an earth ramp had been built running back at a right angle to the slab and rising gradually to a height of ten feet. The ramp had three grooves, spaced about five feet apart at the top of the ramp, but all converging at a point at the exact center of the slab, and at the top of the ramp were three huge, roughly spherical boulders, one at the head of each groove.

At a signal from the priest, the line of water-carriers drew back, and as the slab continued to hiss and splutter, the retaining wedges in front of one of the boulders were knocked away and the massive ball of solid rock came thundering down the groove and smashed into the center of the slab. But to no avail. Thongs were thrown around the boulder, and fifty men leapt to drag it clear, while the water-carriers again dashed forward to soak the rapidly cooling slab. Again the signal was given, and the second boulder came hurtling down the ramp and smashed into the slab at exactly the same spot—and this time, with a mighty crack, the monstrous slab split into two equal halves at exactly the point marked by the priests.

Time moved on—a day, two days, a full circle of the Moon. Ramin was not sure, but now the earth had been dug out from beneath one end of one of the halves of the original monstrous slab, and young whole trees, stripped of bark, had been slipped beneath the rock, and more lay across its end to form a path of rollers. Massive thongs lay bound around the slab, and two enormous drag-lines stretched ahead of the slab. Ramin estimated that there must be over two hundred men on each drag-line, taking up the slack, ready to move.

Around the slab were something like seventy or eighty men carrying earthen pots of animal fat—indeed the rollers and the underside of the slab itself were thick with grease. It was impossible to estimate how many animals had contributed to that supply—perhaps thousands.

At a signal from the priest, the entire assembly broke into a weird, deep-throated chant that echoed across the valley floor—a chant so strange that even though Ramin was not of this scene it gave him a curious jolting, pulling sensation as though some giant hand was plucking his bowels out of his living body—a sickening, vomiting feeling. The reverberations of that strange chant were echoing throughout the inner, and pulling a response from the causative levels that flooded back to the physical in great waves of force that activated everyone present. Deeper and deeper the chant penetrated, and all eyes were glazed with the hypnotic effect of it. A slow, ponderous, crashing rhythm built up in the chant until the whole scene seemed to quiver each time that rhythm was struck, and when it seemed that the terrible buildup of tension could be endured no longer, the senior priest gave another signal, and the men on the drag-lines heaved backward, again and again, in time to the rhythm. Then suddenly, unbelievably, incredibly, the monstrous slab, weighing probably sixty or seventy tons, inched forward along the rollers. Again and again the chant rang out, and inch after painful inch was achieved until the entire slab was actually on the rollers. Men began to drag the tree-rollers from the back and rush them to the front to extend the path. Hour after hour Ramin watched the scene in utter fascination, and by the time the Sun had sunk below the horizon, the slab had traveled a hundred yards or more.

Again time moved on, and Ramin found himself hovering over the banks of the River Avon a mile from the Sarsen quarries. The great slab lay on the north bank in readiness, though whether it was the same slab or another he could not tell. Moored to the bank was quite the biggest raft that Ramin had ever seen, quite sixty feet by twenty, constructed of whole trees lashed together, far larger and thicker trees than those used for the ground-rollers. The pathway of rollers led right to the raft and butted up against its edge. This particular spot on the river had obviously been chosen with care. The north bank was only slightly higher than the water level, and led down to the raft in a gentle slope. The river was quite narrow at this point, and deep, and the opposite bank gave plenty of room for maneuver. The drag-lines from the slab had been increased in length and led down the bank, over the exact center of the raft, across the river, with enough left over to give a clear fifty feet lying on the opposite bank.

Again the chant rang out, its weird rhythm pounding through the inner, and again the men heaved on the drag-lines, and inch by inch the slab moved down the slipway to the heavily greased raft. The trickiest part of the operation came when the slab reached the raft itself and began to inch up onto the floating platform of logs. The raft itself was moored to the bank by a hundred lines, each one heaved tight, wound around a series of deeply embedded posts so that they would not slip. The edge of the raft by the bank rested on the shingle bottom, the far edge jutting out into deep water. It was obvious that while the slab was being inched onto the raft the floating platform must not move by even so much as a fraction of an inch. Indeed Ramin could see several other slabs lying in deep water a few yards away where previous attempts had ended in failure.

There were anxious faces as slowly, slowly, inch by inch, the slab was moved onto the raft. At one heart-stopping point, two of the mooring lines snapped, the loose ends whipping across the water. But the others held, and the slab ground further onto its platform. Ramin could see that the slab was not exactly on the center line of the raft—it was being led slightly to one side—and the senior priest in charge halted the operation as the raft began to tip dangerously at one corner. Half a dozen priests walked onto the raft to examine the situation more closely, and then at a signal one of the drag-lines was left loose, and the other came up taut and inched the head of the slab to one side until it lay exactly on the center line. Then both drag-lines again came up taut until finally the whole slab lay across the length of the raft.

Most of the mooring lines were cast off, leaving five only, and these five were slackened. The drag-lines were removed from the slab itself and fastened instead to the raft. Again the men on the far bank heaved on the lines, while on this side of the river great levers had been thrust under the edge of the raft by the bank, and quite fifty men heaved against them to lever the raft into deep water.

The men heaved, the sweat pouring down their faces, the weird, deep-throated chant booming out across the water, and then suddenly the raft moved an inch, and then another, and then in a moment of seeming pandemonium of snapping levers and whipping mooring lines, with men thrown to the ground,

the raft moved clear, dipped dangerously, righted itself, and dipped again at the other corner. The faces
of the priests were gray with anxiety, and then the
raft with the monstrous slab athwart its length slid
smoothly out into deep water, the five mooring lines
taking up the strain, bringing the raft to a halt, floating serenely on the Avon, ready to be poled down to
Cor Gaur fifteen miles away to the south.

Yet again time moved on—and again—and each
time the scene was the same, the quarry and the
river—and the priest in charge grew old in this service, and died, and another took his place, to grow
old in his turn and so die, his place being taken by
yet another. And so on and on—lifetimes of grinding
labor to furnish the stone for the great circles—and
Ramin was amazed, and the admiration grew within
him until his feelings were those of awe at this stupendous dedication that went on for century after
century. Men died by the score, by the hundred,
crushed and mutilated in a hundred different accidents. Ramin himself saw one such scene when a gigantic slab over a hundred feet long come crashing
down from the cliff face to sweep through the camp,
scattering and crushing the men as though they were
insects, the ground turning red with their blood as it
passed. But still the work went on . . . and on . . . and
on . . . unceasingly.

Yet again Ramin was caught up in that stream of
power, and this time he emerged again above Cor
Gaur a century on in time. All the great Sarsen Trilithons, bar one, were now erect, and the last was now
being prepared. Painstakingly, week after week, month
after month, the grooves were cut into the slabs so that
the great lintel would rest unmoving on top of the two
uprights, to remain so for all time. The two pits had
been dug in readiness for the two uprights, and each
lay in position ready to be hoisted to a standing position—two seventy-ton monsters.

A dozen great wedges had been sunk into the
ground at the lip of one of the pits, butting up against
the end of one of the slabs. A hundred feet away a

great earthen ramp had been built, and the drag-lines ran up at an angle from the other end of the slab to the top of the ramp. Two hundred men began to heave on the lines, and the slab moved against the wedges and stopped. Again they heaved on the lines, and unbelievably the far end of the slab lifted slightly into the air. As it did so, men rushed forward and thrust more wedges under its far end to hold it there. Again the line heaved, and again the slab moved up another fraction of an inch, and more wedges were thrust in to hold its position. Day after day the work went on and, inch after inch, the great slab rose fraction by fraction until it lay on the transverse wedges at an angle of forty-five degrees, its lower end still butted up against the wedges on the lip of the pit. Then one day Ramin saw more drag-lines being fastened to the upper end, splaying out on either side and, when all was secure, further lines were attached to the base wedges. At a given signal they were pulled clear and the great slab slid neatly into the pit, but still lying at an angle. Then again the backbreaking work went on, and inch by inch the great Sarsen slab was hoisted into an upright position, its alignment meticulously checked time and again until the priests were finally satisfied that it was in precisely the correct position, at precisely the correct angle. Once satisfied, work immediately began on the other slab, and day by day, week by week, the whole process was repeated until finally both uprights were in position. Now came the time to hoist the massive lintel into position, and Ramin could not even begin to guess how they were going to do it.

To his surprise the priests and peasants ignored the lintel itself and continued to work around the uprights. Day after day they shoveled earth around the bases of the two Sarsen uprights, stamping it hard, and gradually the level rose, two feet, three feet, six feet. Thousands of tons of earth must have been shifted. Day after day the work went on, and higher and higher the level rose, until the two giant uprights were completely buried with just their grooved tops showing—and then Ramin understood. The whole thing was one vast, earthen ramp—and, sure enough, the drag-lines were then fastened to one end of the lintel and the great stone was dragged up the ramp, inch by inch, day after day, until finally it reached the top and was maneuvered into position athwart the two uprights, fitting into the grooves that were just showing. Then the earth was removed, shovel by shovel, day in and day out—thousands of tons that went to increase the height and girth of the outer earthworks —and the level sank foot by foot until finally, after months of backbreaking work, there stood the last of the great Sarsen Trilithons towering to the sky, the massive lintel across the uprights, stark and titanic against the sky.

Again time moved on and Ramin saw the Holy Bluestones begin to arrive at Cor Gaur and be erected in the same way—though more quickly, since they were smaller and lighter than the massive Sarsens. But here a further incredible fact began to make itself known to Ramin. These bluestones did not come from the quarries at Kna-Put Hill and the Kennet, as did the Sarsens, but from a special quarry to the far north-west, in the land of Cymru, from the Sacred Prescelli, hundreds of miles from Cor Gaur. Mile after mile the Holy Bluestones moved on rollers across open land, and on rafts downriver, hazard after hazard, on their long journey. Thousands of lives were lost in the great work. Decade after decade flew swiftly by. Ramin became aware that one bluestone alone, weighing seven tons, took twelve years on its journey and cost the lives of twenty-seven men before it arrived at Cor Gaur. And perhaps most incredibly of all, one particular stone, the central King Stone, was brought across the sea from the vast, mist-shrouded island of Hiberia, sometimes known as Ei-Ir. But the Hiberians had not given up their sacred stone easily. Ten years the war had raged, and over two thousand Wessex warrior-priests and peasants had died before this one particular stone could be stolen—and then a

further two years were needed to bring it triumphant-
ly to Cor Gaur.

Four hundred years of work had been expended by
tens of thousands of Wessex priests and peasants from
the start of Cor Gaur to its completion. So staggering
was the concept that no priest-mathematician could
even begin to calculate the number of hours involved.
Thousands died in the great work. Tens of thousands
were born to the work, lived and died in its service,
without seeing an appreciable advance in the overall
scheme in their own lifetimes. Four hundred years of
sweat and toil and blood and death, one vast, staggering, dedicated national effort to erect *one* stone
circle called TYRRU CLUDAIR CYFRANGON, later known
as COR GAUR—just *one* circle alone. And Ramin remembered Menahotep saying that there were ap-
proximately *one thousand* stone circles scattered
throughout the realm. No one man could even begin
to grasp the enormity of the Wessex achievement.
Nor could any one man really understand how it was
possible for so magnificent a race to have degenerated so swiftly to the level that could spawn a man
like Mog Agorn and his seven foul sons. It was as
though the supreme, long, drawn-out effort had
sapped the very vitality of the race, leaving it an
empty, exhausted shell to be invaded by forces that
would never have otherwise gained a foothold. But
whatever the foulness the Wessex were now introduc-
ing, nothing could dim the magnificence of their
earlier glory. For thousands of years, to the end of
humanity itself, Cor Gaur would stand as a tribute to
its creators long after the Egyptians, the Druids, and
the Wessex themselves had vanished from the face
of the earth—and Ramin himself, a young, insignifi-
cant priest of Egypt, was present in spirit on that
glorious midsummer sunrise when the whole Wessex
priesthood gathered at the completed Cor Gaur to
perform the first-ever ritual amongst its giant stones.

Paean after paean of joyous chant rose into the
morning air from a thousand exalted hearts, priests and

priestesses suffused with inner glory. The High Priest himself, his face streaming tears of unbridled joy and ecstasy, stood poised on the King Stone, his staff upraised. And as the first ray of the midsummer sun lanced from the horizon, the very Earth Spirit itself moved to meet the downpouring solar force, and the ancient covenant between heaven and earth was fulfilled anew. The circle of force was completed, and spirit and matter met and mingled at the great stone circle at Cor Gaur, and the life-force spread throughout the land to bring the breath of eternity to all that lived!

Chapter Six

The full Council met at the zenith of the Sun, with Menahotep invited as a special guest. The Elder Druids listened with grave expressions to Ramin's recital of his experiences. "And then I awoke in my body," he finished. "While I was actually there the reality seemed sharp and clear—no less real to me than this very room here now—but since leaving the mound at dawn this morning, my memory has grown fuzzy, like a poorly remembered dream."

"We understand," said Druthin. "It takes a great deal of experience to hold the images intact. But you are sure of the names?"

"Yes. Karadoc of the Wessex, and the three visitors were Helios, Melchâdek, and a name that sounded like Netziachos."

"And you have nothing to add? You have told us everything that you can remember?"

Ramin hesitated. Druthin seemed satisfied, and yet at the same time oddly disappointed. "There is one other thing," he said slowly. He looked around at the assembled Druid Council. "But it seems too trivial to mention."

Druthin shook his head sharply. "Everything that happens in an initiation is important. Nothing is trivial." He leaned forward. "Speak. We will judge its value."

"Well," said Ramin slowly, "I was withdrawn from the scene of the dedication ritual at Cor Gaur and returned, as I have said, to the summit of the Green Hill, back to my own time. As I hovered over the

129

summit, my attention was drawn to an island in the marshlands about a mile from Glaeston." He hesitated again. "I did not go to the island. I just happened to notice this one in particular amongst all the others— though why I should do so I don't know. It was no different from the others—a perfectly ordinary little island with no distinguishing feature about it." He spread his hands in a helpless gesture. "And that is all. My attention was on it for no more than a few seconds. The next thing I know I was back in my body."

"And the name of the island?" said Druthin softly. All eyes were riveted on him now, and there was a sudden tension in the room.

Ramin shook his head. "I'm sorry, but I have no memory of its name. It really was only a fleeting moment." Again there was that look of disappointment. "The only thing I remember is something to do with apples . . . The word 'avalon' came to my mind, which is the Druid word for 'apples,' I believe."

Druthin smiled and sat back in his chair, and the tension was suddenly gone. "Well done, my boy!" he said softly. "Well done!" The others of the Council were now all smiling, and Thetan's eyes were alive with warm approval. "And now I think I can explain." He looked around the great carven table, and one by one the Council members nodded their consent. "Unlike Egyptian initiations," he went on, "in Druidry an initiation can be taken at several levels. Knowledge of the first scene that you described grants a first-level initiation, the second scene grants a second-level initiation, and so on. The highest level at this grade is the one in which the secret name of our sacred island is revealed." He looked at Ramin and smiled. "Your initiation was therefore a success at all levels up to and including the highest. For you now know of the Isle of Avalon."

Ramin was still puzzled. "But what is its significance?" he said. "I don't understand."

"As far as the physical plane is concerned," said Druthin, "it is, as you said, a perfectly ordinary island, no different to any of the others, except that it has a grove of apple trees planted by Druids long, long ago, and maintained by us. Hidden in that grove is a small temple called the Temple of Avalon. It is rarely used, for indeed as far as the physical plane is concerned we visit the island only twice a year—once at the Vernal Equinox to tend the trees, and once at the Autumnal Equinox to harvest the fruit."

"And the inner planes?"

Druthin fingered the Serpent Symbol that hung around his neck. "As far as the inner planes are concerned," he said softly, "it is the secret heart of Druidry." Ramin made as if to speak, but Druthin held up his hand. "Enough. I can say no more. Further knowledge and understanding of Avalon can only be obtained by you through meditation. Neither the island nor its name is known to the lower degrees of Druidry. It is known only to those of the Fourth Degree, we of the White, and even we *never* mention its name or refer to the island at all, even obliquely, outside this Council chamber. And *that* is a cardinal rule that will also apply to you! The name, Avalon, may be used silently in your meditations, but it must *never* be uttered aloud, particularly as a word of power. It is a key to unlock the door to the Greater Mysteries of Druidry and admit your soul to our sacred and most secret heart." He looked carefully at the young Egyptian. "Use it reverently," he warned, "and wisely."

Ramin nodded gravely. "I understand," he said. "And the Wessex?"

"They do not have even the slightest inkling of its existence—and never will."

At that moment a knock sounded at the carven door, and the Council members looked suddenly startled. Council meetings, particularly those concerning initiations, were *never* interrupted except for matters of the utmost importance. A senior priestess entered, robed in white with a blue headdress, the Mistress of the Blue, the priestess responsible for the care and welfare of the Bardic Degree. Her face was troubled and her eyes were wet with recent tears. "Forgive the intrusion, Arch-Mage," she said quietly, "but there are grave matters that the Council must know about immediately."

"We have finished our matters here, so it is no intrusion," Druthin said. "What is it?"

The priestess signaled, and Cyffru the woodcutter came in bearing a bundle, followed by his daughter, Brisis. They had never come further into Glaeston College than the great courtyard and the kitchens, where they delivered the herbs and the wood logs that they collected for the Druid priesthood, and certainly not here to the central Council chamber. They were already feeling out of place and a little overawed, and the sight of the grave faces of the entire Druid Council did little to put them at ease. Because of his nervousness, Cyffru's voice was more harsh and abrupt than it would have been. He laid the bundle on a bench. "Here is something you should see," he growled, and pulled back the covering.

A gasp of horror came from many throats, and several of the Druids came to their feet, Druthin included, startled and appalled. For there on the bench was the dead body of the boy, Zelta, his wrists dark with dried blood. There was a horrified silence, and then Druthin came around from behind the great table and slowly approached the body. He put his hand on the boy's breast and then turned to Cyffru. "How came he to his death?" he said quietly.

"By Mog Agorn's own hand," said the woodcutter. "We saw it happen."

"Explain."

Brisis stepped forward. "We were watching Cor Gaur from the nearby hills, as instructed by the Egyptian."

Menahotep nodded. "That is correct. Go on."

"We saw the entire Wessex force move out of Cor Gaur yesterday afternoon," she said, "and make a new camp only a mile away."

"Leaving only Mog Agorn himself, and Asher, the

High Priestess," said Cyffru. "Zelta was still held prisoner in the tent."

"We waited for darkness," the girl said, "and were going to creep down and try to sneak the boy away."

Druthin shook his head. "A dangerous and foolhardy thing to attempt," he said sharply. "The Wessex would have had no trouble in tracking you down before you had covered half the distance. None of you would have reached Glaeston alive!"

"Maybe, and maybe not," growled Cyffru. "If we could have reached the woods we would have stood a chance. I know the woods better than any man alive. It was worth the risk."

"But we could not try it anyway," said Brisis, "because Mog Agorn did not keep to his tent but sat in the center of the great circle for hours, a few yards away from the very tent where Zelta was held."

"But we crept down anyway," said Cyffru. "If I could have got within spear-cast of him, he would have died that very night!"

Druthin threw up his hands. "Cyffru, my friend, you are a brave but foolish man. Your spear would not have reached him." He shook his head helplessly. "Go on, go on."

"But we could not try that anyway. It was too dark to be sure of my aim."

"So we waited for the moon," Brisis said. "It was too dark to see very much, but we could hear Mog Agorn moving about. When the moon rose we saw Asher, quite naked, lying on the King Stone, with Zelta at her head. He was still bound with thongs and seemed unconscious. And then . . . and then . . ."

"Go on," said Druthin quietly. "You must tell us everything."

"It was an evil thing to see," said Cyffru. "I shall remember it all my life. As the moon rose, Mog Agorn lay with his daughter, with Asher, as a lover would."

"He then cut the boy's wrists," said Brisis, "and the blood spurted over both of them!"

"And then he finished what he was doing with his

daughter, crying out strange words that I did not understand!"

There was a deep silence. The horror on several faces deepened as they realized the significance of what they had just heard. Druthin's expression was grim indeed. "And then?"

"The moon was suddenly hidden by cloud," said Brisis, "and we could not see, but after a few minutes we heard a horse ride off, and when the moon rode clear again Mog Agorn and Asher were gone, but Zelta was still lying on the King Stone."

"But he was dead," said Cyffru. "No doubt of that, and so we traveled all night and brought him here to Glaeston."

Again there was a deep silence, and then Druthin said: "Can you remember the strange words that Mog Agorn uttered—even if you do not understand them?"

The woodcutter shook his head. "They were like nothing I have ever heard before."

"No matter," he said grimly. "I think some of us know what they were." He put his hand on the woodcutter's shoulder. "Thank you, my friend. And you too, Brisis. Once again you have risked your lives for us and rendered a service to the Druids. We shall not forget. Go and eat now, and sleep. I will speak to you again when you have rested."

When they had gone, Druthin turned to the Mistress of the Blue. "Zelta will not be buried in any ordinary grave. He and Vordin will be interred in one of the ritual mounds and be granted the honor of the full Ritual of the Dead, as befitting those who sacrifice their lives for the true priesthood. Make the necessary arrangements."

The priestess bowed and then signaled for two junior priests to enter and bear the body away. When they had gone, Druthin resumed his seat at the great table. "Normally," he said courteously to Ramin, "we would now be filled with joy at the success of your initiation, but you will, I know, forgive our preoccupation with these grave matters. Remain with us. It is meet that you know of these things."

Ramin bowed. "I understand, Druthin, and thank you."

Menahotep leaned forward. "We of Egypt, though horrified at such foul deeds, nevertheless do not understand the special significance of what we have heard. Is there some particular horror in all this?"

"There is indeed," said Druthin grimly. "I believe that Mog Agorn and Asher have used an ancient and particularly evil ritual whereby the incestual mating between father and daughter creates the necessary conditions so that the subsequent child of that mating, though having a human body, is ensouled by one of the Dark Ones!"

"A Dark One!" said Menahotep. "Is that really possible?"

"Yes," said Druthin grimly, "though it requires an extraordinary degree of corruption in the vessel used. Asher is depraved enough to possibly qualify for that description. It also requires an adept of a particular type of power, and Mog Agorn might just also qualify. They have very little chance of success, but it *is* possible." He turned to the Egyptian. "It is a very ancient ritual indeed—so ancient that there is a legend that it not only predates both Druidry and Egypt, but also predates even Atlantis, and, before that, even Lemuria—back to a time even before the beginnings of human evolution, when the earth was host to the brief evolution of a nonhuman species that were noted for the depth of their depravity. The old had to make way for the new, but they are forever seeking to remanifest, to begin again their rule on earth, and their way back in is through the depravity and evil of the human soul itself."

"What would happen," said Menahotep, "if Mog Agorn and Asher fail in their attempt?"

"They would die, and I would think that their souls would be totally annihilated."

The Egyptian pursed his lips. "And that would solve all your problems."

"Very true."

"And if they succeed?"

"If the subsequent child grows to adulthood, the Wessex would have an adept of incredible power and unbelievable evil to lead them. It would also open the way for similar rituals, so that more and more of these things could be born into human form. It would not only affect this land but would plunge the whole world into darkness, perhaps for a thousand years, perhaps forever. Neither Druid nor Egyptian could stand against them."

Menahotep's expression became even darker. "And the more that come through, the easier it will be for those that follow. In a very brief space of time, a hundred years or so, we could reach a stage when every single birth on this planet is nonhuman!"

"In theory—yes."

Menahotep rose to depart. "I will contact Egypt immediately, by meditation. They will not be able to help us on the physical plane. There is not enough time for an army to arrive before the birth of the child, particularly as its birth will fall in your winter. But Egypt has its own priests of power, and will do all they can on the inner."

Druthin also rose. "The mother *must* be destroyed before the child can be born," he said grimly, "even if it cost the life of every Druid and every Egyptian on earth!"

"He is mad—raving mad!" Fangorn strode restlessly up and down, fingering his knife. "And why? *Why?*" The seven sons of Mog Agorn were met in a forest glade near Cor Gaur, ostensibly on a hunting expedition. Indeed, one wild pig already lay athwart Fangorn's own chariot. "He is High Priest of the Wessex and controls the whole realm. What greater power can a man want?"

"Spiritual power," said Awrgon. "It is not enough to control men's lives. Our father needs must control their souls as well."

"And he does not control the whole realm," said one of the others. "The Druids still defy him."

"All right, but what he is trying to do is madness. The manifestation of a Dark One will destroy us all. You speak of controlling men's souls, Awrgon. If a Dark One is made manifest, then it will be *our* souls that will be forfeit!" Fangorn's face was dark with anger and a desperate fear. "Admittedly, the Druids will not be able to stand against a Dark One, but then neither will we, the Wessex! Both Druid and Wessex alike will become groveling slaves to some nonhuman obscenity. He is mad, I tell you, raving mad!"

"You are too full of fear too soon, Fangorn," said Awrgon.

"And with good reason! You of all people should know what it means to have a Dark One in our midst."

"Indeed I do—better than most." Awrgon rose and faced his elder brother. "And you know full well, Fangorn—or should—that a priest has to be a powerful vessel, highly trained, before he dares invoke an inner plane force within himself, whether Dark or Light, and the greater the force to be invoked, the greater the vessel he has to be to bear the strain. A Dark One would require a vessel so powerful and of such high quality that it would require a priest or a priestess the like of which has never been seen by any race of Man. Do you *really* believe that Asher is of such high quality?"

The seven sons fell silent, and Fangorn looked at his younger brother with grudging respect. "You are right," he said slowly. "She is a good ritual priestess but she is nowhere near that level."

"I believe that all Mog Agorn has done," said Awrgon, "is to contact the very black depths of Asher's own corrupt soul, and that as such her pregnancy will invite the incarnation of an equally corrupt human soul—but a *human* soul, not a Dark One."

"That's possible, certainly."

"But knowing this doesn't change matters very much as far as we are concerned," said Awrgon. "If the Wessex believe it is a Dark One, then they will obey it without hesitation for fear of what would happen if they didn't. And if the brat is brought up believing itself to be a Dark One, then he will bear himself accordingly. And also, Fangorn, remember this. By our own laws, it should be one of us who takes command of the Wessex after our father's death, *not* the brat of our sister's incest. Why should we bend the knee when it is he who should bend to us?"

"But what can we do about it?" said one of the others.

Awrgon, the youngest, took command of his brothers as he did so easily of late. "Firstly, what we must be clear about is what we *cannot* do. You saw the mood of the assembled Wessex this morning when our father broke the news. The fools are wild with delight, thinking that great power will soon be theirs. We cannot bring them to our command overnight. We could do so gradually by spreading doubts about the possibility of a Dark One manifesting through Asher, but that would take time, and long before we could succeed, word would reach our father's ears and he would order our deaths and say that it was by command of the Dark One soon to come."

"Then why don't we just kill Asher?" said the second brother.

"Because Mog Agorn would still order our deaths, for the same reason."

"All right, then why don't we kill both Asher *and* our father?"

Awrgon shook his head. "No! *Think*, my brothers, try to *think!* If we are held responsible for our father's death, then by our own laws none of us could inherit. The robe of the High Priest would pass to our father's brother, to Sleg Agorn, and *he* would also order our deaths, again pretending that it was by command of the Dark One." He sighed irritably at the stupidity of his brothers. "You don't seem to understand! The Wessex are wild with delight at the promise of unlimited power, and would need only the slightest excuse to turn on anyone who robbed them of that prospect."

Fangorn strode up to his brother. Awrgon's high-handed manner often irritated him beyond endurance. The boy was acknowledged to be the most intelligent of the seven, but he never lost an opportunity to highlight that fact. "All right, Awrgon," he said viciously, "you are the clever one among us. You have told us what we cannot do. Now tell us what we *can* do!"

Awrgon smiled. He enjoyed baiting Fangorn; his brother grew so irritable so quickly. "It is simple. Asher and Mog Agorn must die, and since it cannot be by our hands, then we must delegate the task to someone else, someone who also has a strong motive for wanting them dead."

"All right, who?"

Awrgon looked up at his brother's dark face. "The Druids, of course," he said simply.

Menahotep was with Druthin when Melkor brought the news during the late afternoon. "It is still hard to believe," said the battle-commander, "but Fangorn and the rest of the seven sons of Mog Agorn are at the Great Gates demanding a discussion with the Druid Council."

Druthin raised his eyebrows. "Life is indeed full of surprises," he said. "What do they wish to discuss?"

"They will not say. It is for the ears of the Council only."

Druthin turned to Menahotep. "A trap, do you think?"

The Egyptian pursed his lips. "Possible, but not likely."

"Fangorn thought that might be the reaction," said Melkor, "so he bade me tell you that the Council could bring seven guards—seven against seven."

"I presume he will not come into the College," said Menahotep.

"No, the meeting is to be outside the gates. I fear he does not trust us."

"The feeling is mutual," said Druthin drily. "I am tempted to say that I will not speak with such as they, but curiosity is winning the day."

"And we might learn something," said Menahotep.

"True. Very well, Melkor, tell Fangorn we will come. Gather the Council, Thetan included. Tell them I will meet them in the courtyard in ten minutes. Instruct a guard of seven, four Druid warrior-priests and three Egyptians. There is no harm in re-emphasizing that we have Egypt behind us in this struggle. Besides," he said, turning to Menahotep, "that Captain of yours would daunt the bravest enemy."

Ten minutes later the great gates swung open and Druthin and the full Council moved out to meet the Wessex. The guard fanned out on either side and Druthin stepped forward to face the seven sons of Mog Agorn. "Greetings, Fangorn," he said quietly. "What brings you to Glaeston? Some message from your father?"

"He does not know that we are here," growled Fangorn, "nor do any of the Wessex."

"Vordin said much the same thing when he visited your camp at Cor Gaur, but he was not believed and so died. Why then should we believe you?"

"That was none of my doing," said Fangorn, "or any of us here. It was Mog Agorn who ordered his death."

"I accept that," said Druthin. "Vordin at least was an adult and was aware that he was walking into danger. But the case of the boy, Zelta, is different. The Wessex will pay dearly for *his* death!"

"Again, that was none of my doing," said Fangorn. "The boy died by my father's own hand. The only Druids that I have killed—or any of us here—were in battle, a battle that was sought by the Druids, not the Wessex. However, we did not come here to exchange accusations, Druthin."

"Why, then?"

Fangorn stepped down from his chariot and came closer. "Since the body of the boy, Zelta, is missing, we presume that it was somehow brought here to Glaeston."

"Correct. Go on."

"And we presume that you know the manner of his

death and the ritual in which he was used by Mog Agorn."

"We do."

Fangorn beckoned Awrgon to come forward. "Awrgon here states that a priest has to be a vessel of singular power before he dares to invoke an inner plane force within himself, and that the greater the force, the greater the vessel he must be. What say you to this?"

"Your brother is correct," said Druthin.

"He also says," Fangorn went on, "that Asher is not a sufficiently high-grade priestess to invoke a Dark One within herself, and that if she becomes pregnant from last night's work then it will be from the incarnation of an ordinary human soul."

Druthin hesitated. It was difficult to know how much to reveal. "Normally," he said finally, "a priest invokes a force to indwell his own consciousness such that the consciousness of the force, if I can so express it, fuses with the consciousness of the priest such that they become one. If the priest is not properly prepared, or invokes a force too powerful for him to safely absorb, then the attempted fusion would cause a total disorientation of the consciousness of the priest. The result would be either death or insanity for the priest concerned." He looked from the one to the other. "But Asher's case is different. Certainly she is not of sufficient stature as a priestess, by a long way, to even attempt to fuse the consciousness of a Dark One with her own. But then she isn't trying to. If she becomes pregnant, then her own consciousness will continue to indwell her own body, and the consciousness of the Dark One will indwell the body of the growing child in her womb. There will be no fusion of consciousness, and therefore she does not need to be a high-grade priestess. However," he warned, "the presence of a Dark One within her womb is highly dangerous. Its consciousness would gradually permeate throughout its immediate environment, and it is highly likely that Asher would gradually grow more and more insane from the strain of such proximity."

Fangorn did not really understand what Druthin was saying. He turned to his brother. "And what say you to that?"

Awrgon frowned. "You have a point, Druthin—about the fusion I mean. Do you then really think it possible that Asher could become pregnant with a Dark One?"

"It is within the realms of possibility," said Druthin, "but only just. But we Druids cannot risk even so remote a possibility."

"Nor can we. The physical presence of a Dark One among us would be disastrous to both Druid and Wessex alike."

"And to the whole world."

"Which is," said Awrgon simply, "why Mog Agorn and Asher must die before the child is born."

There was a deep and surprised silence, and Druthin's eyes narrowed. "We are speaking of your father and your sister," he said carefully.

"No, Druthin. We are speaking of a High Priest and a High Priestess who are leading the Wessex down to utter destruction."

"Very well. Though we abhor the taking of human life, we also feel that they must die. We are in agreement then, though I doubt that our motives are the same."

"Ours are clear enough," said Awrgon. "Under Wessex law, in the event of the death of the High Priest, the command of the Wessex is passed to whichever son is considered most fitting. However, if Asher becomes pregnant and delivers a child, whether it is a Dark One or not, Mog Agorn will see to it that the brat succeeds him, thus robbing us of our rightful inheritance."

"Ah!" said Druthin. "*Now* I understand! Well, I can only suggest that you and Fangorn dispose of your father and sister. It is the Wessex who have brought this trouble, and it is the responsibility of the Wessex to rectify matters."

"But we cannot. The Wessex priesthood are besotted at the thought of unlimited power that would be conferred by the presence of a Dark One as their High Priest, and so would turn on anyone who robbed them of that destiny."

"But at least Mog Agorn and Asher would be dead," said Druthin.

"And so, too, would we."

"Perhaps, but no sacrifice would be too great to stop your father's madness."

"Druthin—I would not willingly lay down my life for anyone," he said simply, "nor would Fangorn."

"Now, *that* I believe," said Druthin drily. "What then do you suggest?"

"The matter is quite clear. It must be the Druids who bring about the death of Mog Agorn and Asher —with our help, of course."

Again there was a deep silence. Menahotep looked anxiously at Druthin. It was a very tempting offer. Druthin, however, finally shook his head and said: "We will do all in our power to encompass their deaths and so prevent the dreadful possibility that hangs over us all, but we cannot align ourselves with those whose motives are purely selfish."

Fangorn stepped forward. "The important thing is that they die. The motives of those who would help the killers is immaterial."

"Those who kill without good reason," said Druthin sternly, "are guilty of murder."

"But, Druthin," said Awrgon, "if you refuse our help it may be that you will fail, and thus run the risk of letting loose a Dark One on the world. If that does indeed happen, then the responsibility will be yours."

"Not so! *If* it happens, then the responsibility quite clearly lies with Mog Agorn and Asher."

Fangorn bellowed with sudden anger. "You are a fool, Druthin!"

"Perhaps so," said the Arch-Mage stiffly, "but we Druids live by our understanding of inner plane principles. If we now choose otherwise simply for the sake of convenience, then we would be denying the very reason for our existence." He raised his Serpent Staff and pointed at the Wessex priests. "We will not accept the help of would-be murderers—and that is final!" And he turned and led the Council and the guards back through the gates into Glaeston College.

"How do you feel?"

Asher smiled cautiously. "A bit apprehensive," she admitted, "but otherwise I feel perfectly normal."

Mog Agorn patted his daughter's shoulder. "Good. And why shouldn't you feel normal? It was a perfectly normal thing to do."

She arched her eyebrows. "Father, a mating wherein a daughter lays with her father in an ancient nonhuman ritual, with the express purpose of bearing a Dark One in her womb, can hardly be described as 'normal.' It is not the sort of thing you come across too often."

He chuckled evilly. "True. I meant that the physical act itself was perfectly normal."

"I wouldn't know. I was still out of my body when you entered me."

He looked at her curiously. "Where were you?"

She shrugged. "I don't know. Somewhere in the half-world. There was the usual pulsating beat, and the deep reds of the lower earth, but precisely where in the half-world I couldn't say. Something was holding me down—something quite incredibly powerful—but I could not twist around to see who or what it was."

Mog Agorn grunted. "The Dark One himself, maybe. He probably didn't want you in your body while conception was taking place."

"Maybe. Anyway I could see you and my own body, and the great stones, far above me—so far that you were as tiny as insects—but I could feel absolutely nothing, and that is unusual for me. I usually know what is happening to my body when I am out."

A burst of laughter came from outside the tent. The evening was far gone and dark, and the moon had already risen. He saw her quizzical look and said: "I have ordered a feast tonight to celebrate the most successful ritual ever performed by the Wessex. Fangorn brought two pigs home from the hunt and it seemed a pity to waste them."

"Let's hope they are not celebrating too early." She looked at him. "When will we know for sure?"

"The end of your moon will give us a fair idea, but to be absolutely sure, we ought to wait until the end of your second moon from now before making any announcements."

She sighed. "And then our troubles begin."

"My dear girl, our troubles have already begun. As from this very moment, we are both in perpetual danger every second of every day and every night." His face was dark with determination. "As from tonight your tent will be moved into the center of Cor Gaur and every single night you will sleep in your tent surrounded by the entire Wessex force, and my tent will be next to yours. I have personally handpicked a bodyguard of fifty warrior-priests all known for their fanatical loyalty to you personally. For the next nine moons you will never ever go out of Cor Gaur without those fifty men, and even then you will travel by chariot. Those Arabian mares can outrun anything in the land." He held up his hand. "And to safeguard you from your own irritability at such irksome restrictions, each man in your bodyguard has instructions from me personally, on penalty of death for failure, to refuse to obey any order of yours that contradicts any given previously by me. I might add that I have selected a further fifty men to perform the same service for myself."

She came over to him. "What is it, Father? What has happened?"

"It is nothing. Do not worry yourself."

She stamped her foot angrily. "What is this 'nothing' that has led to such massive safeguards?" She grabbed him by the shoulders. "I am no fool, Mog Agorn, so don't treat me like one! What has happened?"

He threw her off. "All right, I will tell you. Calm yourself." He paced the tent, the worry now clearly in his eyes. "I went back to Cor Gaur this morning to collect the dead body of the boy, Zelta, but it had disappeared."

"Disappeared? How is that possible?"

"An interesting question, and the only answer I could see is that we could not have been alone last night. Someone must have been watching, and so carried the body away afterward. We may never know," he said feelingly, "how close to death we came last night."

"But who? The Druids?"

"Yes, it had to be. So, during my meditation this morning, I looked over Glaeston and there indeed was the missing body. Not only that, but Druthin and the Druid Council know of our ritual and its purpose." He looked at her grimly. "They will now do almost anything to bring about our deaths before the child is born, and such determination from so powerful a cult is always dangerous."

Asher sat down again, obviously relieved. "Is that all? Really, Father, you do get upset about such trivial matters. The Druids are no problem," she said in a voice full of contempt. "We can easily handle them."

"Oh, can we indeed?" he said sarcastically. "If you underrate the Druids, then you are indeed a fool." He waved his hand. "All right, but it is not the Druids who worry me. As I was about to withdraw from Glaeston, I saw your seven brothers arrive with Fangorn at their head."

She came to her feet again. "At Glaeston? This morning? What were they doing there?"

"Offering to help the Druids dispose of you and me." He nodded grimly. "Yes, it appears that Fangorn in particular is worried that the command of the Wessex would not come to him after my death, but will pass to your child, Asher. And oh, he is so right! It also seems that my seven brave sons do not want to be the executioners themselves, for fear that the Wessex would turn on them and tear them apart. And again, they are so right."

"But what will you do?"

He patted her arm. "Do not worry. I have already done it. Come, the feast is waiting."

"Feast? What do I care about feasts!" She grabbed his shoulder again. "What have you done about it, Mog Agorn? Tell me!"

He smiled grimly. "If you want to know that, then come to the feast. Events there will give you your answer."

As they stepped from the tent into the night, a great roar rose up from every Wessex throat, and each man drew his sword and held it high aloft in salute to their High Priest who was bringing them so much. Mog Agorn led Asher into the midst of them to a specially prepared couch of green linen and sat her down. He then sprang onto a rock and held his arms to the sky. Gradually, the salutations died down until there was utter silence, and then Mog Agorn, High Priest of the Wessex, suddenly pointed to Asher. "*Behold the mother!*" he roared, and his voice echoed with power along the emptiness of the silence. A deep roar of approval rose up from the entire Wessex force.

When the tumult died down, Mog Agorn held up his hands again for silence. "Before the feast can begin there is another matter to dispose of, for there is one amongst us who is not worthy of the name of Wessex." The priests looked to each other, the alarm suddenly in their eyes. "Yes," cried Mog Agorn. "There is one here who would betray us to the Druids at Glaeston. What should be the fate of such a one?"

"*Death!*" came the reply from several throats. "*Death, death!*" from a dozen more, and the whole Wessex force took up the cry until the sound of it echoed across the plains. "DEATH!"

Mog Agorn raised his hands. "So be it," he roared. "The Wessex have spoken."

Fangorn was deeply alarmed. Mog Agorn could not possibly know of his visit to Glaeston. But then, suddenly, he caught that particular glint in his father's eye directed straight at him, and Fangorn turned to race for the chariots. But he found himself hemmed in by the milling crowd, and at the rear he could see the guard waiting in readiness for such a break.

Ever one to take the bold course, Fangorn stepped forward and called for silence. "What madness is this? Who here could possibly betray us to the Druids? Name him, *Father*—if you can!"

"Very well. Out of your own mouth be it. It is you yourself who are guilty of this treachery, and name you I will—*Fangorn!*"

The boy calmly folded his arms and sneered at his father. "What nonsense are you planning now, Mog Agorn?" He waved his hand to where Awrgon stood close by Mog Agorn. "I was out hunting all day in the forest. You have me to thank for these pigs that will soon fill your bellies. Nor was I alone. I was with my six brothers—your other sons—all day. Ask Awrgon there, if you disbelieve me. Or is your insanity so great," he sneered, "that you accuse all seven!"

Mog Agorn smiled evilly. "Ah, yes, my other sons. There is always one bad dog in every litter, and you are he, Fangorn. The others will not support your lies."

"Ask Awrgon there," sneered Fangorn. "Ask him!"

Mog Agorn nodded. "Very well. Again out of your own mouth be it! Stand forth, Awrgon, and tell the Wessex what you told me."

Fangorn's eyes narrowed. Not Awrgon, surely not! What could his younger brother hope to gain? He would die along with the rest of them if he opened his mouth now!

Awrgon stepped forward, the other brothers behind him. His face shone in the early moonlight. He spread his hands helplessly as though loath to speak. "We argued with him all morning, my other brothers and I, but Fangorn would not listen." The other brothers nodded in agreement.

Fangorn leapt forward. "You foul liar!" he screamed. "What has he paid you to tell these lies, you whimpering dog!" and he made as if to spring on Awrgon, but the guard stepped between them and held him helpless.

"Bind him and stuff his foul mouth," the High Priest ordered, and Fangorn was dragged down, his rage and fear dying to a sudden gurgle.

Awrgon shook his head sadly. "He was demented with rage this morning and scarcely knew what he said or did. Fangorn has always thought to take command of the Wessex on the death of our father, but now he feared that the Dark One in the High Priestess' womb would supplant him—as indeed we all knew it would." He spread his hands again. "Who would want Fangorn as High Priest when there is a Dark One to lead us?" As he mentioned the Dark One, the boy gave the salute, and many in the ranks of the Wessex followed his example and gave their own salutes. Mog Agorn could not help but smile at Awrgon's coolness.

"We pleaded with him for hours," he went on, "but he would not listen, and so we went with him to Glaeston, pleading with him all the way. And at Glaeston, he offered to help Druthin commit a foul crime against the Wessex."

The boy fell silent. "What crime was this, Awrgon?" said Mog Agorn gently. "You must speak of it so that all shall know."

"He offered," Awrgon said in a whisper, "to help the Druids take the life of Mog Agorn, the High Priest, our own father, and the life also of Asher, and so prevent the coming of the Dark One. So that he, Fangorn, could then take command of the Wessex!"

He turned to Mog Agorn and the Wessex could see the tears on his cheeks. "If the Druids had accepted, we would have killed him there and then, but they refused, and so we held our hands and came to you."

Mog Agorn raised his hand. "It grieves me deeply that my eldest son could be guilty of such treachery. But the Wessex have already decreed the sentence, *death!*" He beckoned to the guard. "Let the will of the Wessex be done. Let the death of a thousand cuts come to Fangorn for his foul crime!"

And the roar rose up from the Wessex, and each man plucked his knife. The guard formed an avenue so that the priests could pass through it in single file toward the bound figure of Fangorn at the other end. As each priest passed the struggling figure, he lightly stroked him with his knife, a stroke so light that only a hairline of blood appeared—and the next man, and the next. The blood began to trickle to the ground, and still more priests joined the line, and those who had gone first now joined the rear to take their turn again. A hundred cuts, a hundred more—and still they came, and Fangorn died in a pool of blood condemned and sentenced by his fellow priests.

Asher plucked the sleeve of Mog Agorn's robe. "Very well, Father. Tell me how you arranged all that."

Mog Agorn grinned down at her. "It was simple. Five of my sons are of no importance. They will always be those who follow, never those who lead. But Fangorn and Awrgon are different."

"What did you promise Awrgon?"

He patted her shoulder. "That when the child is born, I will relinquish command of the Wessex and make him High Priest to rule the Wessex for twenty years—until the Dark One is ready to assume command."

"And he believes you?"

The High Priest shrugged. "He had a choice, of course. It was either that or death. And the Wessex *will* need Awrgon for a few years, as I have always said."

Mog Agorn grinned again and sprang back onto the rock and raised his arms to the sky. "*So die all traitors!*" he roared. "LET THE FEASTING BEGIN!"

Chapter Seven

The word went out along the trackways and the ancient paths throughout the land of what had happened at Cor Gaur, though the story differed depending on whether the messenger was Druid or Wessex. Mog Agorn's couriers cried aloud the news that a Child was to be born to the Wessex at Cor Gaur, a mighty Lord from the inner planes who was incarnating to lead the Wessex to great glory and honor. Druthin's emissaries moved quietly and sadly throughout the realm carrying the grim news that soon an Evil One was to be born to the Wessex who would plunge the whole world into utter darkness, one whose coming had to be prevented at all cost. And when messenger met messenger, their swords rang out, and priests fought and died on the lonely paths with no stone or cairn to mark their passing.

But the reactions to each message were identical. Throughout the realm, priests knelt and made their own obeisance at one last ritual and then set off for the two respective centers of their calling—the Wessex to Cor Gaur and the Druids to Glaeston—leaving behind the merest few to perform the rituals and keep alive the local contacts with the Earth Spirit. And more priests died, and yet still more, as party encountered party and fought bitterly to the death, neither asking nor giving quarter. Deeds of valor came and went unrecorded in the history of Man, though other eyes were there to watch and note the clash of priestly arms. And the survivors moved on and fought again, and yet again, a trail of blood and death that led closer and closer to their journey's end.

And so they came to Glaeston and to Cor Gaur, a living stream to swell the ranks. They came from as far west as Lanyon Quoit, Men an Tol, and the dreaded Nine Maidens at Boscawen-Un, where the angry sea pounds the land by day and night—from as far east as Coldrum and Kits Coty, the mist-enshrouded Vale of Swanscombe Mounds—and some, a very few, came from the Wild Isles to the far far North, from Maes Howe, whose ancient cairns bore the runic words that few would dare to utter. And they came in youth and came in age, some who had barely begun their priestly vows, and some whose wisdom spanned the stars—and still they came, and still yet more to honor or to curse the Child.

Menahotep knocked at the carven door and entered. "Greetings," he said quietly.

"Ah, come in. Greetings," said the Arch-Mage. "Your coming is timely. It gives me the honor to make two distinguished men known to each other: Menahotep, Priest of Re—Vaila, Priest of the Sun."

The stranger rose courteously and stepped forward. "The name of Menahotep is known to me," he said. He was a man past his prime, as old as Druthin himself, but he bore himself well. "I am pleased to meet the man who bears so honorable a name."

Menahotep bowed. "And the name of Vaila of Maes Howe in the Wild Isles is known to me also—a name that bears no small honor itself."

The two men smiled at each other. Druthin waved them to chairs at the table. "I have long wanted you two to meet," he said, "though I would have preferred less ominous times than these."

"Dark days, indeed," said Vaila. "When first I received your message I did not want to believe its significance." He smiled at Druthin. "Forgive me, my friend, but I thought old age had at last warped that fine mind of yours. But I checked on the inner, and sure enough the signs were there, and I left immediately for Glaeston."

"You had a safe journey?" said Menahotep.

Vaila sighed and shook his head. "No, it was anything but safe. Twenty of us left Maes Howe three months ago and a dozen only arrived with me yesterday. The trackways throughout the land are aswarm with priests. It was not so bad in the northlands where there are fewer settlements, but as we came further south, and as the trackways began to converge toward Cor Gaur and Glaeston, so we encountered more of the Wessex, all on the move the same as us. I have never seen anything like it. Every priest in the land, bar a very few, are now here in the South or soon to arrive. Do you know how many are here, Druthin?"

The Arch-Mage nodded. "When we at Glaeston first rose up against the Wessex some months ago, they outnumbered us five to one—five hundred Wessex against one hundred Druids. Melkor tells me that they now outnumber us only two to one—two thousand Wessex against one thousand Druids."

"Ah, that is much better," said Menahotep.

"Maybe, but still a formidable task. All the Wessex have to do is to sit tight at Cor Gaur and deploy their forces in defense, knowing that it is we who have to go to them."

"And we will," said Vaila grimly.

"But carefully, wisely," warned Menahotep, "or they will cut us down one by one!"

"True," said Druthin. "We must wait for a plan, for an opportunity. I am not afraid to sacrifice lives," he said grimly. "Indeed, the loss of every Druid at Glaeston will not be too high a price to pay if Asher dies—providing she *does* die!"

Vaila looked at Druthin. "I suppose there is no doubt that the cursed one *is* with child?"

"None whatsoever, I'm afraid. We have checked and checked again on the inner, and there is no doubt."

They fell silent for some time, and then Menahotep said: "And what do the people think of all this—the peasants, the farmers, the fishermen—the ordinary people?" He raised his eyebrows and clasped his hands thoughtfully in his lap. "Do they understand what is happening?"

Vaila shook his head. "Not the ones I met, anyway. They know that the Wessex and the Druids meet in war at Cor Gaur, and although they have heard tales of the cursed child to come, they do not really understand why it has caused all this fuss."

"But throughout the land," said Druthin, "they are in favor of Druidry and hope to see the Wessex defeated. Or so I am informed."

Vaila nodded. "That accords with our own experience as well. Indeed, some have wanted to join us in our march to the south, but I refused. This is a priestly matter, to be resolved by priests alone. I would not want to see the people at risk in this matter."

"My own feelings exactly," said Druthin, "though Menahotep disagrees. He feels that if a man chooses between two types of priesthood, then that choice is a form of initiation for him, and as such he has the right to undergo the ordeals of that initiation."

"It is a fair point," admitted Vaila. "But, if so, then I feel that these matters are beyond his grade."

"Also a fair point," said Menahotep. "I can only pray that results prove the wisdom of your decision. It would be a pity, to put it mildly, if we failed for want of, say, another hundred men."

Druthin looked at the Egyptian. "You are thinking of Gargan."

"Yes, I am. He has asked me repeatedly to plead with you to allow him to take part in the struggle, if only in a small way, and I fear he grows impatient. He may very well take action soon whether he has your permission or not."

"I hope not," said Druthin sharply. "It would be just like him to go off on some ill-planned venture, and I would not wish to see him dead. You must command him, Menahotep!"

"I have no jurisdiction over him," the Egyptian said, "and in the final analysis, neither do you. He is a free man."

"And a foolish one."

"No, not foolish at all," said Menahotep, equally sharply. "He is brave, powerful, and quite dedicated to Druidry simply because of the many examples he has seen all his life—examples of kindness and wisdom from Druid priests compared to examples of evil from the Wessex. He is of the people, Druthin. This is their land, their realm, their kingdom, and they have a right to partake in the struggle if they so choose." He stared hard at the old Arch-Mage. "Frankly, Druthin, I think you are being a little stubborn in this. And certainly you must agree that he and his friends would be a valuable asset to us."

"Yes, they would indeed. But stubborn or not I still fear to put at risk the ordinary people. I am sorry, Menahotep, but that is my decision."

"I am also sorry, for I feel that Gargan will now make a decision of his own. He, too, is a stubborn man."

At that moment a knock sounded at the door, and Melkor entered. "Cludin has just returned, Arch-Mage, and desires to see you immediately."

"Cludin! Good. Ask him to come in." He turned to Vaila and Menahotep. "Two weeks ago I sent Cludin and an escort to King Arvinus at Caerlon-on-Usk to seek his aid, particularly his men at arms."

"Arvinus!" said Vaila. "That brigand! I thought he was dead."

"No, not yet. Now Arvinus and his men are not of the priesthood, agreed, but they chose to lead a life of warfare and as such continually put their lives at risk. Their case is different to that of Gargan who is a simple stonecutter who has never lifted a sword in his life."

Menahotep acknowledged the point, and then said: "But who is this Arvinus?"

"King Arvinus," said Druthin, "though the word 'king' is too graceful for such a ruffian. He is more of a brigand, as Vaila has said, than a king. He is really the local chieftain of the territory across the Narrow Straits, and his palace is at Caerlon-on-Usk, a gaudy building of gilded roofs—paid for, no doubt, from the proceeds of a lifetime's dedication to the art of robbery!"

"Then how came he to kingship?"

"He had a habit of robbing all and sundry, including the priests of the local Wessex lodge. And in return for immunity against him, the Wessex brought him to Cor Gaur and crowned him on the King Stone —a travesty of justice typical of the Wessex."

"If so, then why should he aid us against the Wessex?"

"He was crowned as King many years ago, and since then the Wessex in his area have grown in numbers and in power, and now it is they who rob him by demanding a tithing at every equinox. He has no love for Druids, but even less for the Wessex. It is a forlorn hope but worth a try."

Cludin came into the room and bowed. "I have seen Arvinus as you instructed."

"And?" said Druthin.

Cludin shook his head. "We can expect no help from him. His dearest wish is that both the Wessex and Druid forces become decimated in the fighting and so leave the land free for him to plunder at will. His remarks on the priesthood in general, and of you personally, Druthin, were somewhat uncomplimentary."

"That I can believe," said the old man drily. "Well, I expected little else, but it was worth the effort. Thank you, Cludin. Go and rest now. I will talk to you later." When he had gone, Druthin turned to his two friends. "Well, that's that. We must make do with what we have, it seems."

Hakin sat staring at the river, his head bowed. Druthin had been kind, tactful, and very gentle, but behind it all lay the ugly fact that Vordin and Zelta were both dead, and that he, Hakin, was responsible

—an error of judgment for which there could be no redress. There was not a single, solitary thing that he could do to correct that error. He would have to live with it for the rest of his life, with every priest at Glaeston aware of his failure. But perhaps the Great Ones would be merciful and permit an early release.

A shadow fell across him and he looked up, startled. "Oh, it's you, Gargan. By all the powers, man, can't you at least cough or something when you approach! You walk like a cat!"

The huge stonecutter dropped to his haunches. "I thought I would find you here," he growled.

"Oh, yes? What made you think that?"

"You come here often since Zelta died."

Hakin raised his eyebrows. "You have been watching me?"

The man nodded. "Yes."

"Why?"

Gargan stared straight into Hakin's eyes. "Druthin will not permit the people to join the fight against the Wessex—so I have come to you."

"Why me? I cannot countermand Druthin's orders."

Gargan shifted his weight. "You sent Zelta to Cor Gaur, and the boy died," he said simply. "Such a man as you might wish to strike a blow on Zelta's behalf."

Hakin's eyes narrowed. By all the sacred powers, even the peasants knew about it! "Perhaps," he said cautiously. "What have you in mind?"

"Horses," he said cryptically.

The Deputy Arch-Mage shook his head. "I don't understand you. What horses?"

Gargan rose to his feet. "Come with me and I will show you."

"Where to?"

"Not far—come."

Hakin hesitated and then rose and followed the huge stonecutter. There could be no harm in at least finding out what this was all about. "All right, I'll come. But where to?"

"Not far. To the old track in the woods—an hour's walk, no more."

Hakin pressed him again but Gargan would say no more. The two men walked in silence—a curious pair to be abroad together: The gray-haired Hakin dressed in the flowing white robes of Druidry, the Serpent Symbol about his neck, carrying the silver-topped staff, the symbol of the Office of Deputy Arch-Mage; and the huge stonecutter dressed in animal skins, swinging a club, stepping as lightly as a cat.

For an hour they walked, and entered the forest at midmorning by the old northern track. "How much farther?" said Hakin.

"Soon," the giant growled.

Another five minutes, and then ten, and suddenly a call sounded from ahead, and Gargan answered it. The track veered to the left and opened out into a glade amongst the trees, and there on the far side were gathered a dozen peasants, most of whom he recognized as having come from Wearyhall Hill, a village near to Glaeston. But what took his immediate attention was the sight of a dozen or more dead bodies that littered the glade, all dressed in Wessex robes, some transfixed by arrows, some their skulls smashed open, and some with gaping wounds presumably caused by swords.

"What is this?" he said sharply.

Gargan grinned hugely. It had been an effort for him to have kept silent until they arrived. "Some Wessex who will fight no more!"

The other men were grinning also, like children. Hakin walked around and inspected the dead more closely. Wessex priests, certainly, but not from Cor Gaur, to judge by the weave of their robes—from the north more likely. Hakin sat himself down on the giant root of an old tree and looked sternly at the men clustered around him. "All right. What happened?"

Gargan folded his arms. "We are not children to hide in our huts," he growled, "no matter what Druthin says. We have had men out watching, and so heard the news of these dogs coming down the track, and so we laid in wait last night, and killed them as they stirred at dawn this morning."

"Did any escape?"

The stonecutter grinned again. "Not one was left alive," he said proudly.

The other men broke into an excited chatter, boasting to each other, reliving their daring, and Hakin listened for a while and then held up his hand. "You should not have shown me this, Gargan. I will have to inform Druthin."

The giant shook his head. "Not until we have done what needs to be done, and not until we have struck a blow, you and I, for Zelta." Gargan's face darkened. "I knew the boy's father, aye, and his mother, and I knew the boy when he was still at the breast."

Hakin's heart suddenly saddened. "I am sorry," he said softly. "I did not know."

"Then you will help us, priest?"

The elder man spread his hands. "Help you to do what? And what has this got to do with horses?"

The stonecutter prodded one of the dead bodies. "Twelve Wessex dogs come from afar, looking to join those at Cor Gaur."

"Yes. From the north probably."

"And took the wrong track and so came nearly to Glaeston."

"Perhaps."

The giant straightened up. "Tell me, Priest, are their faces known to any at Cor Gaur?"

Hakin shrugged. "Probably not, but I still don't understand."

"If their faces are not known, then anyone can don their robes and be welcomed by the Wessex at Cor Gaur."

Hakin looked carefully at the faces around him. "You mean that we put on the Wessex robes and go to Cor Gaur in disguise!" He nodded thoughtfully. "And that is why you need me. Because none of you know how to behave as priests." He rose and examined the bodies. "And what do we do at Cor Gaur, even if we are accepted as true Wessex priests?"

Gargan hesitated and then said: "We steal Mog Agorn's chariots and his horses and drive them to Glaeston!" he said simply. "And maybe kill a few Wessex as well."

It was beautiful. Hakin had to admit that the plan was beautiful—simple, direct, and containing a strong element of surprise. During the day, Mog Agorn always kept his chariots in readiness. At the right moment it would take no more than a few seconds to leap in and drive off. And once on the way, no one could possibly catch them. It was beautiful.

"Druthin would never approve," he said.

"Then why tell him!" said Gargan. "And afterward the sight of the chariots and horses at Glaeston under Druid command may dull his anger."

Undoubtedly it would, thought Hakin. Druthin would be delighted, and so, too, would Melkor. Aloud he said: "And what if we fail?"

"Then we will be dead," said Gargan, "and beyond Druthin's anger." He looked at the old priest and his face softened. "And it would do much to calm your own troubled mind," he growled.

That also was undoubtedly true. "All right, Gargan. I am not yet fully convinced, but while we are here we might as well try on their robes. The sight of you as a Wessex priest is not one that I would willingly miss!"

The men roared with laughter and a sudden exhilaration, and fell on the bodies, chattering excitedly, stripped the robes, and dressed themselves in their disguise. Hakin took the robe of the senior Wessex priest, the one with the purple and gold band at the collar denoting the rank—but he had a little trouble, for the man had been considerably thinner than its new owner. At last he managed to struggle into it and turned to the others, and his eyes widened with surprise. "By all the powers," he said softly, "you actually *do* look like priests! I am beginning to think, Gargan, that this plan of yours is not so crazy after all." Gargan's robe was the worst fit of all, but even his was not too bad. Hakin walked around them slowly. "Stop that grinning," he said suddenly. "It is not enough to look like priests, you will have to behave like priests as well, or else you won't even get past the guards!"

"Do as the priest says," Gargan growled, and the grins vanished abruptly.

"Walk up and down," said Hakin. "All of you!" The men grinned again and sheepishly walked around the glade. "Don't clomp around like stonecutters and herdsmen! *Glide*. Get up on the balls of your feet. Balance yourselves. Tread lightly as though you were stalking a wild pig. A priest doesn't stamp around, he *glides*—softly. That's better. Keep it up. Don't swing your arms. A Priest of the Sun never swings his arms when he walks. Keep them under control. Tuck your elbows in. Clasp your hands together. That's better! Don't turn your heads in all directions—keep them still. And don't bob up and down as you walk. Glide. *Glide!*"

He kept them at it for ten minutes and then called a halt. "Not bad," he said approvingly. "Not bad at all. Now we'll try something else. Now listen. When priests meet each other they say 'Greetings.' Let's try that." Hakin walked up to one of the men and bowed his head slightly. "Greetings," he said gravely.

The man grinned from ear to ear. "Greetings." He chuckled, and then burst into outright laughter.

Hakin waited for him to finish and then said coldly: "You dolt! If you laugh like that tomorrow when meeting a genuine Wessex, then we'll all have swords in our bellies, and *that* will be nothing to laugh at."

Gargan strode over. "Do not laugh," he said menacingly, and the tone of his voice wiped the smile from the man's face instantly.

"All right," said Hakin. "We'll try it again." He bowed his head. "Greetings," he said softly.

The man bowed in return. "Greetings," he replied gravely.

"Good—*good*. Now all of you try it. Walk around the glade, and as you pass each other bow slightly and give the greeting. Go on—try it!"

They shuffled self-consciously around. "Greetings,"

said one. "Greetings," said another, and then another. But it was too much for them. One of them spluttered the greeting, trying to suppress a laugh, and in an instant their control was gone and they roared with laughter. "Greetings!" they shouted, helpless with laughter. *"Greetings. Greetings!"*

Gargan was furious, but Hakin held up his hand. "All right, don't worry. The novelty will soon wear off, and fear will still their merriment tomorrow."

When they had quietened down, Gargan said softly: "Well, priest, are you with us?"

Hakin rubbed his chin thoughtfully. "I don't like the idea of going off and causing Druthin to worry about me."

"One of the men can pass a message to Glaeston that you are called to a sick child."

"And my face is familiar to the Wessex."

"To all of them?"

The Deputy Arch-Mage shook his head. "No, not all. Asher and Mog Agorn know me, and so, too, does Sleg Agorn and Awrgon, but none of the others. However, the seniors will be in their tents, or at the center. It is highly unlikely that they will be at the periphery where the horses and chariots are."

"We can watch from the hilltop to see who is where before we go down to them."

"True, and all we need is five minutes inside those earthworks. If we haven't accomplished our task within that time then we are lost. You may look like priests, but a few minutes' conversation with a genuine Wessex will be enough to arouse suspicion."

Gargan was impatient. "So, what are you saying, priest? Will we try it or not?"

Hakin's eyes were grim. "Oh, yes, my friend, we will try it. Most certainly we will try it!"

Asher lay in her tent writhing with pain. The sweat poured down her body and dampened the skins on which she lay. Her eyes were tightly shut, her hands clenched, and her whole body continually jerked taut at every spasm, the muscles standing out on her arms, her belly rigid. The senior healer rose to his feet and shook his head. "I do not like it. The signs are all wrong!"

Mog Agorn grabbed his arm. "What do you mean?" he growled. "What is wrong with her?"

The healer shrugged helplessly. "I do not know."

Mog Agorn shook him furiously. "You *must* know! You're the chief healer of the Wessex. No one knows more than you. What is wrong with her?"

The healer shook him off. "I don't know, Mog Agorn, and no amount of shaking is going to dredge up knowledge that I do not have. I tell you, I don't know. She has all the symptoms as though she was about to give birth at any moment."

"That's impossible! It is barely four moons since the ritual. And look at her. Look at her! Her belly has barely begun to swell. How can she possibly be about to give birth?"

The healer faced his High Priest. "I just simply do not know, I tell you! It could be a premature birth, but that doesn't make sense either."

Mog Agorn's eyes narrowed. "Premature birth?" he said suspiciously. "Would the child live if it were born now?"

The healer shook his head. "Impossible. It is too soon, far too soon. But there again, who can tell? This is no ordinary birth, Mog Agorn. All the things that are true of ordinary births may simply not apply in this case, I just don't know. Never in the entire history of humanity has any healer assisted at the birth of a Dark One, so there is no precedent, no prior knowledge, and no experience to guide me. I do not know, and, whether you like it or not, you will have to accept that! We can do nothing save wait and watch developments."

"And in the meantime," roared Mog Agorn, "my daughter, the High Priestess, may die—and the child also!"

"Possibly. I do not know."

Awrgon was lounging by the tent opening. "The man is right, Father. You yourself have been at pains to tell the whole Wessex what an incredibly rare event this is, so you can hardly blame the healer when he discovers signs that show how unusual it is. It would have been unusual and even suspicious if he had found everything to be normal."

"All right. But I tell you this—both of you—Asher will live and give birth, for if she dies then she will not be the only one! Do I make myself clear?"

"Yes, Mog Agorn, very clear," said the healer stiffly. "I will do my best."

"And by the powers of darkness, healer, your best had better be good enough!"

A thin, choked-off scream came from the bed. "Father. Father! Oh, by Narada, it hurts. It *hurts! Father!*" Asher flung her head from side to side, her hands white and clenched with the strain. "It's hurting me!"

Mog Agorn strode to the bed and bent over her. "You must hold on," he said fiercely, almost shouting at her. "You must, Asher!"

"It's hurting me!"

"There is nothing we can do. You must hold on."

"It's doing it deliberately," she screamed. "I can feel its mind. It's enjoying my pain. I can't stand it!"

"You must."

"I can't, I tell you. I can't. Oh, Narada—it hurts. It hurts!"

Mog Agorn swung around to the healer. "Can't you give her something?" he shouted. "Isn't there a potion to kill pain?"

"She has already had more than she should. It seems to have no effect whatsoever."

"But surely there is something that will put her unconscious? She cannot take much more of this."

"She has another four months or so to go yet," said the healer. "These are only the early days. It will get worse, far worse, later on."

Mog Agorn looked down at his daughter. "Asher is no ordinary woman. She has more courage than most men. If *she* can't stand it, then the pain must be incredible. Surely there is something we can do."

Awrgon straightened up and strolled nonchalantly to the bed. "Poor old Asher," he said. "A lifetime of whoring certainly made her a suitable candidate, but for what?"

"If you haven't got anything sensible to say," growled Mog Agorn, "then get out!"

Awrgon pretended surprise. "But I thought you wanted something to make her unconscious?"

"You?" said Mog Agorn contemptuously. "What do you think you can do?"

"Simple," said the boy, and he raised his hand and smashed his fist into the side of Asher's jaw. Her head snapped back, her eyes glazed, and she slumped over, unconscious. "You know, Father," he said coolly, "sometimes the simple approach is the best one."

Mog Agorn glared at his youngest son. "You enjoyed that, didn't you?" His hand moved to his knife, and then fell away. "Now get out! And don't bother me again."

Awrgon shrugged and moved toward the tent opening. When he had gone, Mog Agorn shook his head angrily. "In his own way, that boy is as much a thorn in my side as Fangorn was. It may be that he will have to go the same way."

The healer ignored the remark. "Now that she is unconscious, there is something I want to show you." Gently he moved Asher's arms aside and stripped off her tunic until her body lay quite naked. "Watch her belly—closely," he said.

Her legs were young and strong and muscular. Her skin was brown from the sun, and the sweat stood out on her breasts and stomach and ran in tiny rivulets down her sides. Her belly was slightly risen from the growing thing inside her. Not much, but certainly she was not as flat as Mog Agorn remembered. As he watched, he saw her belly twitch, and then again, and again, and at one point the whole skin quivered as though plucked from inside.

"It is moving," said the healer, "but it should not move at all for another month, and even then it should be a gentle twitch or two, not that violent movement. I shudder to think what it is doing to her insides."

"If it's a month too soon for any movement, then it may be born a month prematurely," said Mog Agorn.

"Possibly. I don't know."

"All right, you and your healers watch her day and night. She is not to be left alone. Report any change to me—even the slightest."

At that moment the tent flap thrust aside and Sleg Agorn came in. He looked at the naked girl, his niece. "She is sleeping?"

"Awrgon knocked her unconscious," said Mog Agorn. "It's what she needed. The potions seem to have no effect and she is in great pain."

The healer was gently drawing on the girl's tunic again, and covering her breasts. "I do hope all this is going to work out, my brother," said Sleg Agorn. "If the child dies then you are in an embarrassing position. Apart from having stirred the Druids up in no uncertain manner, your clarion call is bringing every Wessex in the land to Cor Gaur. There are yet another twelve approaching from the West."

"Good—the more the better. Send the senior one as usual to me when they arrive, and see to the welfare of the remainder." He looked back at Asher. "This will not fail. It cannot!"

"But if it does," said Sleg Agorn softly, "it may cost you your life!"

"And yours, probably, brother. Don't forget that!"

Sleg Agorn nodded. "The thought has not escaped me," he said drily.

The two men stepped out into the midmorning sunshine and Mog Agorn strode away to his own tent nearby. Both tents were pitched alongside the King Stone at the very center of Cor Gaur, and the two sets of bodyguards totaling a hundred warrior-priests surrounded the entire central portion of the ancient site, leaving the remainder of the Wessex to occupy the outer circles. Sleg Agorn picked his way through the guard, heading toward the northern point of the great outer earthworks, to the point where the huge, broad avenue came sweeping into Cor Gaur. It was at that same point where the horses were tethered, and where the chariots were kept, ready at any time to race out of Cor Gaur by the broad avenue to deal with anything that might threaten. Sleg Agorn could see that the new arrivals were just coming up to the guard. Their leader seemed to be an old man of high rank, to judge by the purple and gold collar. Sleg Agorn could not remember his name, but at this distance his face certainly seemed familiar. Some of the older ones only came to Cor Gaur once every five years or so, and he couldn't be expected to remember every detail about every one of them. The second man was a huge fellow, standing a clear head above his companions. Now *he* would be useful. Sleg Agorn quickened his pace.

Hakin saw him coming when they were still a few yards away from the guard. "That is Sleg Agorn," he hissed. "Once he sees my face we are lost. It will have to be quick, Gargan, very quick. Don't run, but just walk on past the guards straight over to the chariots and get them away!"

"Very well, priest," growled the stonecutter. "But what about you?"

"Pick me up on the way out. Quiet now!" They came the last few paces to the guard, and Hakin bowed low to the man. "Greetings," he said gravely. "We have come from the far west at Mog Agorn's call. To whom shall we report?"

Gargan and the others, their heads lowered as if from utter weariness, plodded by and into Cor Gaur itself, toward the horses. The other guards, and indeed many of the nearby Wessex, were staring at the newcomers curiously. "Greetings, friends," one of them called out. "Welcome to Cor Gaur—but not that way! The food and drink are at the center."

Gargan waved his hand. "Greetings," he called out, but kept on walking, the others close at his heels.

"Wake up, man!" said Hakin sternly to the guard. "We have traveled long and would rest. Please answer my question!"

"I am sorry, master—and greetings," the man stammered. "Sleg Agorn will see to your requirements. This is he coming now."

"Yes, I know Sleg Agorn, an old friend of mine."

Gargan and the others were nearly at the horses. One of the Wessex took Gargan's arm and tried to guide him toward the center, but the giant shook himself free and kept on toward the horses. The man shrugged—they were a surly lot, these newcomers.

Sleg Agorn was coming faster than Hakin expected. It was imperative that he did not reveal his face. He threw up one arm across his face and pretended to stagger. The guard took his arm, alarmed. "Are you hurt, master?"

"It is nothing—a brief battle with some Druids near Glaeston this morning," Hakin whispered. "A glancing blow on the head—no more. I am all right now."

The guard let him go. Hakin swayed a little on his feet, his arm still across his face. Gargan was coming up to the chariots now, but it was obvious that he would not be able to wheel them about and get back to him before Sleg Agorn arrived. Every second's grace was vital. Hakin pretended to stagger again, fell to his knees, and then sprawled full length, his face buried in his arms.

Sleg Agorn saw the incident and came the last few yards at a run. "What is the matter?" he cried to the guard.

"A battle this morning with the Druids, he said. A glancing blow to the head. He just collapsed."

"I know—I saw. Get someone to carry him, and alert the healers. Quick now!"

At that moment one of the horses whinnied, and Sleg Agorn turned in that direction. The newcomers were in amongst the chariots, climbing aboard, freeing the reins. "What are they doing?" he said angrily. "Mog Agorn will have their hides for that!" As he spoke he saw the High Priest himself come bursting out of his tent, pause for a moment, and then come bellowing toward them. Already the nearest chariots were wheeling about, the whips flailing the horses' flanks—and a dreadful suspicion exploded in his mind. He grabbed the old man's hair and wrenched his head back. "Hakin!"

Sleg Agorn leapt to his feet. "Druids! *Druids! Stop them!*" But already three of the chariots were racing toward the exit, and the other five were wheeling about, their horses rearing at the suddenness of it all. "They are *Druids!*" he bellowed. "Stop them!"

The first three chariots came racing by, then another, and another. Hakin was struggling to his feet. Sleg Agorn grabbed him and pulled him to one side. The dust from the flying wheels filled the air. Another chariot went racing by, and then another. Several spears were whistling through the dust, but their aim was poor. Hakin struggled furiously to free himself, but Sleg Agorn hung on grimly. The last chariot, driven by the giant, was racing toward them.

Gargan was driving with one hand, his sword in the other. He could see Hakin struggling with Sleg Agorn, but a dozen Wessex raced to secure the old man. The scene loomed nearer through the dust as the chariot thundered on. If he was to rescue Hakin, he should rein in now, but there were a dozen men at the exit, with more coming. It was impossible, and Hakin had said time and time again that the chariots must get clear regardless of who was left behind. He saw Hakin's agonized face raise itself up. "Go on, Gargan," he heard the priest cry. "Go on. *Go on!*" Still he hesitated, and more Wessex raced to the exit and turned to face his coming. Suddenly and grimly he made up his mind. The whip lashed out again and again, and the chariot thundered into the Wessex line, scattering men in all directions." *The Great Ones be with you, priest!*" he bellowed as he thundered by, and he saw Hakin raise his arm in salute.

The Wessex were stunned. All eight chariots were clear and racing away up the broad avenue. The guard slackened their grip and Hakin pulled himself free. "The day is ours, I think!" he gasped to Sleg Agorn. He stood upright and his heart leapt with joy to see the chariots wheel about and come to a halt fifty yards away, safe from any pursuit. He walked a few feet to the center of the avenue and turned to face the Wessex, alone.

Mog Agorn came bellowing up the slope. When he reached his brother he smashed his fist into his face, and Sleg Agorn slumped to the ground. "You fool! You bungling, incompetent fool!"

Hakin, a few yards away, bowed insolently. "Greetings, Mog Agorn!"

The High Priest was boiling with rage. "Seize him," he bellowed.

Hakin turned and cupped his hands. "Go on to Glaeston!" he called. "Tell Druthin that Hakin has paid his debt to Vordin and to Zelta!" And he whirled about, and before the guard could reach him he plucked a knife from his robe and threw it as hard as he could straight at Mog Agorn. More by luck than any prowess, the knife buried itself with a sickening thud blade-first and up to the hilt in the High Priest's belly.

Mog Agorn stood stock-still, his whole body rigid with the shock of it, his hands clenching the hilt of the knife.

Hakin folded his arms and stared calmly at the stricken High Priest. "It should have reached your black heart, Mog Agorn," he said, "but even so I am satisfied. If the Great Ones will it so, then you will die—and I, Hakin, Deputy Arch-Mage of all Druidry, will have been the cause!"

Mog Agorn staggered and fell to his knees. "Kill him," he croaked. "*Kill him!*"

A dozen spears flew the air and Hakin fell transfixed to the dust, a smile upon his dead face.

Gargan raised his arm, and the eight chariots wheeled about and headed home to Glaeston.

Chapter Eight

Again Druthin and the entire Council were met in an emergency meeting. It was late evening and the sun had long since abandoned the land to darkness. The tall candles on the great table threw flickering shadows across the faces of the Elder Druids. Druthin's face was particularly grim as he listened to Gargan's tale.

". . . And then Hakin called out to us," the stonecutter said, "and bade me tell you that he had repaid his debt to Vordin and to Zelta."

Druthin nodded. "That he has, and in full measure. He was a man who always accused himself of cowardice, not knowing that he had a heart as big as any I have known."

Menahotep's eyes glinted in the darkness. His command of the Druid language was not perfect, but it seemed to him that Druthin had spoken in the past tense as though he already knew that Hakin was dead.

The Arch-Mage nodded to Gargan. "Go on, my friend. Go on."

"And then with my own eyes," the stonecutter said slowly, "I saw him turn and pluck a knife from his robe and throw it straight at Mog Agorn, and the knife buried itself up to the hilt in the foul one's belly!"

There were startled exclamations from every throat, and Druthin came to his feet. "Hakin never threw a knife in his entire life! Are you absolutely sure of what you saw?"

"There is no doubt of it, my Lord—and we all saw the same thing—right up to the hilt!"

There was a deep silence, and Druthin slowly shook his head. "The Great Ones did not desert him," he said softly.

Cludin also jumped to his feet. "Are you trying to tell us that Mog Agorn is dead?"

A buzz of excitement stirred their calm. The death of Mog Agorn would be a triumph indeed. Druthin raised his hand. "Please be seated, Cludin. Let Gargan tell the tale in his own way."

The stonecutter shrugged. "I do not know whether he is dead or not. I saw the knife enter and I saw him fall to his knees. If he is not actually dead, then certainly he is not overly healthy with a knife in his guts."

Menahotep permitted himself a tiny smile. The giant was certainly not overawed by the august presence of so many Elder Priests. Indeed he seemed to be picking his words carefully as though explaining to a crowd of children.

"Then obviously," said Druthin, "we must establish the state of his health absolutely as soon as possible. His welfare," he added drily, "is close to all our hearts. But what, then, of Hakin?"

"I saw him facing the Wessex alone, his arms calmly folded. And then a rain of spears fell on him—and so he died."

The news was greeted with deep silence, and every Elder Priest there present summoned an image of his lost colleague in his mind's eye and gravely saluted the vision.

At last Druthin sighed and said: "Hakin has rendered a valuable service to all Druidry—and so too have you, Gargan, though you had to disobey me to do it."

"Will you now allow the people to fight alongside the Druids," the stonecutter growled, "now that we have shown that we are not children?"

"Yes, and no doubt we will again have cause to thank you for your service. Go and rest now. You have had an eventful day. The Mistress of the Blue will see to your welfare. Remain at Glaeston tonight as our guest. I will speak with you in the morning as to how best your people can help us."

The giant nodded and left the room. The moment the door had closed Druthin rose and faced the Council. "Before we can make any decisions at all, we must find out if Mog Agorn is dead or not. I will conduct the ritual myself with Vaila, Menahotep, and Thetan to assist me. The full Council will meet again at dawn tomorrow." He bowed to the Council, and beckoned the three to join him, and the Council rose courteously as they left the chamber.

"Lay him there, next to Asher," said Sleg Agorn. The priests obeyed and then hurriedly left the tent. This was no time to be within range of a senior's anger. The Chief Healer bent over the body of the stricken High Priest. "Well? Will he live?" said Sleg Agorn impatiently.

"Give me time," said the healer calmly. Gently he removed Mog Agorn's hands from the knife-hilt. He beckoned one of the junior healers. "Be ready when I pull." He clasped the hilt of the knife firmly—and paused. "Now!" he said, and pulled the knife clear, and instantly the junior healer slapped a prepared swab onto the wound. "Hold it there—firmly!"

The healer bent and put his ear to Mog Agorn's chest. He then rolled up one of the eyelids. He straightened up and moved around to the head of the couch and placed both hands across the High Priest's forehead. He remained like that for some seconds and then grunted to himself. He came around to the side of the bed and took both hands in his own and closed his eyes. He remained like that for a full minute and then opened his eyes. "Let me look," he said to the junior healer. Cautiously, very cautiously, he lifted one corner of the swab, and instantly the blood poured across Mog Agorn's stomach. The junior wiped it again and again, as the blood still flowed. The Chief Healer nodded. "All right, replace it. But hold it firmly. We will look at it again in, say, five minutes from now."

"Well?" said Sleg Agorn.

The Chief Healer turned from the couch. "He is as strong as a pillar of rock."

"We all know that, but will he live?"

The healer hesitated. "At best the human body is a frail thing compared to, say, that of an animal, and no healer likes to commit himself. As far as the actual wound itself is concerned, the knife does not appear to have damaged any vital organs. He will reach a crisis sometime tonight or tomorrow, but I anticipate that he will survive it. The real problem is the possibility of the rotting disease. You know what I mean!"

Sleg Agorn did indeed. He once saw a fairly trivial leg wound go green and give off a foul smell, and as the days passed the foulness had gradually infested the whole leg. It had taken the man fourteen days to die, in the most screaming agony, and during those last few days the smell of him had been vile, so much so that no one could come within a few yards of him without wanting to vomit. "Yes," he said slowly, "I do indeed. When will we know?"

"If he is still alive in seven days from now, and if the wound heals cleanly with no rotting, then he will regain his full health and strength."

"And then," sighed Sleg Agorn, "will come my day of reckoning!"

The healer had seen Mog Agorn strike his brother down. "If anyone is to blame," he said sympathetically, "it is the guard for allowing them through without establishing their identities."

Sleg Agorn shrugged. "And who can really blame the guard. Our number was a mere five hundred, now swollen to two thousand—an additional fifteen hundred Wessex priests from throughout the land. No guard can recognize them all. And who would believe the Druids to be sufficiently cunning for such a ploy." He shook his head. "But it's no use crying about it now!"

A sound came from the other couch and the two men turned. Asher had raised herself to one elbow. "So. He is going to live, is he?" she said. "Well, at least he also now has a pain in the belly. Perhaps now he'll appreciate what *I've* been going through!"

Sleg Agorn went over to her. "I thought you were unconscious," he said softly, "or asleep. How is your pain now, Asher?"

She slumped back on the couch. "It's gone—for the time being. I don't suppose even *he* can keep it up all the time!"

"He?"

She pointed to her belly. "Him!" She sighed and closed her eyes. "I'd sooner have a knife in my guts than *him*—any day!" Her eyes flickered open again. "I tell you, Sleg Agorn, if I had known what it would be like I would never have allowed my father to talk me into this." Her mouth creased in a vicious smile. "I would have given a great deal to have seen the Druid bring him down! By all the powers, it must have been a nasty shock to feel that knife ram home." She looked up at the two men. "Who did it?"

"Hakin," said Sleg Agorn briefly.

The girl smiled. "Now there is a priest I salute with all my heart! What happened to him?"

"Dead. A dozen spears brought him down."

She nodded. "I guessed as much, but what a way to go! I almost wouldn't mind dying myself if I could bring Mog Agorn down."

The healer stepped forward. "Quiet now," he said gently. "Get some sleep before the pain returns."

She looked up at him. "I tell you, healer, I do not know whether I can endure this for another four months."

"You must."

She grunted. "Yes, I must, but not for the reason you suppose." She put her hand on her belly. "I tried to kill him this morning. I won't tell you how—it might offend your delicate ears—but it was no use. *He* wouldn't let me." Sleg Agorn and the healer exchanged glances. "You don't believe me?" she said. "It's true. There is the rod I was going to use." The two men looked to where a ritual rod lay on the cabinet. "But when I raised it up, he made me drop it. He commands my mind. Did you know that? No, I don't suppose you did—or that you even believe it! The ravings of a woman in pain, you'll say! Oh, who cares any more? There's nothing that you or I can do about it anyway."

"Hush now," the healer said. "Go to sleep."

She closed her eyes. "Yes, sleep—sleep—and tomorrow another day of pain. There is one coming to lead the Wessex indeed, but the Wessex are going to get more than they bargained for. Believe me, I *know!*"

The healer beckoned Sleg Agorn away. "Do not place too much significance to her words. Pain does strange things to a human mind."

"She seemed rational enough to me."

The healer shook his head. "Forget what she said, Sleg Agorn. Forget it. We don't have much choice now anyway. Mog Agorn, your brother, has led us onto this path, and there is no turning back now. Come, it's time we had another look at his wound."

He walked to the couch where the junior healer was still holding the swab firmly against Mog Agorn's belly. The Chief Healer cautiously lifted a corner, and the junior wiped away the blood, and again, and again, but although the blood was flowing freely, it was not quite so copious as it had been earlier. The healer nodded. "It's easing off," he said to the junior. "It will probably stop altogether soon. Keep that swab in position." He turned to Sleg Agorn. "Your brother is a lucky man. Another inch in any direction and he would probably be dead by now. I will remain here until the bleeding stops."

"Very well. Report to me if there is any change." He took one last look at the sleeping Asher and then left the tent. Awrgon was leaning against the King Stone, obviously waiting for him. "You will no doubt be filled with joy, Awrgon," he said sarcastically, "to learn that your father will probably live and return to full health."

Awrgon smiled. "I have been praying to the Great Ones," he said.

"No doubt you have, but the signs are that your father will *not* die."

"You misunderstand me, Sleg Agorn."

"I doubt it."

"I was praying for his recovery."

Sleg Agorn grunted. "You surprise me," he said drily.

"Do you think that I would pray for his death?"

"Yes. I do. You would bend the knee to every god you could think of if it meant your taking over the Wessex."

Awrgon shrugged. "You judge me too harshly, my uncle."

"Perhaps ... but I doubt it."

Awrgon straightened up. "Be that as it may—what now?"

Sleg Agorn looked around the ancient site. "Already we are very crowded, and there are two hundred more at Abiri." Tents had sprung like mushrooms all over Cor Gaur between and around the ancient stones, filling every circle right out to the great outer earthworks. "And without Mog Agorn's horses, we cannot command the avenue to Abiri, nor the road to Glaeston."

Awrgon nodded thoughtfully. "It will be some hours before the Druids at Glaeston learn of what has happened, but once they do it will not take them long to realize that our people at Abiri are now too isolated."

"Agreed. I do not like making decisions in Mog Agorn's absence, but I dare not wait even a week to consult him. We must abandon Abiri immediately and bring everything here to Cor Gaur."

"And then what?"

Sleg Agorn pursed his lips. "Neither will it take them long to realize that the Wessex have no alternative but to remain here at Cor Gaur until the child is born. Also, now that they have the chariots and can command the roads, it means that they can leave their cursed College virtually unguarded."

"A siege, you mean?"

Sleg Agorn nodded. "It is what I would do if I were commanding the Druids. I would seize Abiri and lay siege to Cor Gaur. One thousand Druids laying siege to two thousand Wessex."

"And the Wessex cannot risk venturing out to battle," said Awrgon, "lest our rear be taken and Asher killed."

"Exactly."

"But with those numbers surely we can successfully withstand a four-month siege?"

"Yes, I think so. Food is no problem, though it will not be plentiful. We have a good stock of corn and dried meat at Abiri, and we can slaughter all our cattle and so add to the store. Two thousand priests and priestesses will eat a great deal of food in four months, but even so I think we will survive." He looked to where the great water barrels lay. "Our real problem is water." He pointed to the barrels. "Every day the carriers bring their water skins from the Avon nearby to keep those barrels full, but we cannot do that under siege conditions."

Awrgon pointed beyond the earthworks. "The hills, Sleg Agorn—the rain must come down from the hills. There must be any amount of water right under our feet."

"A well, you mean!"

"Why not? We could have one dug in a matter of days. This whole area is one mass of magnetic spirals, a good indication of the presence of water underground."

Sleg Agorn looked doubtful. "A well might upset the magnetic pattern—might disturb the Earth Spirit."

"But we must have water. The Earth Spirit will just have to put up with being disturbed!"

Sleg Agorn frowned. "Not the remark I would expect from a dedicated priest, Awrgon," he said sternly. "But what you say is true enough, though I don't like it. Very well—send your messenger today. Tell them to abandon Abiri and bring all the food stores and cattle here to Cor Gaur. Get the diviners to discover the best place for a well and commence the digging at dawn tomorrow. In the meantime I will remain in Asher's tent, all night, probably. There are other things that worry me."

"You mean the seals?"

"Yes. Mog Agorn had his personal seals over the whole of Cor Gaur to prevent the Druids from watching us. All they could see was a cloud of black fog. But as he is stricken, those seals are gone. The first thing the Druids will do on learning the news is to pay us a visit, to overlook us from the half-world. I will put my own seals on, but I doubt that they will be enough to keep them out—my seals are not as strong as Mog Agorn's."

Awrgon shook his head. "They will not learn anything that they could not deduce."

"Perhaps. I just don't like the idea of having our every move carefully watched by Druids. Anyway, we will see. I will leave you to your tasks. Let me know if you run into any problems."

Sleg Agorn returned to Asher's tent just as the two healers were leaving. "The bleeding has stopped," the Chief Healer said. "We will not disturb him by further probing. Let him sleep now. I will return when he regains consciousness."

Sleg Agorn nodded and entered the tent. The swab had been left on Mog Agorn's belly, held in place by strips of cloth wound completely around his torso. He was still unconscious, but his face was no longer contorted. His expression now was more like that of natural sleep. Asher, too, was asleep, though she had kicked the coverings off the couch. Her body was completely naked, and he studied it thoughtfully. She was, no doubt, a magnificent specimen of a woman —those breasts alone would weaken a strong man's resolve—but Sleg Agorn had never felt the desire stir in his loins for Asher, though he could understand why few men had been able to resist her bed. She was too strong a personality for his taste. He liked a woman to look at him adoringly, to be demure in his presence, to melt in his arms. Asher's attitude to men was one of contempt, and her sexual grapplings were more in the nature of contests, of fights. Asher was a woman who liked to dominate her men, both in bed and out of it. She had tried her wiles on him many times over the years, but always he had resisted. He had never even kissed her, or touched her breasts, let alone anything else, and he counted himself fortunate to be so seemingly immune to her charm. He placed his hands on her breasts now, and gently ran his fingers down her body, caressing every part of her. He bent over and pressed his loins to her body, but then smiled to himself and drew back. Her body held no attraction for him at all. He drew the covers across her nakedness and left her to sleep in peace.

He pulled the brazier into the middle of the tent and threw on some incense. He then settled himself amongst the cushions and waited a few seconds. The fragrant smell of olibanum began to waft through the tent, and as it did so Sleg Agorn rolled back his eyes and in an instant he was above Cor Gaur looking down at the seething hive of activity beneath. To the North he could see the runner that Awrgon had dispatched already half a mile away on the avenue to Abiri. He looked to the West, but so far there was no sign of any approach. Below he could see the diviners with their sensitive rods beginning the survey of the site.

Beginning in the East, he began to move around the circle, drawing the lines of force that would define the area, and putting the seals on at the four cardinal points. This done, he then, as it were, drew the threads together so that a "blanket" lay over the whole of Cor Gaur, a screen that would be difficult for any but a very senior priest to pierce. He then withdrew and awoke in his own body. The whole operation had only taken a few minutes, and he felt more at ease now that it was done. He rearranged the cushions more comfortably and settled down to a long wait. The chariots would not reach Glaeston until early evening at the outside, and it would be late evening before the tale was told, the situation assessed, and the ritual prepared for a half-world journey. It was still only late afternoon now—it would be another three or four hours, at the earliest, before the visitors arrived.

As late afternoon wore into evening, the bustling sounds of activity from outside gradually died down. The sun was already below the horizon when Awrgon came to report. "The strongest indication for the well," the boy said, "is at the Hele Stone, right where the avenue begins, almost in the exact spot where Hakin died. But as that is right at our outer defenses, I have chosen a less strong but more suitable site in the center, a few feet from the western trilithon, and as the West is under the dominion of Water I feel that site to be singularly appropriate."

Sleg Agorn nodded. "Very well. Get some sleep now. The work must commence at dawn."

When the boy had gone, Sleg Agorn heard the guard being changed at the outer perimeter, and also heard a guard take up its position right outside the tent. There was no point in guarding the central tents during the day, but Mog Agorn had insisted that his own and Asher's tent be watched at night—a reasonable precaution, and one that would ensure that Sleg Agorn was not disturbed.

When the time drew near, Sleg Agorn again slipped from his body and hovered over the center of Cor Gaur. He could see the lines of force radiating out across the land along the trackways, and below him he saw the circles of force marked by the great standing stones. His own circle of force, ensouled by his personal seals, lay just outside the outer earthworks. The whole scene was like a huge red and silver web, with himself as the spider at the center.

He did not have long to wait. Suddenly there was a "movement," and his visitors had arrived. Sleg Agorn had been a priest all his life—the number of times he had journeyed through the half-world were uncountable—but he had never lost his sense of amazement at the speed of travel. It could be as slow as one wished, or so fast as to be an instantaneous transfer. He had not seen his visitors approaching, even though he had been watching for them. They must have come at full speed. The scene had merely "shimmered" slightly, and there they were.

There were three of them. Two of them were Druthin himself and that cursed Egyptian, Menahotep. The third one was not known to him. There were rumors that Vaila had traveled down from Maes Howe in the Wild Isles—and this might be he. Although he could see his visitors quite clearly, he knew that they could not see him. To them Cor Gaur was completely hidden in a blanket of fog.

He saw Druthin raise his arm and cry out an invocation—and the line of force quivered, but held firm. Sleg Agorn saw them confer briefly and then separate to the three senior cardinal points, East, West, and South. When they were in position, all three raised their arms, and all three cried out the invocation in unison, and Sleg Agorn's seals cracked and fell apart, and the line of force vanished. Now that they could see him, and the whole of Cor Gaur spread out below, they came to him swiftly.

"Greetings, Sleg Agorn," said Druthin coldly. "We have come to see whether Mog Agorn lives or not."

Sleg Agorn drew himself up with as much dignity as he could muster. "Since you have broken my seals, Druthin, and so will be able to learn all you want, there is no point in my attempting to prevaricate. Mog Agorn lives, though sorely stricken—but he will certainly return to full health."

"That is sad news," said Druthin gravely, "for both Wessex and Druid alike. If Mog Agorn had died, there might have been a chance of persuading the Wessex to abandon this insanity."

The other Druid stepped forward. "I am Vaila of Maes Howe. Greetings!"

Sleg Agorn nodded briefly. "I had guessed as much."

"You do realize," said Vaila, "that every Druid in the land will lay down his life to prevent Asher giving birth to that thing?"

"I do—and I hope you realize that every Wessex priest will lay down his life to protect her." Sleg Agorn turned to Menahotep. "But what has Egypt got to do with this?"

"I am a guest in your land," said Menahotep, "and if it were simply a question of one priesthood at variance with another, it would sadden me deeply but I would not interfere. But this matter is so grave I have already alerted my Elders in Egypt and have sought their aid. The birth of this child must be prevented at all costs, and Egypt too will use all its powers against you—and those powers are formidable!"

Druthin raised his hand and pointed a long, bony finger at the Wessex priest. "The future of this land is, for the time being, in your own hands, Sleg Agorn. Before Mog Agorn recovers, you and Awrgon could retrieve the situation before it is too late. I beg of you. Put an end to this evil pregnancy!"

"I could not even if I wanted to. Asher herself has already tried to abort herself but the thing will not permit it, and I fancy the same control would extend to me if I tried."

The three visitors exchanged glances. "So already the thing controls the Wessex," said Vaila, "and it is as yet barely half-formed in her belly."

Sleg Agorn nodded. "You are beginning to see, at last. Mog Agorn has come more and more under its control these past few years. How else could it have persuaded him to adopt a course that will inevitably bring the Wessex under total domination? Mog Agorn has become a puppet led on by visions of unlimited power—guided to a point whereby he provided the means for its incarnation. Already it has Asher under control, and those who come near her. How many more days or weeks will it be before it is able to reach out and control every soul at Cor Gaur? And how many more days after that before its influence reaches Glaeston?" Sleg Agorn looked at his visitors. "Don't you understand? Even if you attack tomorrow, and kill every Wessex priest at Cor Gaur and capture Asher herself, not one of you will be able to lift a finger to harm either it or her. The thing will not permit it—and then the control will grow stronger until even you, Druthin, will crawl to do its bidding."

They were silent for some time, and then Druthin said quietly: "Knowing all this, why continue to serve your own destruction? To participate in such evil is to invoke the inevitable annihilation of your very soul. Go back to your body. Walk out of Cor Gaur and join us at Glaeston."

"I cannot. I have served the Wessex all my life, and I am not going to recant now simply because things aren't entirely to my liking."

"Very well," said Druthin. "It is your choice, and may the Great Ones have mercy on you!" And the three visitors turned and left—and Sleg Agorn awoke in his own body, sweating profusely, his hands trembling.

He snatched up a knife, raced to Asher's couch, and flung back the covers. Asher woke up, startled, to see him towering above her. She stared into his eyes and knew his mind. She shrank back on the couch. "Go on," she whispered. "Do it. Do it now!"

Sleg Agorn poured all his strength into his arm to bring the knife down and ram it into her body, but he could not move.

"Go on," she screamed. "Kill me!" She sprang up and grasped his arm and tried to pull it down. "Go on, Sleg Agorn—go on! Kill me! *Kill me!*" But his arm would not move. Suddenly he collapsed, his strength gone, and he hurled the knife away. He flung himself across the tent and rushed wildly into the night—and Asher fell back on the couch, screaming in absolute agony as wave after wave of intolerable hatred and pain flooded her body, her mind, and her very soul.

It was dawn at Glaeston and again the full Council was met. "The time to attack is therefore now, immediately, before Mog Agorn recovers and before that thing gains further control."

Cludin raised his hand. "If the thing already has sufficient control to prevent those nearby from causing it harm, then how shall we kill it even if we prevail against the Wessex and get close enough to do so?"

"A good question," said Druthin, "and one for which there is no comforting answer. We will destroy the Wessex first, I hope, and then conduct the full Seventh Degree ritual and call down the Fourth Aspect of the Great Ones upon the child. I do not see how it could survive such an invocation."

There were startled glances amongst the Council. The Fourth Aspect! Only once throughout the entire history of mankind had that aspect ever been deliberately invoked, and even that occasion had become a legend. It was said that in ancient times in Atlantis the priesthood had grown so corrupt that Kumara, the High Priest of the Withdrawn Temple, and Helios, High Priest of the Sun Temple, had performed a joint ritual invoking the Fourth Aspect—and the result had been the utter destruction of the whole of Atlantis, a destruction so complete that not one single shred of evidence remained to show that Atlantis had ever existed. *

"I know," said Druthin grimly. "We will try all other methods first. The Fourth Aspect will only be invoked as a last resort."

"What of Glaeston itself?" said Cludin.

"The aged and those unfit for travel will remain at Glaeston. All others will march on Cor Gaur as soon as humanly possible, including all the priestesses and seeresses, Thetan."

The High Priestess nodded. "It will be done, Dru-

*See *The Seedbearers*, the first novel in this trilogy, also published by Bantam Books.

thin. But who will care for the aged while we are away?"

"Gargan, and those able-bodied men of the surrounding villages who wish to do so, will march with us. I have already spoken to Gargan accordingly. It was a condition of his coming that the womenfolk of his villages move into Glaeston after our departure to help care for those left behind. I have already appointed a priest-healer and two seeress-healers to remain and take charge of all matters at Glaeston." He turned to the Egyptian. "Your men will presumably march with us, Menahotep."

"Myself and Ramin, and the twelve soldiers of my personal guard, yes—but the sailors will remain with the ship. If we are defeated, my ship-master has instructions to bear the Druid survivors to Egypt to carry on the struggle from there."

"A wise precaution. I hope it will not be necessary." He turned to the young battle-commander. "Well, Melkor, once more your hour has come."

The younger man sighed. "Then let's hope I do better than last time."

"That was not your fault," said Druthin. "Indeed, the fact that we were able to get so many away to safety was attributable to you personally. As to this present venture, I want the Druids to march from Glaeston at dawn on the day after tomorrow. That gives you two clear days."

"It will be enough."

"Very well. As from this moment, you are in command of all physical plane matters to do with this war. All will obey your commands, even we of the Council."

"So be it. My first move is to appoint the captain of Menahotep's guard as my advisor, to remain with me at all times. His experience will be invaluable."

"It will be done," the Egyptian said. "I will send him to you."

Druthin rose to face the Council. "We are priests of the Sun, knowing the sun to be but a symbol of the Most High whom even the Great Ones serve. The thing that is being born to the Wessex is a Dark One, the extreme antithesis of everything we represent." He took the symbol of his Office in his right hand, the carven staff with the Serpent Symbol. "We march to our destiny." His voice was vibrant and full of power. "And I tell you this, Priests of the Sun. We will not rest until our land is cleansed and returned to honor!"

Menahotep strode into Ramin's chamber, and the boy was startled to see the grimness on his mentor's face. The older man quickly explained the situation, ". . . and so we march at dawn the day after tomorrow. We must, however, report immediately to Egypt —now! Prepare the couches."

"To Egypt!" Ramin said. "But I am not skilled enough to reach Egypt in a meditation. Look what happened the last time I left my body."

"You will be with me, under my protection. And anyway, we are not going to Egypt. We are going to the Egyptian inner plane Lodge."

"It's still a long way."

Menahotep shook his head. "Do try to think before you speak. The inner planes are states of consciousness, not places." He pulled a small container from his robe and dropped a few pieces of Egyptian kyphi onto the glowing brazier. "It is a long way only in the same sense that it is a long way between, say, love and hatred, even though they may coexist in the same human heart, a love for a friend and a hatred for an enemy. And, also, there is no distance at all between two who share a love, though they stand a thousand miles apart." He pulled the brazier into the middle of the chamber. "You know all this, Ramin, so why allow foolishness to escape your lips. Think before you speak."

, Ramin pulled the couches around, one in the East and one in the West. "It sort of slipped out unguarded," he apologized.

The older priest grunted. "An undisciplined tongue is the tongue of a fool. It serves only to advertize his ignorance." He adjusted his robe and looked around the room. "If everyone kept . . ."

"I know, I know!" said Ramin hastily. "If everyone kept their mouths shut until they had something worthwhile to say, the whole world would be deafened by the silence."

"And don't you forget it. Right. You take the West —and stick close to me."

Menahotep performed the deosil circumambulations and put the seals on. He then took his place in the East and began the opening invocation. Ramin felt the rush of power, just as it had been during his initiation, and then suddenly he found himself standing in the center of the inner Lodge, a grove of black pillars, polished, symmetrical, the floor of black and white paving. In the center was the black altar with a light upon it, and in the East were the three carven thrones of the High Magi.

The Lodge was empty, but Menahotep stood patiently, facing the East—and Ramin stood just behind him. Suddenly the Eastern Portal shimmered and three figures appeared on the carven chairs, and Ramin's eyes widened with astonishment, and with awe. The two on either side were the High Priest and High Priestess, familiar sights to Ramin though he had never been privileged to speak with either of them. But the one in the center was the Venerable High Master, he whose name was never mentioned —a being so august and so withdrawn that few priests even in the Temple of Re in Egypt had ever even seen him. The younger initiates, like Ramin, were never quite sure whether he existed at all, and even if he did, they were not quite sure whether to think of him as an incarnated human being like themselves or a great inner plane being shadowed forth in human form.

"You called us, Menahotep of Egypt, and we have come." The voice was soft, but full of power.

Menahotep raised his head. "The Dark One has incarnated in the womb of Asher, the High Priestess of the Wessex, and already it controls the minds of those in its immediate vicinity. The Druids will lay down their lives to destroy it, and the Wessex will lay down their lives to protect it." Ramin had always thought that Menahotep had the gentlest, the softest, and yet the most powerful voice that he had ever heard, but it sounded harsh and ugly in comparison with the voice of the Venerable High Master. "We come, therefore, to advise Egypt of the situation and to seek her aid."

"We already know of these things and grieve for the foolishness thereof." The voice seemed to emanate from a vast distance rather than from the figure in the East. It was as if the very walls, the very inner Lodge itself was speaking to them. "We control the inner such that the Evil One will not be able to seek aid from others of its kind. But we cannot and will not interfere in human activity on the physical plane. Humanity has been granted the task of working out the factor of free will in the manifested universe of the Most High Logos, and any interference in that work would be a denial of human destiny. The effect of the cause is on the physical plane and must be dealt with on that plane. The Gate was opened by incarnated human beings and must be closed by them alone."

Menahotep stepped forward a pace. "But if the Dark One prevails, the world will be plunged into darkness for century upon century, perhaps for a thousand years!"

The inner voice was even more gentle now, though with a touch of reproach. "A thousand years is but a drop in the ocean of forever, Menahotep, as you well know—and ultimate harmony is assured, as you also well know, though perhaps not in your lifetime. Do not let your tongue deny your innate knowledge of these matters." The figures on the carven thrones began to fade. "Return now to your own plane and work out your destiny by your own efforts, according to the Law that governs all things."

The Lodge began to shimmer, to fade, and Ramin felt himself caught up by the rush of power, and the last thing he heard was that vast voice ringing in his heart. "The Great Ones are with you, Menahotep of Egypt, and those who stand with you. If the Evil One prevails, it can only do so for a little time—the merest flicker in the vastness of eternity. Have faith in your calling. Ultimate harmony will prevail—be assured of that!"

And Menahotep and Ramin awoke in their own bodies in the great Druid College at Glaeston.

Chapter Nine

In the gray half-light of that hour before dawn, one thousand Druid priests and priestesses were drawn up in rank and file outside the great gates of Glaeston College—waiting. At their head were the eight chariots and horses that had been Mog Agorn's pride. The horses were restless in the early wind, and the muscles stood out on the drivers' arms as they fought to control them. Immediately in front of the gates were the ranks of the white-robed senior priests of the Druid grade, their arms patiently folded, their expressions calm but grave, their headdresses blowing in the wind. Behind them were the green-robed Ovates, amongst whom here and there were the green headdresses of the seniors of that grade, the Ovate Druids. At the rear were the ranks of the Bards, the blue-robed youngsters, their eyes dancing with excitement, barely able to keep their bodies still in order to appear seemingly grave in emulation of their seniors, but the day contained too much prospect of adventure to maintain the composure of their youthful serenity. To one side were drawn up the ranks of the priestesses and seeresses, robed in the blues and greens of the sea, their silver headdresses whipping in the wind. To the left, outside the priestly ranks, was the giant figure of Gargan, the stonecutter, and with him were over a hundred men from the surrounding settlements, together with a train of the huge lumbering draft-horses laden to capacity with the needs of their exploit.

In front of the chariots stood Melkor, the battle-commander, his arms folded, waiting for the Elders to appear. His was the leading chariot, just behind him, and its driver was the captain of the Egyptian guard. These two, from the command chariot, would direct all operations of the coming struggle. With Melkor stood Ramin and Cludin, each designated a place in one of the chariots. Ramin was to command the east flank, and Cludin the west. Each had protested that they had neither the qualifications nor the experience to command in battle.

"For that matter, neither have I," Melkor had said. "I am, like yourselves, a priest more at home in a ritual than on a battlefield. But, also like yourselves, I have a trained mind, a developed imagination, and an awareness of what is at stake in this affair. How can I refuse to accept the responsibility thrust upon me by pleading inexperience? Every priest at Glaeston is a stranger to war. Someone has to command, and the choice has fallen on me. Now I place some of that responsibility on you."

"But at least you and Cludin are of the Druid Council," Ramin had said, "and your authority in priestly matters is recognized and honored. I am an Egyptian, a guest in your land, a stranger to Druidry and only newly initiated into your Mysteries. Who am I to command a wing of Druids in battle?"

"You are one of those chosen to command, *that's* who you are, and all will recognize that authority and honor it!" Melkor had said. "Do you wish to abrogate the responsibility I lay upon you?"

Ramin had hesitated. "Put like that, no. How can I refuse? But I take no pleasure in it!"

"Pleasure," Melkor had said drily, "will be conspicuously absent in this affair. Anyway, Ramin—and you, Cludin—the stones are cast and your parts are decreed. Fulfill your roles as best you can, as indeed will I." And so Ramin and Cludin stood at Melkor's side at the head of the Druid force, each enburdened with the weight of care that events had thrust upon them.

With them stood Thetan, High Priestess of all

Druidry, Pythoness to the Order of Theutates, her black hair streaming in the wind, her eyes unusually grave. "The sun will rise at any moment," she said suddenly. "If I live another thousand lives, I will never forget this day!"

"Nor, too, will any here," said Melkor.

Cludin gathered his robe more closely around him. "I feel as if a million eyes were watching my every heartbeat—as if the whole of eternity was holding its breath!"

At that moment Druthin, Menahotep, Vaila, and the rest of the Elder Druids came slowly through the Great Gates toward the specially prepared litters. The Arch-Mage paused for a moment and then raised the Serpent Symbol to the sky, and as if on command the first rays of the day came lancing down from the hilltops. "Priests of the Sun!" he thundered. "This is the day of our destiny. Let us discharge our tasks with courage and with honor."

The three commanders saluted and sprang to their chariots. The banners of the Serpent Symbol and also of Awen, the three rays of Light upon which all knowledge is inscribed, were hoisted aloft, and the ranks of Druidry wheeled to the east and began the long march to Abiri and to Cor Gaur.

And thus the Druids went to war—and on the inner, the Great Ones drew near to watch with compassion as humanity yet again struggled with itself to fulfill the destiny that would lead them to eternity.

Awrgon stood on the outer earthworks at Cor Gaur staring toward the west. He had been there since dawn, and now it was the zenith of the sun. Three days had passed since Mog Agorn had been struck down, and he felt it in his bones that today was the day that would see the Druids arrive. Everything that could be done had been accomplished. Even the well had struck fresh, clean water—though they had to go to thirty feet to find it. All the priests and all the supplies from Abiri were now here at Cor Gaur, and that most ancient of all stone circles at Abiri now lay

empty and abandoned to await the Druid advance. It
would now be a straight siege, and for the life of him
he could not see how it was possible for one thousand
Druids to storm these massive earthworks successfully
against two thousand determined defenders. He
looked around the earthworks and down into the circle of Cor Gaur. Five hundred warrior-priests were on
guard on the earthworks themselves, and no fewer
than one hundred guarded their weakest point where
the broad avenue came sweeping through the earthworks into Cor Gaur itself—though the barricade of
boulders even now being hastily erected would make
that entrance equally impregnable. The children had
been herded into a stone compound at the very center, near the King Stone, with a dozen priestesses
designated to care for them. Fortunately, there were no
more than a score of them, the children of the original
five hundred Wessex at Cor Gaur. The fifteen hundred Wessex who had responded to the call, and who
had come from throughout the land, had naturally
left their children behind. But that, too, had its dis-
advantages, because for the most part they had left
their priestesses behind as well. In all, the Wessex
could boast no more than fifty priestesses and seeresses, and of these only twelve were trained in the arts
of healing. And of the total force of two thousand
priests, only five were healers—seventeen healers in
all. Awrgon shook his head. "Seventeen may sound a
lot," he said to himself, "but it will prove too few
when the battle begins!"

Five hundred mountain oxen were penned rump to
rump in a stockade in one of the outer circles. It
would have been fine if they could have been kept
alive—fresh meat would have been welcome—but
there was too little grass within the circle. Awrgon
had reluctantly given orders for their slaughter and
for their meat to be cut into strips and laid in the sun
to dry. All morning the butchery had been going on,
and the dwindling survivors were frenzied by the
smell of blood and death. The noise of their continual

bellowing made it difficult for a man to think. Dried meat, corn, and water would be their diet for four months, worse than peasants' fare. But at least it would keep them alive until the child was born.

Awrgon saw Sleg Agorn beckoning to him, but he ignored the signal and made the older man climb up to him. He was panting quite heavily by the time he made it to the top. "You're an old man already, my uncle," Awrgon sneered. "You had better hide when the Druids come!"

Sleg Agorn paused for a moment to regain his breath. "Mog Agorn is conscious," he said at last, ignoring the taunt, "and wants to see you immediately."

"Let him wait."

Sleg Agorn raised his eyebrows. "He is still the High Priest, Awrgon."

The younger man turned on him furiously. "While he lies in bed, I have a battle to fight—a battle that will decide whether *his* ambition is fulfilled or not. He had better treat me with a little more honor and respect than he has of late, or else I will wash my hands of the whole affair and he can command the battle from his bed!"

"He cannot do that, and you know it."

"Aye, but does *he* know it? I tell you this, Sleg Agorn. I am fast coming to the point where I am no longer prepared to tolerate his arrogance! Whether he likes it or not, he is now very dependent on *me*. I will *not* be ordered hither and thither like a newly initiated neophyte. I said let him wait. I will come when I am good and ready!"

Sleg Agorn was silent for a moment. "You speak of Mog Agorn's arrogance, but you have a fair measure of it yourself—and so, too, did Fangorn, and look what happened to him."

"Mog Agorn did not need Fangorn, but he does need me. *That* is the difference."

Sleg Agorn sighed. "Very well. It looks as if once again I must act as peacemaker between my brother and his sons, though the Great Ones know it is a thankless task. Give me fifteen minutes to speak with him, and then come. I will try to curb his arrogance at least long enough for the two of you to speak together without actually coming to violence." And he turned and made his way back down into Cor Gaur.

Awrgon smiled to himself. Sleg Agorn was no man of power. Let him play at diplomacy if it pleased him; at least he was useful as a messenger boy.

A guard shouted and Awrgon turned to see a lone figure appear on the hilltop to the west and come down to Cor Gaur at a steady run. Yesterday Awrgon had sent a dozen men to hide themselves at various points along the road from Glaeston to report back on any Druid movement. This must be one of them. He waited patiently, ten minutes, fifteen minutes, and then finally the man arrived and Awrgon went down to meet him. "Where are the Druids?" he said harshly.

The man was panting heavily. He pointed to the north. "They are passing Cor Gaur by, obviously heading for Abiri."

"How many?"

The man shrugged. "I do not know. It looks as if every Druid in the land is on the march. There must be a thousand of them! All the priestesses are with them, and the draft-horses, a great mass of supplies, and something like a hundred peasants as well. Druthin himself is at their head."

"And our chariots?"

"Oh, yes, they are there, too, all eight of them, and our Caspian horses as well."

"Very well. Get yourself some food and drink. I will question you again later." And Awrgon turned and headed toward Mog Agorn's tent.

What had been worrying him all day was now clear. Awrgon had *known* that the Druids were on the march today, and yet that feeling had not made sense. Tomorrow was the Autumnal Equinox. It would have been more logical for the Druids to have remained at Glaeston, to have conducted the Equinox ritual there, and *then* to have marched straight to Cor

Gaur. It was now obvious that Druthin wanted to use Abiri for his ritual, presumably at dawn tomorrow. After all, Abiri was the greatest power-center in the land after Cor Gaur. It meant that the Druids would not arrive at Cor Gaur until midday tomorrow at the earliest.

Then, suddenly, the most significant fact of all struck home in Awrgon's brain. All this meant that the Glaeston College was, at this very moment, lying virtually empty and unguarded—and the Wessex had nearly twenty-four hours to take advantage of that fact!

Awrgon broke into a run and burst into Mog Agorn's tent in a flurry of excitement. His father lay propped up on one elbow, his face ashen with pain. The Chief Healer was winding a clean, fresh cloth around his torso. Mog Agorn looked up as his youngest son came bursting in. "Ah, there you are at last! Sleg Agorn has been telling me how much you have accomplished. It was well done. Thank you." He grimaced with pain as the cloth was tied and made firm. "We can now withstand a siege for months—especially now that we have unlimited water."

Awrgon shook his head. "Forget all that, Father. Something has happened that will change all our plans." He quickly explained the Druid march to Abiri. "So we must strike camp—immediately—this very minute, and march the whole Wessex force to Glaeston. Every priest, every priestess, all the children —everything! Glaeston is empty and virtually unguarded. We can arrive halfway through the night and take possession unopposed. Once behind those great gates, the Druids will not be able to touch us. We can live freely and comfortably until the child is born. We've won, my father—we've won!"

The Chief Healer shook his head immediately. "You would not survive such a forced march, Mog Agorn. It will be your death."

The injured man grunted. "Maybe—maybe not. I'm tougher than you think."

"The Druids are watching Cor Gaur," said Sleg Agorn, "and will see us depart and pursue us—and don't forget they have the chariots."

"So what?" said Awrgon. "How many men can eight chariots carry—sixteen, twenty? What danger are they to us? The main body of the Druids are two hours forced march from Cor Gaur, and then they will have to strike westward to Glaeston. With a two-hour start, they will never catch us."

Mog Agorn sank back onto the couch. If anything, his face was grayer than before. "You are all missing the real point at issue," he said heavily. "Cor Gaur is the spiritual center of the land. The Child has to be born here, on the King Stone itself."

Awrgon could hardly believe his ears. "But that's ridiculous. Why? What does it matter where the thing is born? Why on the King Stone—why?"

"Because I said so," Mog Agorn suddenly flared. *"That's* why! Who are you to question it? Just because you've made yourself useful for once in a few trivial matters doesn't give you the right to question my decisions."

"A few trivial matters," shouted Awrgon. "If it weren't for me, five hundred Wessex would have been trapped at Abiri and slaughtered. If it weren't for me, there would be no water at Cor Gaur—forcing a surrender within a week of the Druids arriving. Trivial matters! I have made Cor Gaur safe for you."

Mog Agorn struggled to prop himself up again. "If Cor Gaur is as safe as you say," he bellowed, "then there is no reason to leave it."

"By all the powers," shouted Awrgon, "are you really that stupid? Of course, Cor Gaur is safe. Of course, the child can be born here. But if we march now we can have Glaeston College as well!"

"Am I really surrounded by imbeciles?" bellowed Mog Agorn. "Do you really think that Druthin is that stupid as to leave Glaeston unguarded, if there was the slightest chance of it being taken in his absence? Hasn't it yet occurred to your tiny brain that Druthin *knows* that I cannot leave Cor Gaur, and knows as well as I that the Child *must* be born on the King Stone? Have you really not understood *any* of the significance of all this?" He glared at his youngest son ferociously, but then his face sagged and he fell back on the couch.

The Chief Healer bent over him. "You really must not carry on like this. If the bleeding starts again I cannot guarantee your life. You must rest."

The sweat stood out on Mog Agorn's brow. "How can I rest when no one, *no one*, seems to understand the staggering importance of what we are doing?" he whispered. "How can I rest knowing that the ignorant can bring us all to ruin?"

Awrgon looked at Asher, but the girl was still unconscious. He flung up his hands. "All right. I admit that you and Druthin are more experienced in priestly matters than I. So tell me, Father—help me understand—why Cor Gaur and nowhere else?"

Mog Agorn shook his head weakly. "Cor Gaur is the spiritual center of this land," he said slowly and carefully, "and as such the Child *has* to be born here, on the King Stone itself. If you cannot understand that by your own insight, then any explanation of mine would be meaningless to you. You will have to accept that what I say is true, even if you do not understand it."

"And also," said Sleg Agorn, "since all the evidence points to the fact that Druthin is of the same mind, surely that is at least some form of confirmation that what your father is saying is correct."

Awrgon shrugged helplessly. "Very well. So be it. But it still sounds crazy to me." And he turned to go.

"Awrgon!" Mog Agorn called. "I will keep my promise to you. On the day the Dark One is born, I will announce you to the Wessex as the new High Priest, and I will withdraw into the background—and Sleg Agorn here is a witness to my word." He pointed at his son, and his eyes were anxious, even pleading. "Until then, keep the Druids at bay. *Nothing* must endanger the culmination of all my work. Since I lie stricken here, I have to rely on you. Don't fail me!"

The Druids arrived at Abiri during the late afternoon, and Druthin in particular was relieved to find it empty. He drew Menahotep and Vaila to one side. "Good," he said. "This is the first concrete evidence that our reasoning has been correct. Mog Agorn has indeed withdrawn all the Wessex to Cor Gaur."

"Let us hope they stay there," said Vaila.

"Mog Agorn *has* to remain at Cor Gaur. The Child cannot be born anywhere else."

"And they will," said Menahotep, "providing Mog Agorn still commands."

"Yes," sighed Druthin. "*That* is the gamble. If he still lies unconscious, then Awrgon will not be able to resist the temptation to march on Glaeston once he knows that we are here—and surely he must know that by now. If the Wessex march to Glaeston, then the Child cannot manifest, and all their plans will have been brought to nothing."

"But the Druids will lose Glaeston," said Vaila.

"A small price to pay to avert such a disaster. Anyway, we will see—we will see. If the Wessex intend to take Glaeston, then they will have to march today. If they are still there at sunset, then we will know that Mog Agorn commands and that we will have to march on Cor Gaur tomorrow."

The Arch-Mage summoned his commanders, Melkor, Cludin, and Ramin. "We will rest here until sunset," he said, "but we must be ready to move at a moment's notice. We will make the decision at sunset as to whether we stay or go. Advise your men accordingly. See to it that all are fed. If we move we will have to march all night."

They did not understand, but they saluted and turned to obey unquestioningly. When they had gone Druthin shook his head. "It is not right that men should be shunted hither and thither without knowing the reason why, especially priests." He turned to Menahotep and Vaila. "I would be grateful if you would move amongst them and explain why it is that we must wait."

Menahotep looked at him thoughtfully. "Tell me,

Druthin, in your heart of hearts, do you believe that the Wessex will march on Glaeston?"

"No, I do not—and for one very good reason—the Covenant. Vaila knows what I mean."

The Elder from Maes Howe pursed his lips in surprise. "Oh, yes, the Covenant! Strange that I should have forgotten that." He turned to the Egyptian. "When Glaeston was first constructed, Menahotep, a Covenant was given by the inner-plane adepti to the priests-in-earth, and amongst other things that Covenant guaranteed that Glaeston would never ever be attacked by force of arms and that it would function unmolested until it was time for the Old Order to give way to the New Age—and even then it would not be destroyed by violence, but would be dismantled carefully and lovingly and its very stones used to build the new Temple—and that its dismantlement would be so complete that not one single shred of evidence would remain to show that Glaeston College had ever existed."

"Doesn't that sadden you?"

"In a sense, yes," said Druthin. "But it must be so and I accept it. When that time comes, it will mean that the Druids will have fulfilled their destiny, will have contributed to the march of human evolution, will have fulfilled their guardianship of the living truth, and will have handed on the flower of our contribution to the New Age for the next phase of development—and that, surely, is occasion for joy, not sadness."

"*The living truth!*" said Vaila. "There is no such thing, Menahotep, as an absolute truth. All existence is life, and all life is growth, change, development, evolution. Even the Most High is changing, developing, evolving—and as such the truth of these things must also change. This means that the teaching, the philosophy, must also be continually evolving in order to adequately express the living and evolving truth. Our function during this phase has been to preserve what is already known, to encourage the growth of that knowledge, to add a new understanding, and to hand on the seeds of our efforts to those who follow. The use of the stone of Glaeston College to build the new Temple will be a symbol of that continuing, living, and evolving truth expressed in the new forms to come."

Menahotep sighed. "Would that Egypt could accept the march of evolutionary change with equal grace. But I fear that there are already signs that our ritual forms and our philosophy have become too rigid, and that we are resistant to change."

"Now that *is* sad," said Druthin. "Egypt's contribution to human evolution is almost immeasurable. They have deserved much honor, and it would be a pity to mar that honor by denying or resisting the New Age to come. However, that is Egypt's problem. Our own problem at the moment is to resist an evil change, to resist a devolution in order to preserve the opportunity for evolution. The birth of a Dark One would be a retrogressive step, and one that we must resist at all costs." He looked at the sky. "It lacks about two hours to sunset. I will meet with you again then." And he turned and climbed a knoll to the west of the ancient circle of Abiri, obviously wishing to be alone.

"A fine man and a fine priest," said Menahotep.

"Yes," said Vaila. "He is without doubt the finest Arch-Mage that the Druids have yet produced. Come, let us explain matters to the others."

Ramin was standing alone, leaning against one of the stones of the outer circle. Thetan came up to him. "You look worried," she said softly.

"No, not at all," he said hastily, but she looked at him quizzically. "Well, perhaps just a bit. I've had a brief training in the use of the sword and the spear—all the young priests have to in Egypt—but I have never had to put that training to the test. When the moment comes, I don't know whether I *could* kill a man." He avoided her eyes. "I have been trying to imagine what it would be like, to plunge a sword into another human body, to see the blade slice into living flesh, the blood, the pain . . . I don't know whether I could."

"You will do what you have to do when the time comes," she said.

"I hope so. But even that's not the worst fear—I won't even speak about *that!*"

"You don't have to. I know." She looked at him gently. "You will not run away. Men like you never do."

He smiled wryly. "I will never be able to keep many secrets from you, will I?"

"Not many," she admitted. "Does it worry you?"

"Not really, but it does make one feel sort of . . . naked."

She laughed. "And being naked with me makes you feel nervous, does it?" she said archly.

He looked at her seriously. "Don't tease me, Thetan. It is bad enough that I must remain silent until all this is resolved." The wind was blowing from the west and flattening her robe against her body. "If you tease me too much, I may forget my promise."

She stepped closer to him. "I was wrong, Ramin, and you were right," she said softly. "You recognized the reality between us immediately, and being a good priest you wanted to express that reality. I closed my eyes and tried to deny my heart, thinking that it had to take second place to all this." She took his hands in hers. "If you were to die without knowing what is in my heart, I don't think I could ever forgive myself."

"And what is in your heart, Thetan?"

"You," she said simply.

"And you in mine." He pulled her close to him. "I think I could take on the whole Wessex force single-handed now!"

She laughed softly, and then suddenly clutched him hard, her hands digging into his back. "Stay safe for me!" she whispered fiercely.

He was taken aback by the ferocity of her sudden resolve. "I will," he said thickly. "I promise you—I will!"

She looked up at him. "Lay with me tonight," she said simply. "Just in case . . ."

He stroked her hair. "I am not going to die."

"Lay with me!" she said fiercely. "Lay with me to-night. Promise me—*now!*"

He nodded. "I promise. I promise!"

An hour later Druthin came down from the knoll and sought out Vaila and Menahotep. "It was not ideal conditions today for contact," he said, "but as far as I can judge the Wessex are still at Cor Gaur. We will therefore remain here tonight, conduct the Autumnal Equinox ritual at dawn, and then march on Cor Gaur. I would be grateful if you would make the necessary arrangements."

Menahotep pointed to where Ramin and Thetan stood, their arms around each other. "There are two who will welcome a night's rest here at Abiri."

"Ah! I am glad that they have declared to each other. It seems that Egypt may have lost a priest, Menahotep."

"Or the Druids a priestess."

Druthin chuckled. "We will see. He will be welcome to stay here with us."

"And she would be welcome in Egypt."

The two men looked at each other. "All right, Menahotep!" The Arch-Mage laughed. "A pact between us then—we will let *them* decide!"

"Agreed."

Vaila and Menahotep passed on the commands, and the Druid force settled down to sleep. Fortunately, the night was clear and the air warm enough to dispense with tents for this single night. Menahotep and the Egyptian soldiers picked a spot just outside the main circle to lay their beds of skins. Menahotep was trying to settle himself into a more comfortable position when Ramin came up to him. "When I get back to Egypt," the old man grumbled, "*if* I get back to Egypt, I think I will retire into graceful old age. No more foreign lands for me. I fear my bones do protest too much!"

Ramin smiled. "I have some news that may make you forget your aches and pains."

The old man cocked an eye. "You mean Thetan? I should think the whole of Druidry knows it by now!"

The boy grinned wryly. "Were we that obvious?"

"No, no, not at all! You *may* have been practicing some art of healing massage on each other."

"Do you approve or not?"

Menahotep caught the note of anxiety in the boy's voice. "Yes," he said seriously. "I do indeed approve, and so, too, does Druthin. You have our blessing, both of you. And now leave me to find a piece of ground that is not littered with stones. I never saw such a country as this for stones—and all of them seem to be gathered beneath my bed!" The boy grinned and turned to go. "Ramin!" the old man called. "Try to get at least *some* sleep tonight. We have a battle tomorrow—remember?" The darkness hid the boy's blush, and the old man chuckled to himself.

The sounds gradually died down as the Druids settled to sleep. By and large, the priestesses and seeresses slept in a group at the center, and the priests occupied the outer circles. But here and there the couples who had declared for each other lay together. The guards stood on the high ground surrounding Abiri, particularly to the south, and every two hours the guard-commander slipped silently through the sleeping camp to wake their relief.

Only one tent had been erected, and that for Druthin himself. He waited until the camp was quiet and then slipped from his body to verify for himself that the Wessex were indeed still at Cor Gaur. He had been receiving impressions all day from the Elders left behind at Glaeston, but it had not been easy to keep himself receptive during the rush and bustle of the march—he could so easily have been mistaken. It was therefore with some relief that he came to hover over Cor Gaur and saw the tents, and the night fires, and saw the guards nervously pacing the outer earthworks. He lingered only long enough to verify that Asher herself was still there, and then withdrew back to Abiri. He had been gone only a few minutes. He woke and stepped to the tent opening and watched the sleeping Druid force. His face was gray with sadness, for he knew that some would not sleep an earthly sleep again, not in their present life anyway. He sighed and returned to his couch and composed himself to natural sleep. Let the morrow bring what it would. There was nothing further he could do except lead them where they had to go.

Two hours before dawn, Awrgon slipped from his tent and sniffed the early air. Already there was a tinge of gray in the eastern sky. He picked his way through the tents to the outer circle to the guard-commander. "Any signs?"

The man shook his head. "No, nothing—quiet as a ritual mound."

Awrgon grunted and returned to the center. A priestess slipped naked from a tent, and thinking herself unobserved she stretched her full length and yawned. Her body glistened with oils and there were red marks on her breasts and thighs. Suddenly she saw him watching her and was at first confused, but then she smiled archly and came toward him, stepping delicately in the morning air. "You are abroad early, Awrgon," she said softly.

"So, too, are you, priestess," he said. For the life of him he could not remember her name. She had only recently been appointed to the position of senior priestess. "You had a busy night?"

She tossed her head and snorted. "Him! He busied himself for an hour, no more! The strength of a man rarely matches his boasting." She looked at him and smiled. "I have to prepare the oils for the dawn ritual," she said, "but I could delay it a little."

He laughed softly. "I would need more than an hour."

"Another boast?" she said.

He touched her breasts lightly. "Not now, priestess, but when this is over, I may prove my word."

"I look forward to it." And she smiled and slipped nakedly away.

He walked over to the Chief Healer's tent and

shook the man awake. "I want you to look at Mog Agorn and tell me if he is strong enough to attend the ritual—and Asher."

The priest rubbed his eyes and looked up at Awrgon. "Very well. How close to dawn are we?"

"Close enough. Get moving."

He stepped out into the air and looked around him. The sky was rapidly lightening. The priestess had awakened two of the junior seeresses, and the three of them stood washing themselves down at the water-butts. One of the seeresses laughed, and he saw her point to the red marks on the priestess's breast. The older woman slapped her face and the girl cried out. Soon they slipped to their tents and reemerged robed for the day. Others, too, were now awake, and Awrgon saw Sleg Agorn emerge from his tent and go to Asher's. The guard was noisily changed, and some of the tents were already coming down to be stored away. Soon the fires were freshly fed, and the smell of cooking began to drift on the air.

Awrgon went to Asher's tent. "How are they?" he said.

"I am not dead yet," growled Mog Agorn.

The Chief Healer nodded. "He is well enough, though he won't be leaping around too much."

"You open the ritual, Awrgon," said Mog Agorn, "and conduct the cardinal invocations, but by the Dark One you had better see to it that the seals are put on properly! We cannot afford any errors, today of all days!"

"I am no novice. How's Asher?"

The girl stirred and sat up. "Better than I expected," she admitted. "He seems to have quietencd down. What Office do you wish me to serve?"

"None at all," said Mog Agorn. "I want you on the King Stone. Tell the senior priestess to take over as Pythoness for this one ritual."

That would not tax her too much, thought Awrgon —she's been practicing all night. Aloud he said: "Very well. I will take the East, Sleg Agorn the West, and the Pythoness the South. The Healer can guard the Northern Portal. The King Stone with Asher on it can be the Altar. I will see to it." And he left the tent to supervise arrangements.

A priestess brought him a platter of food and he ate hungrily, watching the preparations that he had instructed the previous day. Occasionally he beckoned a priest, or a guard, or one of the seeresses, and issued fresh instructions. All the tents, except Asher's, were now cleared away, the cooking fires demolished, the children herded into their compound, and the Master-of-Weapons and his assistants were already setting up their platform, laying out the rows of spare swords and knives. In an hour it was done, and the Wessex were as ready as they would ever be to hold Cor Gaur against any who would march against them.

The sky was now quite bright; the dawn was only a few minutes away. Awrgon threw off his day-cloak and donned his ritual robe, black as ebony with the five-pointed gold star on the breast, the emblem—so legend said—of the Temple of the Sun in lost Atlantis. He walked to the eastern trilithon and stood there facing the center, the King Stone itself. At that signal the priests, priestesses, and seeresses began to gather in a circle, following the line of the great Sarsen Trilithon circle. Sleg Agorn came from Asher's tent, bearing the girl on his arm. She was robed in the blue of the sea, a circlet of silver about her neck. Her face was pale but her eyes were bright with anticipation. Sleg Agorn led her to the King Stone and the High Priestess of all the Wessex, Mother of the Child, lay on the stone, her head to the East. Sleg Agorn took up his position in the West, and the senior priestess hers in the South. The Chief Healer came out of the tent and took his position in the North.

There was a moment's delay and then Mog Agorn stepped forth and paused for a moment, his body upright, his eyes glittering, his ritual robe flowing about him. As he did so a murmur rose from the assembly. Few there had expected him to attend this ritual. The senior priestess in the South—as was the custom—stepped forward and raised her arm. "Behold, brethren of the Wessex, the High Priest after the Order of Karadoc!" And the entire assembly raised their right arms in salutation. "*Hail the High Priest!* ALL HAIL!"

As the tumult died down, the High Priest stepped forward, strongly, upright, with no trace in his expression of the wound that he carried. Behind him the juniors hastily struck the last of the tents and hurried it away. Mog Agorn came slowly and with dignity to stand at the King Stone at Asher's head.

Awrgon in the East raised his arms wide. "Brethren of the Wessex," he cried, "the Sun is at the Gates of the Mighty Ones. Let the celebration of the Autumnal Equinox begin!"

The entire assembly gave the response in unison. "*So let it be!*" and as the sound of that response echoed around the ancient site of Cor Gaur, the first rays of the morning sun lanced across the Hele Stone at the outer perimeter and struck the King Stone at the center.

Awrgon turned to face the East and traced the opening pentagram seal in the air, and cried aloud the ancient invocation to the Guardian of the Eastern Portal. Then, with his arm still outstretched, he traced the line of force around to the South, traced the same pentagram again—this time the invocation ringing out to the Guardian of the Southern Portal. He then traced the line to the West, then to the North, putting on the same pentagram seals, and then finally he traced the line back to the East to complete the circle. He then turned to face the Altar. "Brethren of the Order of Karadoc, I declare this Lodge open in the Fifth Degree. Let all here enter upon their duties, and may the blessing of the Great Ones be upon you all!"

He then exchanged the standard ritual responses with the Officers of the South, West, and North, and then declared the governing principle of the East. This done, he then raised his arms again. "Brethren," he cried in a ringing voice, "the Lords of the Manifested Universe are drawn near to this, the celebration of our most honored and ancient rite of the

Autumnal Equinox. Let all here open their hearts to the Great Ones!"

This concluded the standard opening, and Awrgon stepped back. Mog Agorn now raised his arm and pointed dramatically at Asher. "Behold the Mother of the Child—the Vessel of the Dark One! Behold!" He paused for a moment, and the assembled Wessex thrilled at the power in their High Priest's voice. "He is coming from behind the Veil to lead the Wessex to greatness and to honor." He paused again. "But," he cried, "there are those in the land who seek to destroy the Mother, and to deny life to the Child, and already these false ones have raised the hand of violence against your High Priest! Even now they are gathered to the north at Abiri, desecrating that holy place with their vile presence, and soon they will come here to Cor Gaur seeking to destroy us all!" His fierce and glittering eyes swept the assembled Wessex. "Brethren of Karadoc," he suddenly thundered, *"this must not be permitted!"*

Again he paused for dramatic effort. "Do not fear the coming struggle, my brethren, for it is given by the Great Ones that the Wessex *will* prevail against those who stand against us, providing we face their coming with courage." Again his fanatical eyes swept the crowd. "In order to help you face the ordeal that lies before us, all here, every priest and priestess, will come to the Altar and lay their hand on the Mother and so draw power from the Child within." He turned to the East. "The Hierophant in the East will lead the procession, followed by the Officers of the Gates, and then those of the Lesser Degrees. Let the procession begin!"

This announcement took Awrgon by surprise. Mog Agorn had made no mention of any procession. He was, however, an experienced ritualist and he stepped solemnly to the Altar and laid his right hand on Asher's belly. "The Powers of Air in the East serve the Child," he cried, and as he did so he felt the rush of power through his body and he looked down at his sister in surprise. Could his father have been right all along—that Asher really did have a Dark One in her belly? He paused there for a moment and then returned to the East. Sleg Agorn came forward and laid his hand on the body of the High Priestess. "The Powers of Water in the West serve the Child," he cried. Then came the turn of the senior priestess, who declared in the name of the South and Fire, and then the North for Earth. And then every priest, priestess, and seeress there present filed past the Altar and laid their hands on the Mother and declared their service to the Child, and as they did so the fear disappeared from their faces and they were filled with a resolve to discharge the tasks of their ordeal with honor.

When all had returned to their places, Mog Agorn turned to face the East. "Most Honored Adeptus," he cried, "have all the brethren declared their loyalty?"

"They have so declared," he replied.

"Then in the name of the Great Ones I command you to close the Lodge."

Awrgon bowed to the High Priest and turned and placed the closing pentagram seal on the East, and the mighty inner portal closed with a rumbling crash. He then repeated the procedure in the South, West, and North and then led the closing circumambulation. When it was over, the priests and priestesses took up their positions in the outer circles and on the earthworks to await their ordeal. A special litter was brought forward and Asher was helped into it. "How do you feel?" said Mog Agorn.

"Peculiar," she said. "I can feel him moving but there is no pain. When you all laid your hands on me I felt wave after wave of triumph pour through me." She looked up at him. "He is anxious to get out. I feel as though he will not wait for a normal birth but will claw his way out through my living flesh!"

The Chief Healer had come up and heard her words. He put his hand on her belly and frowned. "I don't understand it. She is—what? Four months, five months? It is impossible for the birth to be near, and yet he is certainly vigorous enough! And her belly is still barely risen."

"There is much here that is beyond our understanding," said Mog Agorn. "I have the strongest premonition that he will manifest within the next week whether you feel that to be impossible or not. There is nothing that is impossible to a Dark One." He put his hand on Asher's shoulder, almost affectionately. "And I have the strongest premonition that he will not harm the Mother."

"Well, you have been right in everything else you have said," the Chief Healer sighed. "So let us pray that you are right in this also."

"Stay with her, healer. Don't leave her side."

Awrgon came up and drew Mog Agorn aside. "What was all that about the Great Ones' guarantee that we will prevail against the Druids? *Have* you had such assurance?"

"Not in so many words," his father said, "but I feel it in my bones."

"Then let us pray it's not just old age creeping on," the boy retorted. "We can only wait. The Druid ritual at Abiri will have been completed, and they will even now be gathering for the march."

An hour passed, and another, and the morning gradually wore on. The fervor of the dawn ritual had now dissipated and the fear had crept back into Wessex faces as the guards anxiously scanned the land to the north. Another hour passed, and another, and then one of the guards shouted and pointed to the north. Awrgon raced up to the top of the earthworks and there, from the direction of Abiri, he could see the advancing horde like a dark river spreading across the land toward Cor Gaur. He signaled below and he heard his father's bellowed commands, and the Wessex priests came streaming up to take their positions. As the horde drew near, he could see the eight chariots out in front and behind them the cloud of marching priests. The whole of Druidry was marching against them—a thousand men—and Awrgon knew in his heart that each and every one would lay down their life if necessary to destroy the Child. The enemy was implacable. The Wessex would need to destroy them to the last priest and priestess before the Wessex could be said to have prevailed against them. Such resolve, of itself, was enough to be a herald of a deadly fear.

The Druids arrived at the zenith of the Sun and came to a halt in line abreast, the eight chariots to the fore. The traveling-litter was brought to the front and Druthin stepped forth, accompanied by Vaila and Menahotep. The three Elders came closer to the earthworks. The Arch-Mage drew himself up. "I am Druthin," he cried. "High Priest of all Druidry! Who commands the Wessex?"

Mog Agorn stepped forward. "I command here, Druthin," he bellowed. "What do the Druids want of the Wessex?"

"We come to destroy the Child. Give Asher up to us. We will abort the child and return Asher to you unharmed. If you do this, then many lives will be saved, and the Druids will return to Glaeston and seek no further war with the Wessex!" The Arch-Mage pointed his bony hand up at Mog Agorn. "I must, however, warn you that, if you refuse, then every Druid here will lay down his life if necessary to take the Evil One by force. What is your answer?"

Mog Agorn glanced at Awrgon. "Give the old fool a suitable answer," he growled.

Awrgon nodded and stepped forward. "I am Awrgon, son of Mog Agorn," he cried. "My father tires of your foolish babble. If you feel you must throw away your lives, then do so. But the Wessex will not give up Asher to you or to anyone! Take her by force, if you really think you can."

Druthin turned to Vaila and Menahotep. "Even now I am reluctant to commit so many men to their deaths, and yet I fear it must be so. Are we agreed?" And the two men nodded. Druthin sighed and turned back to face the Wessex. "So be it then," he thundered. "Let the Dogs of War decide this issue!" And the three Elders withdrew.

A few minutes later the Wessex saw the entire Druid force split into three wings. "That is Melkor leading the center wing," said Awrgon, "and Cludin the west, but who is that leading the east?"

"It's the boy-Egyptian, Ramin," said Mog Agorn. "What is an Egyptian doing, leading Druids? They must indeed be short of commanders!" Awrgon turned to bellow an order, but Mog Agorn restrained him. "Wait! Wait until we are certain of their plan. Do not commit us too early."

Awrgon glanced down to where the broad avenue swept into Cor Gaur. The entrance was sealed by a barricade of boulders that rose to twice the height of a man and more with a third of their entire force, seven hundred men, committed to its defense—but even so it was their weakest point. "It has to be there, Father. Let me draw more men from the earthworks."

"Not yet, not yet. You are probably right, but let us be certain."

The center wing of the Druids took up their position on the broad avenue itself, with the two flanking wings on either side. The Elders, the priestesses, and the very young Bards were grouped at the rear. They saw Melkor draw his sword and give the signal, and all three wings started forward, each led by its command chariot. The attackers broke into a trot, and then into a full charge as they drew nearer, and all three wings were heading straight for the barricade at the northerly point of the defenses. "Now, Father. It must be now!"

"No—wait!"

Suddenly, the two flanking wings broke away and headed for the earthworks around the circle of Cor Gaur, obviously intending to attack at the east and west. "Ah, I *thought* that was a possibility," Mog Agorn growled. "Three simultaneous attacks at three different places—though little good it will do them. It never pays to be too impatient, boy!"

Awrgon grinned. "And now they really are doomed. Their center wing cannot contain more than three hundred, and we have seven hundred behind that barricade."

But suddenly the two flanking wings veered sharply inward, so that all three wings were now headed for the barricade with barely fifty yards to go—one thousand against seven hundred.

Awrgon did not wait but turned and bellowed his orders instantly, and Wessex priests began to stream back down the earthworks, heading for the barricade. But it would take some minutes for them to arrive; precious minutes had been thrown away by Mog Agorn's delay. "It never pays, Father," Awrgon hissed furiously, "to be too patient!"

"Forget it," he growled. "There is no real danger."

Sleg Agorn commanded the Wessex at the barricade and met the first onrush. Melkor and a dozen priests, plus the giant Gargan, were the first to arrive. As planned, the Druids leapt upward, hacking and thrusting at the defenders, while Gargan used his giant strength to pluck the boulders away from the base and so weaken the barricade. Then Ramin and Cludin's wings arrived on either side, and the barricade became a seething mass of struggling priests. Two of the defenders fell, their bodies gushing blood, and already three of the Druids were gasping their lives away, clutching frantically at fatal wounds. Hacking, stabbing, the Druids stormed the top, and Melkor heaved himself up over the last boulder. Sleg Agorn swung his sword at him, but Melkor ducked under the swing and smashed his shield against the man's head. Sleg Agorn grabbed Melkor's sword by the hilt, but his eyes glazed from the blow he had received and he fell backward off the barricade and crashed to the ground below, still clutching Melkor's sword. More Druids swarmed to the top and shielded their weaponless commander.

Melkor snatched a sword from a dead defender and paused to look around. Cludin and his men held the top in his section, though already a dozen priests lay dead and dying at his feet. Melkor turned and saw Ramin smash his shield into a defender's face and slash the man's legs sending him crashing backward. But then, to his horror, he saw a Wessex sword swing wildly in an arc and bite into Ramin's chest and shoulder, and the Egyptian fell, his body pouring blood. "Get his body to the rear," he bellowed. "Get him clear!" It was a bad sign for warriors to see a dead commander. If he were carried away, they might think him merely wounded.

Gargan and the village men were still frantically hauling boulders away, and already they had breached a gap, cutting the barricade in two. A Wessex leapt to cut the giant down, but Gargan grabbed him and smashed his head against a rock, splitting the skull, and Melkor saw the brains spill out and stain the ground.

But more of the Wessex were arriving every second, and still more, and the Druids found themselves unable to press downward on the inside of the barrier, though they still held the top. A rain of small boulders hurtled against the attackers, and one smashed into Melkor's chest. He staggered, slipped sideways, and a defender reached up and slashed his legs, and Melkor, battle-commander of the Druids, came crashing down and smashed into the middle of a group of Wessex, alone. His crashing arrival took them by surprise, and Melkor was on his feet before they could recover. Two more Druids deliberately leapt down to their commander's aid, and then two more, but even five was not enough, and the Wessex surged against them and Melkor died from a dozen thrusts, his body spraying blood as he fell. The four who had leapt to his aid tried to regain the barrier, but one by one they were cut down until all were dead.

Cludin, still on top of the barricade, now found himself in sole command with two of his fellow commanders already gone—and still the Wessex were arriving, and yet still more. He fought desperately, frantically, with a maniacal strength, the memory of Zelta's death burning his mind. But the Wessex, sensing that the tide had turned, pressed forward, yelling and screaming, shields up, stabbing and thrusting as they pressed upward to retake the barricade. Two more Druids died, and then two more, and still the

Wessex came on. Gargan was screaming with rage, his massive arms hurling boulders into the thick of the Wessex. He had hated the Wessex all his life, and like Cludin he, too, had a memory to drive him on, the memory of his wife and two daughters who had been dragged away to be foully used in obscene rites before being finally murdered. Four dead Wessex lay at his feet in partial appeasement of that memory, but even his giant strength was not enough to hold the flood that pressed against him, and he found himself being driven back away from the gap.

Cludin was fighting desperately, but already the Wessex had regained the top in several places and he knew that it was now only a matter of time. Suddenly, from the rear, he heard a Druid horn sounding—the recall signal. Druthin had obviously seen their plight and knew it to be hopeless. Cludin barked a command, and the Druid warrior-priests leapt down from the barricade and began to stream away to the rear.

A howl of Wessex triumph filled the air, and on the earthworks Awrgon was jumping up and down with excitement. "We've won. We've won!"

Over a hundred dead Druids littered the barricade on either side, and over fifty Wessex. Mog Agorn's eyes glittered fanatically. "Yes, the day is ours. The Druid dogs will never recover from this. Nothing can stop us now!"

Chapter Ten

The living and the dead, and those who were neither, were gathered in the Inner Lodge. Ramin and Melkor and a score of Druids were grouped to the North of the Altar. The two Druid Elders, Druthin and Vaila, together with Menahotep, stood at the Altar itself. A whole phalanx of Priests of Re from Egypt were in the South, and in the West were High Priests and High Priestesses and Elders from a dozen different groups, cults, and religions from throughout the known world. This was the Universal Inner Lodge. It owed its allegiance only to the Most High. No cult, human or otherwise, could claim the Lodge as its own. Anyone who knew of its existence, and who was able to reach it, had the right to enter, and all such were welcome. Its formulation was such that it could only be reached and entered by the activation of a certain state of consciousness, which of itself thus automatically excluded any whose motives were not in harmony with the principles it represented. It was not a Lodge created on the inner by the group-mind rituals of a physical plane human cult, nor was it an inner Lodge created to project certain concepts onto the physical plane that would draw incarnated human souls together to form a cult. This was the Universal Inner Lodge administered by those Intelligences whose task it was to guide human evolution, and the evolution of the Planetary Being itself. It was, as it were, the Master Lodge of all the inner Lodges.

In the East, clad in human form, were those very senior inner plane entities. With them were those who had known the Earth in the very early days of human existence, those who had been involved in the Polarian and Hypoborean ages. There, too, were those who had incarnated during the Third Era, the Lemurian Age, and those, too, from the Fourth Era, the Atlantean Age. There were human entities there who had been priests in Shamballa, and later in Ruta, and some there had once been known by names that had become merely legends to those currently experiencing incarnation. Yen K'Ing of Shamballa was there, though he had borne a dozen names in earth since— and there, too, was Kumara of the Withdrawn Temple in Atlantis—and many an honored and famous name besides. And in the East also were those of previous evolutions who were as Lords to the current human swarm, in particular the simulacrum of Narada, a being so mighty that many could hardly differentiate between him and the Most High. Lords of Flame were there, and Lords of Mind and Lords of Form, all gathered at this critical point in the evolution of those who would in due course be known as the Lords of Humanity.

And all the faces were grave, both human and nonhuman alike, and the silence lay deep within them. And then, into that stillness, there drifted a clear, harmonious voice intoning the simple and perhaps most ancient invocation of all time:

Holy art Thou, Lord of the Universe!
Holy art Thou, Whom Nature hath not Formed!
Holy art Thou, the Vast and Mighty One,
Lord of Light and Darkness!

Konx om Pax!
Khabs am Pekht!

The echoes of the invocation died away, but before the ripples were fully extended, another voice drifted into that stillness—a deeper voice, soft and gentle, and yet vibrantly powerful:

Behold, the Light shineth in Darkness!
May the Blessing of the Prince of Countenances
Rest upon you all!

A silvery, soft, yet brilliant light began to pervade
the Lodge, and the silence descended yet again. Then
another voice sounded, this time from the East, though
none could discern from which figure it emanated.
It was as though a voice had been created to represent them all.

"We are gathered here," the voice said gently, "to
hear the petition of those in Earth. Let the petitioner
stand forth!"

Druthin raised his head. "I am Druthin, Arch-Mage
of all Druidry in Earth," he said quietly. "Those whom
I represent seek your counsel, even as Menahotep
sought the counsel of the inner Egyptian Lodge."

The silence was once more in evidence, and then
the voice said: "The counsel given by the Egyptian
Lodge was born of Wisdom. We of the inner are not
permitted to live your lives for you by telling you
what to do, for such would not be in accordance with
the Will of the Most High. Our sole function is to
represent causative principle and to make available,
as it were, the states of consciousness wherein those
principles may be apprehended by any who seek
them."

"I understand," said Druthin. "We seek your counsel by asking you to state the principles that are involved in the Druid's struggle to prevent the Evil One
being born to the Wessex."

Again silence pervaded the Lodge, and then the
voice came again. "The manifested universe was created by the Most High in terms of polarized duality
—active and passive, positive and negative, male and
female. The work of creation was carried out by the
first three swarms in accordance with that Will. These
swarms are known to some as the Lords of Flame,
Form, and Mind—and to others by other names. The
function of the fourth swarm, that of humanity, is to
achieve a synthesis of this apparent duality such that

all is one in harmonized balance. And at the same time it is their task to work out a new factor in the universe, the factor of free will, and it is because of this factor that we on the inner are not permitted to interfere.

"Humanity achieves the synthesis of apparent duality in the universe by achieving that same synthesis within its own nature. Much has been achieved since human evolution first began, but much of the nature of humanity is still in a state of duality with little or no synthesis, and the two facets, instead of complementing each other, are persistently in opposition, even at war.

"Humanity in Earth sees itself in terms of separate groups and, sadly, we have a situation where one group is at war with another. We on the inner, however, see humanity as one entity struggling with itself to achieve the balance of a harmonious whole."

There was a pause and then the voice went on: "The petitioner has used the word 'evil.' Humanity makes much of these terms, good and evil, but in truth they are merely the reflection of the apparent duality of the universe. The universe is force in action. There is balanced force, and there is force that has yet to be brought to a balanced equilibrium. There is no difference in the essential nature of the so-called forces of good and evil: The difference lies purely in their balance or imbalance. As far as human activity is concerned, the majority live out their lives haphazardly, pulled hither and thither by the positive and negative forces in their environment and in themselves. A few either unconsciously or deliberately seek to perpetuate the state of imbalance because its apparent freedom and lack of discipline strikes a sympathetic response from the imbalance in their own nature. Still fewer consciously seek to achieve an equilibrium of forces, a harmony, because the beauty in such balance strikes a response from the essential underlying nature of their being. These two attitudes are described in terms of 'good' and 'evil.' We cannot tell you what to do, but we can say that the solution does not lie in the destruction of 'evil' by 'good,' because only forms can be destroyed, not the force that indwells them. The solution lies in the recognition of the essential wholeness of all that exists—and the manifestation of that solution lies in the ability to create the correct forms that will encourage force to manifest in harmony.

"There are some here who are due to return to the Earth sphere to complete their current incarnations, and some who have already had their present incarnations terminated by this present struggle. To all of you we say: Meditate on these things and thus seek your own answers. But be assured that ultimate harmony will ultimately prevail!"

The voice ceased and the silvery light began to fade. The forms of the Lodge, the symbols and furniture, even the Altar itself, began to shimmer and become indistinct, and Druthin, Arch-Mage of all Druidry, returned to full consciousness in Earth. It was late evening and the inside of the tent was dark. He stepped to the opening and stared out into the night. The sky was clear and the stars were as bright as he had ever seen them. The tents of the Druids were gathered in a circle with a strong guard posted around the outer perimeter. Here and there were cooking fires, and several priests and priestesses were still moving about. To judge by the moon it was about three hours after sunset. To the south, a mile away, he could see the guard-fires of the Wessex on the earthworks at Cor Gaur. Suddenly a priestess came hurrying by. "Thetan!" he called softly.

The High Priestess stopped and then came toward him. Even in moonlight he could see that her face was ravaged by tears. "I have just seen Ramin in the inner Lodge," he said gently.

"Was he . . . was he . . . ?"

He shook his head. "No—he was numbered amongst those still in incarnation." He took her hand. "I will stake all my knowledge and all my experience that he will live, even though he is dreadfully wounded." She paused for a moment and then suddenly collapsed against him, the tears pouring down her face. "Shhhhhh!" he whispered. "This is no time for tears! He will bear a livid scar for the rest of his life. But live he will, that I promise you!"

She looked up at him. "Druthin, Druthin, you should have seen the blood on him! And the gash was so deep and his heartbeat so weak! Are you sure—are you really sure?"

"Yes," he said gently. "I am sure."

A great shuddering sigh racked through her and then she became calmer. "Thank you," she whispered. "I had not dared even hope. Thank you!"

He nodded. "Go back to him now. He will want you there when he awakes."

She squeezed his hand gratefully and hurried away.

A sound came from within the tent and he turned to see Vaila and Menahotep also returning to full consciousness. He gave them a few seconds to become aware and then he said: "Well, my friends, before the experience fades too much into memory, let us discuss what we have seen and heard."

They talked together for an hour, and then Druthin sighed and said: "The destruction of form does not destroy the force within, but at least it would deny that force a vehicle for manifestation. Clearly the form which is Asher and the Child must be destroyed, and once the force is free of the incorrect form we can then begin to create more suitable forms for its expression. Are we agreed?"

The two men nodded. "Yes," said Vaila. "Asher must die. We were correct in that determination but we had not carried our thinking beyond that point."

Menahotep rose to stretch his limbs. "If Asher is a corrupt body which has attracted an unbalanced force, then what we need is an incorruptible body to house a force perfectly balanced."

The two Druids looked at him. "Taking that thought to its logical conclusion," said Druthin softly, "do you realize what you are saying?"

"That we need a perfect human being," said Vaila, "to act as a vehicle for the incarnation of the Most High itself!"

There was a silence, and then Menahotep said: "Very well. I will face the idea squarely. We have seen a corrupt mother. Why not an incorrupt one? We have seen that it is possible to incarnate a dark force from the inner. Why not one representative of light? And if that is possible why not the incarnation of Deity itself?"

The two Druids looked at each other. "I do not see how it is possible," said Vaila.

"There is an ancient teaching," said Druthin, "that says that what can be conceived by Man can be achieved by Man."

"But the incarnation of Deity?"

Druthin shook his head. "I do not know. But if it *is* possible, then we have already taken the first step to its achievement by giving the idea expression in Earth by speaking of it. If it can be done, it will not be in our lifetime, or in many to come. It may take a thousand years—two thousand. Who knows? But the Great One said that ultimate harmony will prevail ultimately, and I can think of no finer example of ultimate harmony than the concept of Deity in Earth."

The three men were silent for some time, and then Menahotep said: "But first we have to destroy the incorrect form—Asher!"

"You are right, my Egyptian friend," said Druthin. "You are so right! But how that is to be achieved I do not know. A hundred Druids and more lie dead, including Melkor whom we saw in the Inner Lodge. We will not repeat that error again. I suggest we take the advice to meditate on these things and thus seek the answers. Let us sleep now. We will meet again in the morning."

Scream after scream came shrieking from Asher's mouth. "It's trying to claw its way out! Stop it! *Stop it!*" She writhed on the couch, her hands clutching her belly. "Father, Father—stop it! By all the powers, *KILL IT!*"

The four men in the tent were staring at her in horror. Mog Agorn's face was ashen. The whole of Asher's belly was writhing hideously as though some monster was indeed tearing its way out through her living flesh. "I can't," he whispered. "I *can't!*"

The girl's face was livid with bruises where Awrgon had unsuccessfully tried to knock her unconscious. At one point, in desperation, Mog Agorn had struck her with a piece of wood as thick as his arm, but to no avail. The pain in her belly was so great that she could not be driven from her body.

Much as Awrgon detested his sister and held her in contempt, even he was appalled at the incredible agony that she was suffering. "Is there *nothing* we can do?" he said fiercely.

The healer shrugged helplessly. "It is beyond my powers. I have never seen or heard of anything like it."

Mog Agorn spun around. "Can't you cut the child out?" he hissed.

"I could try—but it would kill her!"

Mog Agorn pointed at his screaming daughter. "It's killing her, anyway. We have got to do something!"

The healer shook his head. "You started this, Mog Agorn. You can't now put the responsibility onto me. I will attempt to carry out any order you care to give me—but it's up to you. As far as I can judge, she is already past the point when normal birth should have taken place. But you know, and I know, how ridiculous that is. It is only five moons since conception. By all the powers, how do you expect me to give a normal assessment when every sign is so abnormal that I begin to doubt my own sanity?"

Mog Agorn looked fiercely from one to the other, his expression raging and desperate. He spun back to the couch and smacked his open hand across the girl's face. "Stop that screaming!" he yelled. His voice had risen to a shriek to match her own. "I can't think straight with this screaming filling my ears! Stop it, I tell you, stop it!" and he smacked her again and again.

Sleg Agorn grabbed his brother's arm. "That will serve no purpose," he said grimly.

The High Priest staggered against him, clutching suddenly at his own belly. His wound must have re-opened, for blood was beginning to seep through the cloth strips wound around his body. "Get her outside," he whispered. "Put her on the King Stone. Who knows, perhaps that's what it wants."

Awrgon leapt forward eagerly. *Any* action was better than just standing there listening to those screams. Her body was entirely naked. She had long ago torn off her robe in her agony. He scooped her up and carried her outside to the King Stone and laid her down, but her shrieks were still echoing amongst the ancient stones.

Inside the tent, the healer was hastily stripping the bloody cloths from Mog Agorn's body. He wiped the fresh blood from the wound and peered at it anxiously. "Not as bad as I thought," he said. "I will put fresh strips on, but you must take it easy, or I will not answer for your life either."

Mog Agorn was quiet now, and he sat seemingly patiently as the fresh strips were wound in place. They could still hear Asher's near-demented screams from outside. "What can I do, healer?" he whispered. "It is beyond your powers, I know, but it is beyond mine also. Like you, and Asher herself, I can only wait it out and hope that it will come right."

"You have another problem, too," said Sleg Agorn.

"The Druids?" The High Priest almost smiled. "Believe me, my brother, they are the *last* of my problems."

Sleg Agorn shook his head. "Not the Druids—the Wessex! How do you think the Wessex priesthood feel to hear their High Priestess shrieking in agony hour after hour?"

Mog Agorn frowned. "What do you mean?"

"When the healer has finished, come outside and

look at them closely. Feel their mood. You will soon see what I mean."

"I am finished now," said the healer. "But keep him quiet. He must not undergo any violent exertion."

Mog Agorn walked outside with his brother. Asher was still screaming and rolling about in agony, but he seemed to detect a slight lessening in her intensity. Perhaps she would quiet down altogether during the rest of the day.

The Wessex priesthood, almost without exception, were facing in toward the center, all watching Asher on the King Stone. Mog Agorn walked slowly amongst them, noting their expressions, sensing their mood, and he began to frown. The priestesses and seeresses were mostly in tears, a helpless expression on their faces, but it was the priests who were causing Mog Agorn's concern. There was fear there and worry, but the predominant expression was one of anger. "You are not popular," said Sleg Agorn quietly.

"Me? I am not causing her agony. It is the Dark One."

Sleg Agorn shrugged. "Maybe, but they cannot vent their anger against him as they can against the man who brought their High Priestess to all this!"

"What do I care what they think?" he grunted. "I command the Wessex, not they."

His brother shook his head. "Asher is very popular, particularly amongst the priests—though admittedly her popularity owes more to her sexual prowess than to her qualities as a High Priestess. She is also popular amongst the priestesses, because of the example she sets in being beholden to no man, and many follow her example." He looked at his brother. "As to command, you command because they permit you to command. If they turn against you, Mog Agorn, then you are a dead man."

The High Priest stopped short in his tracks. "Oh, am I?" he growled ominously. "We shall see!" He strode to the King Stone and leapt up and stood straddling the body of his daughter, his arms akimbo, glaring at the Wessex. "Priests and priestesses of the Wessex," he bellowed. So powerful was his voice that it carried clearly even to the outer circle and to the very top of the earthworks. "No one grieves more than I at the suffering of my daughter, your High Priestess. It is a price that she is willingly paying—for *you*—so that the Wessex will have the opportunity for greatness! She knew the danger and knew of the suffering that would come to her, but she accepted it gladly —for *you!*"

One of the priests stepped forward. "Why is the Dark One hurting her?" he shouted. "Is this his reward to her for giving him life?"

Some of the others began to call out, and one in particular raised his voice above the others. "If he is so uncaring of Asher's agony now while still in her belly, what will he do to the rest of us when he stands amongst us as a man?"

"Why can't you stop it?" cried another.

"You're the High Priest. You have no right to subject anyone to such agony."

"You have no right. It's up to you to stop it!"

A score and more were now calling out, and the expressions on their faces were growing more ugly. Mog Agorn raised his arms. "You fools!" he bellowed. "Don't you think I would ease her suffering if I could? This is no ordinary birth. This is a Dark One coming through. Are you so stupid, all of you, that you cannot grasp the enormity of what is happening?" He glared around at them. "No ordinary woman could even contact a Dark One in her meditation without risking her sanity, let alone offer herself as a vehicle for its incarnation. At this very moment, the entire living force of a Dark One is confined in Asher's belly, and that force is so great that her very flesh can barely take the strain. The Dark One is protecting her as far as possible, but even he cannot shield her completely."

"Why is her belly writhing like that?" shouted one of them.

"Because he is seeking to be born as quickly as possible so as to shorten the duration of her agony."

"And then what will happen?" shouted another.

Mog Agorn raised his arms to the sky. "And then, my brethren," he bellowed fanatically, "Asher will be free of pain and will stand before you smiling and triumphant, the Great Mother herself, and in her arms she will be holding the Child, the Dark One made flesh. And then, my brethren, the Wessex will rise to a power and greatness that is beyond your ability to imagine!"

Asher suddenly doubled up yet again, her hands clutching her writhing belly, and her piercing shrieks echoed and reechoed amongst the ancient stones of Cor Gaur.

"Priests of the Wessex," bellowed Mog Agorn, pointing down at his daughter. "Hear the voice of the Dark One struggling to be with you. Prepare yourselves for his coming . . ."

Thetan had erected a special tent for Ramin, and the boy lay weakly on a pile of skins. Menahotep pushed open the flap and came in. "Ah, I see you are still with us," he said gruffly. "You had us worried there for a while."

The boy's face struggled with a ghost of a smile. "I was a little concerned myself," he said faintly.

The old man chuckled. "How is he?" he said to Thetan.

The girl's face was taut and strained after a night of tears and worry. "The healer says he will be fine but he must not exert himself, and not attempt to walk for at least three days."

"Then see to it that he obeys the healer's orders. He can be a stubborn youth. How extensive is the wound?"

"From his left shoulder right down across his chest to his right side."

The old man gently moved the boy's robe aside. His entire torso from neck to belly was swathed in strips of white cloth. "You look as though they were preparing you for the tomb," he grunted. "A bit early to embalm you yet. How do you feel?"

"Weak," said Ramin. "With all this swathing around me, I feel as though I cannot breathe—trapped, as though I can't get out. They've wound them too tightly, I'm sure."

A thought flitted across Menahotep's mind. He strove to capture it, to fix it, but it escaped. Something to do with embalming methods in the House of the Dead in Egypt. He sighed. Perhaps the thought would return. "If the healer has wound it tightly then it is because it must be so. Stop grumbling. You are lucky to be alive."

Ramin's expression changed. "How many were not so lucky?"

"A hundred Druids," grunted Menahotep, "and about thirty or forty Wessex, as far as we can judge."

"Then we have lost?"

"We have lost a battle—that is all. The Druid Council met again this morning, and the orders have already been issued for the next phase in the struggle."

Ramin shook his head. "We can't beat them in a straight battle. There are too many of them. Many more will die. Surely Druthin has learnt a lesson from the first fiasco!"

"He has. We are not going into battle. We're going to smoke them out."

Awrgon stood on the earthworks surveying the scene to the north. He shook his head. "I don't understand. What *are* they doing?"

"You say this is the third lot they've brought from the woods?"

"Third or fourth. They started yesterday at dawn. About fifty marched off, led by two of the chariots. They were gone for hours. They came back about midafternoon with a whole pile of dead wood tied with vine-ropes, dragged by the chariots. Then they went back for more, and then more." He pointed to where the pile of brush and branches, logs and trunks, already rose thirty feet high. "Surely they don't expect to use fire against us?"

Mog Agorn looked thoughtful. "No, not fire. Smoke."

"Smoke? That's all dead wood. It'll go up in flame, not smoke."

"Not if they add green wood as well. Or wet grass. Then it would smoke."

Awrgon shrugged. "All right. So what?"

"You have no imagination, boy. Imagine a wall of wet wood thirty feet high, pushed close to the earthworks completely surrounding Cor Gaur—and then set on fire. It wouldn't matter which way the wind blew. The smoke would come rolling in."

They were silent for a moment, and then Awrgon said: "A bit of smoke won't hurt us."

"No, but great giant rolling clouds of it pouring into Cor Gaur would be quite another matter. I don't like it. I don't like it at all. I was once very nearly caught in a forest fire many years ago before you were born. At the height of the fire there was a brief shower of rain, not enough to put it out but enough to make everything damp. I shall never forget the smoke, great clouds of it blotting out everything. You can't breathe; you can't see. You just run. Your eyes are streaming, and there's only one thought in your brain: how to get clear of the smoke, because you know that if you don't get clear, and quickly, you are going to die." He waved his arm around Cor Gaur. "If that happens here, they'll run, and the Druids will cut them down one by one as they stagger out."

"Do you think Druthin knows?"

"I don't see why not. He's an old man. He's lived a long time, seen many things. If I've seen a forest fire, he may have as well."

Awrgon grunted. "Well, that decides it. We can't just tamely wait here for it to happen. We will have to go out and finish them once and for all."

"No!"

Awrgon knew it—the same old argument. "Why not?" he shouted. "We have two thousand against one thousand. It would be a simple matter! Asher can stay in Cor Gaur on the King Stone, if that's what worries you."

"And who will guard her?"

"A hundred men—two hundred. As many as you like. The Druids will be too busy to think of Asher."

Mog Agorn shook his head. "You still don't understand. The Druids are only interested in battle as a means to get at Asher. They will consider it a victory if Asher dies, even if every Druid dies with her, even if it means leaving the Wessex as undisputed masters of the realm. They are not at war with *us*. They are at war with the Dark One in Asher's belly."

"So what? It amounts to the same thing in practice."

"But it doesn't. By all the powers, are you so stupid that you cannot grasp the simple fact that the Druids only have to kill just one of us to have triumphed, providing that one is Asher?" Mog Agorn flung up his arms in despair. "If you take two thousand out to battle, leaving Asher unguarded, how can you guarantee—*guarantee*—that a score of Druids will not slip by the battle and race into Cor Gaur and kill her?"

"All right, we'll leave a hundred warrior-priests to guard her."

"Then how can you guarantee that a hundred Druids will not evade the battle and come here?"

Awrgon threw his hands wide in exasperation. "All right, you old fool. We'll leave a *thousand* men to guard her!"

Mog Agorn grabbed his son by the throat. "You stupid, yapping puppy! If you do that, you will only have one thousand to fight the battle—one thousand against one thousand. You will have split our force in two, and will have played right into Druthin's hands!"

Awrgon broke free. "You bungling, incompetent old man," he gasped. "This whole thing has addled your brains. You are no longer fit to command the Wessex!"

"And what do you think you're going to do about it?"

Awrgon straightened up. "I shall put the matter before the Council and before the whole Wessex priest-hood—and demand that you be brought to ritual trial. Every Wessex priest has the right to challenge the High Priest."

"Oh, yes," sneered Mog Agorn, "but if his challenge is unsupported then the challenger forfeits his life."

"Unsupported! You really are crazy. The whole Wessex will rise against you when I tell them of your latest madness." He adjusted his robe and looked at him coldly. "Your time has come, Father," he said calmly. "For too long have the Wessex followed your insanity!" And he turned to stride away.

A great bellow of rage burst from Mog Agorn's throat, a roar of bestial ferocity. He snatched a knife from his belt, sprang on Awrgon's back, and rammed it up to the hilt in his son's chest. He dragged the knife clear and plunged it in again, and again, and again—and Awrgon, son of Mog Agorn, fell to the ground and his blood seeped into the earth of Cor Gaur, and his father stood over him, panting furiously like an animal at bay, his hands red, his eyes glaring fanatically, insanely.

Day after day the Druid plan came inexorably to fulfillment. Every day, twice a day, a consignment of dead timber was dragged from the forest to swell the wall that was growing steadily around Cor Gaur. The first pile had been pushed close to the earthworks, built to a height of thirty feet and then extended on either side—inexorably, foot by foot, day by day—until it had begun to encircle the ancient site. And the Wessex could do little but watch helplessly as the final day drew nearer and nearer. The Druids guarded their wall every minute of every day, firstly to protect it against Wessex attempts to fire it prematurely, and secondly to take advantage should the Wessex decide to venture out. A special force of two hundred war-rior-priests was kept permanently on the alert with the instructions that, should the Wessex venture out in force, they were to seize the opportunity, ignore the battle, and drive straight into Cor Gaur against the depleted forces within, and fight straight through to Asher and kill her.

Menahotep shook his head. "I would not have believed it possible." He looked wryly at his friend. "When you and Vaila first mooted the plan, it seemed to me to have been born of desperation, doomed to an abysmal and embarrassing failure."

Druthin smiled grimly. "Had this been a normal warfare, I would have agreed with you, but over these past few weeks I have come to understand Mog Agorn's obsession. He would willingly sacrifice the life of every Wessex in the land to secure the birth of that thing, even as we would sacrifice every Druid to prevent it."

"As such," said Vaila, "he cannot afford even the smallest risk to Asher."

"He cannot send out a small force to destroy the wall," said Druthin, "because we could easily deal with them, and so whittle his forces down."

"And he dare not send out a large force," said the Elder from Maes Howe, "because it would leave Asher vulnerable to direct attack. This is why we have openly paraded our special force. We want him to know that we are ready to ignore any battle, and to go straight for Asher if the opportunity presents itself."

"And the beauty of it," said Menahotep, "is that the longer he leaves us in peace, the more demoralized the Wessex will become. It cannot be pleasant for them to stand there day after day and watch our preparations advance—and not be allowed to do anything about it."

"Yes, the fear must be in their eyes by now, and that fear will grow in them hour by hour, and fearful anticipation is always more dreadful to endure than the actual event that is feared."

"When will we strike?" said Menahotep.

"When the weather is right," said Vaila.

Druthin smiled. "Vaila and I have been talking to the younger seeresses who tend the cooking-fires."

"They must have thought us mad until we explained."

The Arch-Mage pointed at Cor Gaur. "It is surrounded by earthworks that would form a natural barrier against clouds of smoke. The danger is that no matter how large our fire, or how smoky, the clouds of smoke may rise straight up into the sky and leave the Wessex perfectly safe at the center, laughing at us."

"But we have been watching the cooking-fires," said Vaila. "On some days the smoke goes straight up, and on others it hangs low and is blown unpleasantly throughout the camp.

"So we talked to the seeresses, to search their memories. Between them they have tended thousands of cooking-fires over the years. What we need, apparently, is a day when the clouds hang low in the sky— a dark day—not necessarily raining, but a damp, overcast, cloudy day. And this is the right time of the year for such days, the period immediately after the Equinox.

"So we will wait," said Vaila.

Menahotep looked thoughtful. "We cannot afford to wait too long. Mog Agorn is also waiting. The only reason he is entrenched at Cor Gaur is so that the thing can be born on the King Stone. Once the birth takes place, he can then come out in force, and we will not be able to stand against him—and if he defeats us here, he will then march on Glaeston."

"What you say is true," said Druthin, "but since we have no alternative, we can only wait with as much patience as we can muster."

The wall grew foot by foot until the day came when it formed a complete circle around Cor Gaur, but the Druids continued to drag more material from the forest and the wall grew thicker and thicker. The days were infuriatingly fine and sunny. One day it did rain, and the sky was indeed dark, but the wind was judged to be too strong, and so the Druids waited, and their anxiety grew with each passing hour. Inside Cor Gaur, Mog Agorn also waited, growing more and more demented as Asher continued to scream with agony hour after hour, her belly still writhing. But, as yet, no birth. Almost every hour of every day would see him rush to the top of the earthworks to check on the Druids' progress, and then rush back to Asher. Time and again he would rail at the Chief Healer in demented fury, quite literally insane with rage, but there was little that could be done, save wait. On one occasion, under Mog Agorn's goading and much against the healer's will, they massaged Asher's belly, hoping to induce the birth, but, unbelievably, Asher's shrieks rose to an even greater pitch and they had to desist.

Then one day, just before dawn, Menahotep stepped from his tent. There was a light drizzle of rain, so fine that it was almost a mist of water. The day was dark and the whole sky was gray and ominous. The Egyptian watched the cooking-fire and saw the smoke blowing into the seeress's face. He almost ran to Druthin's tent, and burst in just as the Arch-Mage was rising. "The day has come, Druthin. The waiting is over!"

The Arch-Mage paused, then stepped to the tent-flap and looked out. "You are right, my friend. It has indeed!"

The dawn ritual was more than usually solemn, almost ominous . . . The Officers were too aware of their immediate destiny and, as such, their human personalities tended to obtrude too much on their ritual functions. Druthin's invocation from the East was the most heart-lifting cry of impassioned humility that Menahotep had ever heard, and in the South the tears were quite clearly visible in Thetan's eyes. After the ritual, all were fed, the guards withdrawn, and Druthin rose to address the Druids.

"Today is the day," he said quietly, "that will decide the future of this land for centuries to come. We all know what is at stake in this matter, and all here will, I know, conduct themselves with courage and with honor." He looked around at the assembled

Druids and they could see the tears in his eyes. "May the Great Ones be with you this day!"

An hour later, the entire Druid force—every priest, priestess, and seeress—were drawn up in a circle around Cor Gaur. All the grades were there from the most senior to the most junior. There was no question of the women or the younger ones being kept safely at the rear—this was a total confrontation. The priestesses and seeresses, and the younger Bards, were not able to wield the heavy swords, but they all carried knives and would if necessary use them to the death. Only the sick and wounded, with Ramin amongst them, remained in the rear, and even then they had insisted vehemently that they be brought up immediately behind the fighting line. Ramin alone had no fewer than four knives hidden beneath his blanket, and he was not the only one. If the Wessex broke out and overwhelmed the Druid line, then Ramin was determined to take at least two of them with him through the Gate into the Hall of Osiris!

Druthin, Vaila, and Menahotep stepped forward in front of the line. "Mog Agorn," thundered Druthin. "Show yourself!"

A figure appeared on top of the earthworks, but it was Sleg Agorn, not the High Priest. "My brother chooses not to speak with you," he shouted.

"Then let Awrgon speak for the Wessex."

The figure hesitated. "Awrgon is dead," he shouted, "a traitor to the Wessex."

The three Druid Elders looked at each other in surprise. "A good sign," whispered Vaila drily, "that the Wessex are not of one mind."

"Very well," cried Druthin, "then we will speak with you, Sleg Agorn. The hour has come when this matter must be decided once and for all. But before we embark on our irrevocable course, we must in honor give you one last chance to yield and thus save the lives of many, both Druid and Wessex alike. Do you yield, Sleg Agorn, or do you stand?"

The figure on the earthworks stepped forward and raised its arms to the sky. "The Wessex yield to no one!" he cried. "Embark on your course if you must, Druthin, but embark prepared to die."

Druthin sighed. "Very well. So be it." He looked at the sky and snuffed the wind that blew from the north. Around the circle at four separate points, east, west, south, and north, were priests poised ready to fire the wall on the given signal. It was unnecessary to fire the whole circle, only that quadrant in the path of the wind. Druthin raised his arm and from behind him came a single blast on a horn, the signal for the northern sector to be fired. A dozen priests ran forward and soon the wall began to blaze. At first it blazed in flame as the dead wood caught, but soon the wet grasses and the green wood began to smoke, and the Druid Elders eyed it anxiously. Thicker and thicker the smoke grew until great billowing yellow-gray clouds of it poured from the wall of fire, and the Druids pointed excitedly as the wind rolled it up and over the earthworks into Cor Gaur itself.

Vaila nodded in satisfaction. "It is not rising too much. It must be rolling down to ground level inside, surely!"

"We will see," said Druthin grimly.

More priests rushed forward, their shields up to protect their faces from the heat, and hurled more damp grass and green wood onto the fire. And then others rushed forward, and then still more, and the smoke grew thicker, and the light wind from the north rolled it inexorably into Cor Gaur.

Inside Cor Gaur, Sleg Agorn pulled the guard away from the top of the earthworks in the northern sector and repositioned them around the rest of the circle. There was no danger in leaving that sector unguarded; if the Wessex could not breathe in that smoke, then neither could the Druids. Sleg Agorn had assumed full command of the defenses, for it was impossible to get any sense out of Mog Agorn. His brother was a raging, demented madman, quite incapable of commanding even himself, let alone others.

The healer had to bear the full brunt of Mog Agorn's rage. "For the hundredth time, Mog Agorn, there is nothing I can do. You are the High Priest. If you don't know, then how do you expect me to?"

"Get the Dark One out," he screamed. "Get it out before it is too late. Cut her open. Slit her belly. Anything! But get him out!"

"I can't. I can't!"

"Get him out!"

The healer snatched his knife and flung it on the ground at Mog Agorn's feet. *"You* get him out. *You* slit her belly. She's your daughter, not mine!"

Mog Agorn was beside himself with panic. His lifelong dreams were fading with every minute, the years of preparation wasted. He kicked the knife away. "All right, squeeze him out. I'll hold her legs."

The healer threw up his hands. They had tried that a dozen times already, but it was better than doing nothing. He straddled Asher's chest, facing her belly. Mog Agorn spread her legs wide. "Go on, squeeze him out."

The healer put his hands on her belly and pressed inward and downward, again and again, and Asher's screams rang through Cor Gaur. "It's no use," he shouted. "It's not ready."

"It must be!"

"It will kill her."

Mog Agorn jumped up, his mouth foaming with rage. "What do I care if she dies or not? Get him out!"

The whole Wessex could hear their screaming argument, and the priests began to look at each other angrily, frightened. This was not what they had been led to expect. The dreams of power and glory seemed so remote from all this.

One of them pointed with his sword. "Look," he shouted, and there, rising above the top of the earthworks, they could see the flames of the Druids' wall of fire reaching to the sky—and then came the smoke, rolling over the earthworks pushed by the northerly wind. "Stand fast," bellowed Sleg Agorn. "It will roll over our heads."

But it didn't. The thick, yellow smoke poured down

the inner slope of the earthworks and began to roll through the camp. Those in the northern quadrant began to pull back to the center, coughing, spluttering. "Down on your faces," Sleg Agorn bellowed.

The clouds rolled inexorably throughout Cor Gaur, and the ancient stones loomed like giants wreathed in smoke as they stood glowering over the demoralized Wessex. The priests on the earthworks to the south saw the clouds engulf their companions, and they could hear the screams rising through the darkness. They saw Sleg Agorn come bursting out of the smoke. "Stay at your posts," he screamed up at them. "Get down on your faces. Let it blow over you." But they could see across Cor Gaur to where more and more smoke was pouring over the northern earthworks.

Some of them flung themselves to the ground, but others took a pace backward, and then another . . . and then they saw the smoke engulf Sleg Agorn and begin to billow up toward them—and some threw down their swords and stumbled down the outer slopes and through the unlit southern wall of wood to where the Druids were waiting for them.

In the center where the smoke was thickest, the Wessex hugged the ground, their robes wrapped around their heads, gasping for every breath. The children yelled in terror and Asher's screams continued unabated. Mog Agorn bellowed with futile rage. A priestess made a run for it, and then another. One young seeress, blinded and spluttering, ran at full speed in blind panic and smashed straight into one of the giant Sarsens and cracked her skull. A priest collapsed, and then another, and then a dozen more. Some ran in panic, coughing and spluttering, scrambling up the earthworks to get away.

In a demented rage, Mog Agorn stood at the center, his sword drawn. "You fools!" he bellowed. "The Dark One is coming to lead us to greatness and honor!" A priestess crashed into him and he smashed his sword at her, slicing open her belly like an overripe fruit, and she fell, her entrails spilling out onto the ground. Priests were stumbling in all directions, and he slashed at them whenever they loomed near enough for him to reach them. "Fools! You fools!"

The healer had collapsed over the body of Asher, his lungs rasping in agony, and he pressed his mouth to her belly. "Fool," he whispered. "You're too late . . . too late."

In one of the outer circles, to the south, Sleg Agorn crouched behind one of the giant stones, momentarily shielded against the smoke. He was still as calm as ever. He even smiled to himself as he listened to the utter rout of the Wessex around him. Slowly he pulled a knife from his belt and raised his arms aloft. "Let it be known," he whispered, "that Sleg Agorn remained loyal to the Wessex to the end, his only claim to honor. As to the rest, he acknowledges his foolishness and bows to your judgment." And he swung his right arm down with all the force he could muster and rammed the knife into his own belly. He fell to the ground and the smoke rolled over him. In extremis, he smiled a challenging smile. "At least I come to you for judgment of my own volition!" And the blood spilled from his mouth as he died.

Outside Cor Gaur, Druthin stood grimly, his arms folded, his eyes brimming as he listened to the reports that came every few minutes. "My soul is stained for having been the cause of so much suffering," he said quietly. "I will have to toil for many lives to repay such a monstrous debt."

"It was necessary," said Vaila.

Druthin turned to him. "Was it?" He shook his head. "I cannot believe that such horror can ever be necessary."

Menahotep came over to him. "Over six hundred have now fled out of Cor Gaur. It is done, Druthin. It is done!"

The Arch-Mage nodded. "And now for Asher. Pull down the fire, douse the flames. Report to me when it is clear enough to enter."

But it was not easy to undo what had been begun. They pulled away the unburnt sectors of the wall in the east and west so that the fire could not spread. Then they began hauling away the burning logs from the main part of the fire and dousing them with water. But it took two hours before the fire was low enough so that no more smoke rolled into Cor Gaur.

It was midafternoon before the Druids could move in. The main force climbed the earthworks and stood in a grim ring looking down at the scene of devastation below. The barricade was pulled down and the three Elders, together with the entire Druid Council, walked slowly past the Hele Stone and into that ancient site.

Bodies lay everywhere, doubled up, their eyes wide open, their faces black. But here and there were some still alive, those who had found pockets of air that the smoke had not reached. Druthin signaled for the healers to move in, and gradually the stricken were led or carried away, still gasping painfully. "No one will ever convince me that this horror can ever be necessary," he said grimly.

"That is your human compassion speaking," said Vaila.

"Yes, it is. And it has the right to speak, and loudly."

"But the alternative, Druthin, would have been more dreadful by far than this."

"I know. Tomorrow I may be able to take a detached view and recognize the necessity, but right now my heart is filled with the horror of all *this!*"

They came to a small compound and peered in. There was a tangle of bodies in a heap at the far end. There was not a single movement—all were dead. Vaila drew in his breath sharply. "Oh, no—the children!"

Menahotep's face went suddenly gray and haggard. "There must be twenty of them."

Druthin pointed the Serpent Staff at them. "Was this necessary?" he hissed, his eyes blazing angrily.

Vaila remained silent, his very soul sickened at the sight. Druthin strode grimly on toward the center. As they drew near the King Stone, they saw a naked woman crawling painfully across the ground, a knife in her hand. "It's Asher," said Menahotep suddenly.

Mog Agorn himself sat on his haunches near the King Stone, rocking backward and forward, muttering to himself. Druthin made as if to dash forward but Vaila restrained him. "Let me go," Druthin hissed.

"No." Vaila's eyes were quite calm. "This has to be." Druthin struggled but Vaila held him firmly. "Let me go! There shall be no more deaths today."

Vaila shook his head. "Two more must die. Let Mog Agorn come to his destiny. If there is any responsibility, then it shall in part be mine for preventing any interference."

Vaila held Druthin firmly, and they watched Asher creep painfully up on her father. She raised her arm and struck, but she was so weak that the knife hardly penetrated. Mog Agorn did not stir. He sat there completely oblivious of his surroundings, muttering to himself. Again she struck, and again, and the blood began to run down the High Priest's back. But, incredibly, he still ignored the knife. Again she struck, and again, until at last his body sagged sideways and, his eyes closed, Mog Agorn lay in a widening pool of his own blood. Again she struck. "To honor and to greatness," they heard him mutter. "The Dark One is coming . . ." Again she struck. "Behold the Mother," he whispered. "Behold the Child!" Again Asher struck, and at last his mutterings ceased. His chest gave one final heave and then he was still. Incredibly, he was dead at last. Mog Agorn, High Priest of the Wessex, was dead at last!

"And now for the final act," said Vaila. "Menahotep, do what has to be done."

Menahotep beckoned two healers and they went to Asher. The Egyptian pulled the knife from her hand and threw it away. The healers brought forward two bales of cloth strips, and they began to bind the High Priestess from her neck to her feet. They wound the cloth around and around her body, pinning her arms to her side, strapping her legs together. More and more cloth was wound on until at last she was completely enveloped, her entire body swathed in cloth strips, leaving only her head free. And during the whole time Asher had not moved a muscle, or cried out, or in any way given a sign that she knew what was happening to her.

When the task was done they laid her on her back on the King Stone. A party of Druids hurried forward and began to strew dead wood around her body, piling it high about her, and when that was done they withdrew, and the whole Druid force waited for the final act.

For an hour they waited, and then another. The ring of grim-faced Druids lined the earthworks and stared down at the bizarre scene below. The Druid Elders, and Thetan the High Priestess, stood in the East, and the great Sarsen Trilithons towered above them, mute witnesses to the enactment of this grim justice. At the edge of the Bluestone circle stood Ramin, supported by a healer, his eyes fixed on Thetan. He knew of her part in this, and his heart marveled that he had been the choice of such a woman.

Suddenly Asher's head rolled back and a hideous scream came bubbling from her lips, and as the Druids watched, they were horrified to see the tightly bound strips around her body begin to heave, rippling obscenely, her whole body straining upward. Druthin's face was white with horror. Vaila nodded to Thetan and the High Priestess of all Druidry, Pythoness to the Order of Theutates, stepped forward. A young seeress came up bearing a flaming brand of wood and handed it to her with a bow.

Thetan stood at the King Stone, her head thrown back, her arms raised high in mute invocation, the flaming torch in her right hand. Druthin stepped forward and raised the Serpent Symbol, and as he did so the entire Druid force lining the earthworks raised their swords to the sky in response.

The tableau was maintained for a moment, poised, frozen—and then Druthin brought the Serpent Staff down, and as he did so Thetan plunged the burning torch into the wall of dead wood around the body of Asher.

The flames leapt up and Asher's screams echoed and reechoed throughout the ancient site. Her hair caught fire and the skin of her face blackened with the heat, but still her screams rang out. The strips of cloth began to smoulder and catch fire, and her whole body disappeared in a sea of flame. With one last, hideous scream of pure agony, Asher, High Priestess of the Wessex, gave up the struggle and died, and her soul fled shrieking down into the darkness to meet its grim judgment.

And through the flames the Druids saw the cloth strips burst asunder, and something reared up, enveloped in fire, struggling hideously against the flames that was consuming it—and wave after wave of pure hatred swamped the minds of the human watchers. Druthin felt himself take a pace forward, and then another, a burning rage within himself to rescue his Master. Thetan took a pace, and so, too, did Vaila—and the thing radiated its commands from amidst the sea of flames.

But then the fire roared up and the thing collapsed, writhing horribly—and the waves of power faded, and the Druids came to a stumbling halt, their faces dripping with sweat.

For an hour the fire raged, and then died down. The three Elders approached the King Stone but all they could see were charred lumps of bone. It was over; it was finally over.

Druthin turned and raised his Serpent Staff. "The evil has been averted," he thundered. "Let the races of Man so conduct themselves that never again can humanity be brought so close to disaster." He pointed to the ancient stones. "This place was once the Holy heart of our land. I, Druthin, Arch-Mage of all Druidry, hereby decree that never again shall this ancient site be used for ritual purpose. Pull down the outer circles and scatter the stones throughout the land. But let the great Sarsen Trilithons remain, and let the King Stone remain, to remind those who follow of the glory that was once Cor Gaur. I, Druthin, have spoken. Let all here heed my command!"

The Druids withdrew to Glaeston, and during the following months the outer stones were wrested from the holes in which they had stood since time beyond measure, and scattered throughout the land. And the winds blew and the rains fell, and winter followed summer, and spring followed winter, and the years passed and the power that was Cor Gaur faded until it was nothing but a few tumbled stones with no life within them.

And one day an old, white-haired priest came to Cor Gaur and sat amongst the stones, quite alone. "Do you remember, Menahotep, my dead teacher?" he whispered to the wind. "Do you remember, Thetan, my dead wife? Do you remember when we three stood here with thrice-honored Druthin and Vaila and cast out evil from the stones?"

He cocked his head but no answer came. "You are silent," he whispered, "but I know that you *do* remember. But will others?" He was silent for a while. "How transient, how fleeting are the deeds of Man!" He sighed and rose shakily to his feet. "Who knows, perhaps in a thousand years or so men will come and wonder why these strange stones are standing here in the middle of nowhere—and their questions will go unanswered. They will never know." He looked up at the sky and smiled. "But you know and remember, and so do I."

And he set his face to the east and walked slowly away, his staff tapping the ground before him.

ABOUT THE AUTHOR

PETER VALENTINE TIMLETT was born in London in 1933. A former jazz musician Mr. Timlett has traveled widely, living for several years in Australia. *The Seedbearers*, his first novel, was prompted by his interest in the occult. *The Power of the Serpent* is the second in this fantasy trilogy. At present he works for a large British publishing house and lives in Bedfordshire, England, and is completing the third novel of this trilogy.

Bantam Book Catalog

It lists over a thousand money-saving best-sellers originally priced from $3.75 to $15.00 —bestsellers that are yours now for as little as 60¢ to $2.95!

The catalog gives you a great opportunity to build your own private library at huge savings!

So don't delay any longer—send us your name and address and 25¢ (to help defray postage and handling costs).